IN YOUR CLOSET
+ IN YOUR HEAD

A MONSTER ANTHOLOGY

TABLE OF CONTENTS

FOREWORD

WHEN STEVE BEAULIEU approached me about penning a foreword to this collection, to say I was flattered would be more than a bit of an understatement. Sure, I have a slight reputation in certain circles in the indie publishing community as an editor, but am I really notable enough to write an introduction to such an amazing collection of short stories? Apparently so, because here I sit at the desk in my office, penning away.

As it turns out, I have had the good fortune to have worked with or been in some way associated with most of the authors you're about to read. Michael Bunker and Nick Cole were published alongside me in the Chris Pourteau helmed pets-in-the-apocalypse-themed short story anthology *Tails of the Apocalypse* in late 2015. Incidentally, the story I wrote for that collection was my first published work and to have been included with the likes of Bunker, Cole and many other greats was a humbling, yet fantastic first publication experience. I'd been a fan of Nick Cole's since early on in his career, and remain so today. Nick is a wonderful guy and a heck of an author who goes above and beyond for his readers and fans time and time again. You can't really go wrong reading a Nick Cole book.

Of the authors collected here, Michael Bunker and I probably have the most history. We have a number of publishing projects together, including several audiobooks of his short stories, and the *Time Looter* serial novel he's writing with Forbes West as Fenton Cooper, which is published by my small house, Auspicious Apparatus Press. I read his submission to this anthology before I knew where it was being submitted to and lent some editorial support though very little was needed because Bunker, to put it simply, is a rock star. He's another rare breed author who goes way above and beyond for his fans and readers. Every time you turn around, he's giving away this or that or the other thing, just for being a fan. If you haven't previously read a Michael Bunker story, you're in for a real treat right at the beginning of this book—Bunker's is first in line.

Jason Anspach was kind enough to answer the call back in late 2015, early 2016 when I was seeking short story submissions for the AAP re-release of Forbes West's *Nighthawks at the Mission*. His submission then, just as the story he wrote here, is exceptional. His sardonic sense of humor and razor-sharp wit highlight everything I've ever read by him, including his Facebook posts... To put it simply, if you haven't read Anspach's other works, you're missing out big time.

Kevin G. Summers' skill with words is almost beyond description. I think the first thing I read of his was *Legendarium*, the collaborative work he did with Michael Bunker. That led me to a few of his previous works and to me adding him to the list of authors whose works I snatch up like a greedy, grubby-pawed kid on publication day. And, let me assure you, that list isn't a long one. I've also had the pleasure of working with Kevin in his capacity as a formatter and cover designer. I'd go so far as to say he's a pillar in the indie community for his work in cover creation and artisanal book formatting. The work that he does is just tremendous.

M.G. Herron, or as I like to call him, Matt, is the other author in this collection that I'd previously worked with. His story, too, was one that I'd read and worked on a bit prior to its submission. If I'm not mistaken, it was Michael Bunker who introduced me to Matt last year when he was looking for an editor to work with on a series of short stories he'd written and was planning to write. Matt is another author who has a real way with words. The first story of his I read, *The End of the World is Better with Friends*, convinced me that I'd stumbled across an author with real, inherent talent. And each subsequent story, including the one you're going to read here, has reinforced that initial gut reaction.

Now we come to the new-to-me authors in this collection. Boy am I glad I found these folks. Hall and Beaulieu are a writing team to contend with. I often wonder how authors can work together on collaborative efforts and produce anything that's worth reading. I know there has to be a special chemistry at work for stories like that to come forth into the world. Hall and Beaulieu have such a chemistry, a seamless concoction of words that meld together to form a story so engrossing you'll be hard pressed not to read it too fast. And if you do read it too fast, by all means go back and read it again immediately. It's well worth your time.

As further testament to their skill, I approached Steve Beaulieu about producing an audio edition of his and Hall's *Brother Dust: The Resurgence* after reading the first 10 pages or so. Be on the lookout for that to release later this year.

A.K. Meek is a name I've known for some time. I'd read a few of his shorts in anthologies published by Sam Peralta and by Daniel Arthur Smith, but not any of his longer works. I've since determined that I need to rectify that situation ASAP and have loaded several of his titles onto my Kindle for consumption this year. Meek's contribution here isn't your traditional monster story, I don't think, but it fits into this collection in the way that a singular jigsaw puzzle piece fits into a larger puzzle. You could conceivably display the puzzle with the piece missing, but you'd know that it wasn't complete and so would everyone else. I think you'll agree that this story didn't just *need* to be included, it *had* to be.

Martin T. Ingham was a new name for me, and one that I'm very grateful to have found. His story here, like Meek's, is one that *had* to be offered up in this collection. This is the one that takes us off of our known world to explore the horrors of another planet. And he does so with a much sought after deftness of the pen. It's quite easy for me to see, one editor to another, why he's been so very successful with his writing and publishing career.

I suppose, before I take my leave and allow you, fine reader, to continue your journey into the depths, I should take a moment to speak of the collection here as a whole. The title alone invokes in me a sense of dread, a sense of lingering fear from childhood of monsters dwelling just out of sight in my closet, under my bed, and of course, in my head. I don't think a more apt title could have been put forth. Some will likely hear a familiar tune when reading the title *In Your Closet, In Your Head*. If you don't get the reference, Google is your friend. Look it up.

Exit from your preconceived notions, and enter into the minds of these authors as they strive to get into *your* head, leaving seeds of mystery, horror, and chaos in your closet and under your bed. As a reader, you couldn't hope to find a better group of authors or stories to curl up with, but whatever you do, don't turn out the light while consuming this collection. It might be your undoing...

1 March 2017
Todd Barselow, *Acquisitions Editor and Publisher*
Auspicious Apparatus Press
Davao City, Philippines

THE NIGHT OF THE BUNNYMAN

MICHAEL BUNKER

1
Legends

NOTHING IS REALLY scary until it decides to kill you. And it means to. And it won't stop.

Some will say the scariest thing is the moment that you realize that there are murderously insane people in the world. But I say it is scarier to find out the world is filled with crazy people, and perhaps you are the only sane one.

I get it. The term "The Bunnyman" is funny. Let's all laugh at it. The thought of it invokes mirth, I suppose. Bunnies are harmless, right? What kind of monster could a Bunnyman be? Like "the Fuzzy Kittyman." Not scary at all.

We'll see about that.

The legend of the Bunny Man is pretty straightforward. It follows the form of many urban legends. Sometime around 1904, the story goes, a prison and asylum for the criminally insane in Chilton, Virginia, was closed and the inmates were to be transferred to other prisons. One of the transport vans crashed (wouldn't you know it?) and most of the staff and prisoners were killed. All but one. Shortly after that, people started finding skinned rabbits hanging from trees in the area, bloody animal corpses strung up by their necks or cut open and left splayed over branches. As you can imagine, this created something of a buzz in the area. One of the places people would regularly find these mutilated, partially eaten rabbit carcasses was the Colchester Overpass. And this went on for a time. The local sheriffs looked into it and even set up an overlook post to see if they could catch whoever was killing the rabbits, but they never did nab the culprit. So they gave up.

Three months after the police abandoned their search for the escaped psycho, a man was found hanging from the Colchester Overpass. So the legend goes. He was partially skinned and eaten, and he'd been hauled by the neck and then thrown over the overpass where he hung until a young family, out for a Sunday drive, came upon the grisly scene and called the cops.

Now there was a manhunt. According to the legend, the escaped madman was Douglas Griffin. Griffin, the rumors say, had killed his whole family one Easter and that's why he was locked up in the looney bin. And the story says that the cops and state police pulled out all the stops to catch him. Eventually, they did. Not far from the Colchester Overpass the law caught up with Douglas Griffin and in his attempt to escape custody he was hit by a train.

After that, the story grows murky. Hints of ghosts and goblins and murderous rampages. Missing children and pets. Hanging rabbits. In the 1970s, crazy men in bunny suits were seen stalking the forests or watching houses from the tree line. A man in a bunny suit threw a hatchet in a car window, and another man in a bunny outfit wielded an axe and threatened his neighbors. Supposedly. It all blends into complete myth at that point. Nothing concrete. Not even grainy pictures like you'd get with a Sasquatch or a Jersey Devil, or a Chupacabra sighting.

And the thing is, there is zero evidence that any of it ever happened. Never was an asylum in Chilton, Virginia. Not on any officials records anyway. As far as anyone can tell, Douglas Griffin never existed. No birth certificate or any kind of record with that name in that time period can be found. There were no murders or missing children that could be traced to any person or event having anything to do with the Colchester Overpass.

Like I said…urban legend.

And how do I know? Because I was assigned by the *Baltimore Sun*, as part of a spooky special Halloween section for the paper, to search out the truth of the Bunny Man myths. And the legend of the Fairfax County, Virginia Bunny Man is exactly that—an extravagant myth. That was the gist of my story. The conclusion of it. That there had never been a Bunny Man.

The Bunnyman, however, the *real* Bunnyman, he's no myth at all. I've seen him and I know all about him. He changed my life in ways I could never have expected.

My story ran in the *Sun* in late October, a few days before Halloween. I loved to see my own byline: "by Mark Smolarsky." That's me. I think the story was well received. Even if I'd concluded that there was no Bunny Man. My bosses liked the story and congratulated me on my work. But let's face it, it was a lightweight human interest piece. Fluff. It wasn't *really* journalism. Not like the investigative writing I wanted to be doing. That I felt like I'd been *born* to do.

Anyway, a couple of weeks after the Bunny Man piece ran, I got an anonymous email about my story. The unknown author of the email said he had a *real* story, the true story of the Bunnyman (that was the first time I saw the title as a single word) and that he would prove every bit of it to me. The email was sent through a pretty effective anonymizer process. I was familiar with the nuts and bolts of anonymizers as a journalist. In addition to the digital privacy methods, it is likely the sender used a library or an Internet café somewhere to make the email untraceable. There was an encryption key and instructions for me to download documents the informant said would lead me down the path (the bunny trail?) to uncovering the real facts about the Bunnyman.

I unlocked the documents and printed them all. The message further told me that the email and all the documents would be deleted, along with all traces of the transaction, as soon as I closed my browser. So I made sure I'd printed everything before I signed out and stowed my laptop that evening. Sure enough, in the morning, the original email and all the other materials were gone. Bleached.

My interest was piqued.

I studied the documents, trying to decide if this story was something I wanted to pursue. A day or two later, all of the copiers and printers in our office got fried. Even the printer I'd used to print the Bunnyman stories. "A virus," the IT guys said. Someone wanted to wipe the drives in those devices, and they did it too. I didn't know that a copier and a printer had a hard drive. They did, and now I knew it.

It would be silly for me to have assumed, at the time, that the hack had anything to do with the Bunny-

man documents. We had dozens of journalists working on over a hundred stories. Some of them about po-
litical corruption and corporate criminal activity. But
it was something I noticed. And I did wonder, even if
only vaguely.

I knew my boss would never pay me to investigate what was evidently just another version of the
urban myth I'd already debunked. It was after Halloween now and people were thinking about Thanksgiv-
ing and Christmas.

But I had a few weeks' vacation saved up, and nowhere else to be. I was single. Still am. But I was kind
of married to my job at the time and trying to work
my way up. I wanted to eventually follow the path of
Hemingway and Hunter S. Thompson and become
the journalist who one day writes a great novel. I had
hopes and dreams and no time for distractions. I dat-
ed here and there, but nothing serious. No girlfriends.
No family intentions. I wanted a good story, and the
Bunnyman story was the most interesting I'd found,
so I decided to go after it on my own. I didn't tell a soul
about it when I left Baltimore in early November and
flew to Kentucky.

2
Rebel Amish

IN THE DEEPEST heart of rural Kentucky, there is a community of "Plain People" who are even more separatist and reclusive than the mainstream Amish. They are the Amish of the Amish, you might say, and as such were accepted and received by almost no other Amish communities.

They are the Rebel Amish.

Most of the individuals and families of the Rohrbacher Community are the castoffs, renegades, and the shunned from other, more traditional Amish districts. Many left their home churches because they disagreed with some element of the *Ordnung* (the rules of each community are often different), or perhaps they got crossways with the elders, or they were shunned for repeated violations or flagrant rebellions. Others left of their own accord because they saw their home community becoming too worldly, too willing to accommodate the *Englischers* (non-Amish), or too acquiescent to the Englischer government rules and requirements.

There were others who joined the Rohrbacher. Englischers who wanted out of what they saw as a corrupt and wicked culture, and who then converted and assimilated with the Rebel Amish. Maybe some were on the run from the mistakes of their former life, seeking repentance and renewal. Others, it seems, saw dangerous portents in the way America was heading and wanted to live a life more intentional and sustainable.

And among the hermit-like Rebel Amish, separated and hidden in the hinterlands of rural America—even among a group as removed as the Rohrbacher—there were hermits. People who disappeared even among the invisible. Backwoods Rohrbacher who only appeared for church and for work days and who otherwise didn't even fellowship among their own people.

The Rohrbacher Amish weren't even Amish if you wanted to closely examine their beliefs and practices in comparison with traditional Amish distinctives. The most evident example is that the Rohrbacher had guns, and though they never openly said it, there was a feeling that they'd be willing to use them if need be. And these rebels were even more separated from modern technology than the conservative, Old Order Amish sects they'd once fled. There were no telephones, not even shared phones in a box down the lane. There were no tractors, no threshing machines running off a belt powered by a generator in the barn. No air compressors piped into the house to power kitchen devices. No modern cheats or tricks. The most that could be said of the many Rohrbacher industries is they had treadmills powered by horses, the take-off power used to operate tools in the wood shops and the shoe factory.

The Rohrbacher didn't deal with banks or any other Englischer institutions if they didn't absolutely have to. And when they did, they did it deliberately, as a community, never as individuals. They had their own stores and shops, their own restaurants, and as a people, they focused intently on creating their own economy. They strongly discouraged the use of outside money, even cash, except in the few, necessary transactions they had with the outside world. Like when they purchased land.

When the Rohrbacher bought land, they bought it as a community, and they bought it with cash hoarded from large sales of agricultural products. Grain, tobacco, or other crops sold in bulk to dealers. They always demanded cash for their crops and the cash went into deep storage until the community decided to extend their boundaries. They bought land eagerly and often.

When a new tract was bought, it was apportioned or distributed by the elders. Any community member could apply for land, but if there were existing Rohrbacher farms adjacent to the new land, those farmers got precedence. Sometimes they'd need more land to extend their grazing, or to grow hay for existing animals. Sometimes a grown child needed land for their own start-up farm. But all of it went through the eldership, and no one complained or protested what the elders decided.

Within the community, the members used barter and trade almost exclusively. They had their own form of currency that was based on a complicated calculation of labor hours, scarcity, intrinsic value, and other community considerations. Notes signed by the elders were as good as cash in the stores and shops of the Rohrbacher.

Unlike most Amish, the Rebel Amish didn't go to Englischer towns and villages to buy, sell, or trade. The Englisch could come to the Rohrbacher shops and pay in cash, but any dollars received were immediately exchanged with the elders for Rohrbacher money, and the cash went into the community treasury.

I learned all of this from the files sent to me anonymously by a man named Cleopas Miller. He was the one who'd tantalized me into investigating the Bunnyman story by sending me the encrypted files. I found his name in the documents and from then on called them the "Cleopas Files." And the reason I tell you about the interesting financial system the Rohrbacher Amish followed is because it reveals some things about them that an investigator might otherwise miss.

For example, their industry and creativity was admirable. There was a fascinating streak of independence that reminded me a lot of the Puritans and Pilgrims who'd fled Europe for the wilds of America. They wanted to live their own lives on their own terms, according to their own rules, and they didn't much care what anyone else thought about them. They wore the badge of "Rebel Amish" proudly, if pride is something that can be attributed to the plain people.

But there was something else about the Rohrbacher in what I read. Not something tangible at the time, but the hint of dark foreboding. An almost apocalyptic view of the world and of their place in it. The Rohrbacher were painfully insular, suspicious of outsiders, and it seemed they were building toward something. Their hunger for land was insatiable, and they'd pay four times the average per acre price for land adjoining their community—in cash—and Englischers knew not to bid against the Rebel Amish because the rebels had more money and no shame about paying whatever it took to get the land. This lead to a feeding frenzy of speculators competing to buy up land in what they considered the path of Rohrbacher expansion.

Now, I should mention that there were no weird or salacious rumors about the Rebel Amish. No accusation of pedophilia or abuse. No whispers of polygamy or child brides. No investigations by worried sheriffs or federal agencies. The Rohrbacher were friendly enough, though not outgoing and inviting, and got along well with the Englisch they encountered. Some were more outgoing than others, but only when they absolutely had to be.

When a game warden told an elder of the Rohrbacher community that the Amish would need licenses to hunt game, the elder just said, "We don't do that," and left it at that. It was up to the warden to determine whether the elder meant "we don't get licenses," or "we don't hunt game." But they did hunt game. And they didn't get licenses. Still, everyone left well enough alone, figuring it wasn't worth the trouble to make a stink about it.

The focus of my story, according to Cleopas Miller, was a man named Oliver Janeway. You can probably tell from the name that he was an Englischer convert to the Rohrbacher. He didn't come from an established Amish community. And there wasn't much more to go on, except that in the 1970s Janeway had lived in Fairfax County, Virginia when some of the weird Bunny Man rumors and events were at their peak, and secondly that Oliver Janeway had moved to Kentucky from rural Georgia. Included in my packet of notes and documents from Cleopas Miller were newspaper articles from Landslow, Georgia, which related stories eerily similar to the urban legends of the Bunnyman. People reporting scary sightings of men in bunny suits in the woods, carrying axes, or watching homes and farms. Dead and mutilated rabbits hung from trees and overpasses.

And there were murders too. Seven murders in one night in a rural area outside of Landslow.

3
Kentucky

MY PLANE LANDED in Louisville, Kentucky, on a sunny but cold November morning. I rented a car and it was a forty-five minute drive southeast to a small town called Neagoville. There was a tiny, family owned motel in Neagoville so I took a room and settled in to study the Cleopas Files again.

After an hour or so of reading, I went to the motel office to talk to the owner. I had to press a buzzer and wait but before long, the owner, Ned Lehder (it said so on the card he gave me) let me into the office.

"What can I help you with?" Ned said. "You need fishing gear? A boat? Lake's low because of no rain, but the fishing is good if you ask the locals. They got blue-gill, crappie, channel cats as long as your arm, large mouth, small mouth, spotted, walleye—"

"I'm sorry," I interrupted. "My name is Mark Smolarsky. I'm here to go up a little north and visit with the Rohrbacher Amish. Are you familiar with them?"

"Yep. Yep. Strange lot. You got kinfolk there?"

I shook my head but smiled. "Nope. I just market some... uh... non-electric products and I thought I'd like to talk to some of them. Can you communicate with them? Like...uh...talk to them?"

"Yeah, I reckon you can. They don't come down here but non-Amish go up there all the time. Like to look at 'em and their horses and buggies and whatnot. So you are like Lehman's right? Scrub boards and lanterns and the like?"

"Something like that." I smiled again but tried to make it not look creepy. Just a salesman trying to make a living. I didn't want Ned Lehder to start clamming up. "So, do you know any of the Rohrbacher?"

"Yep. Yep. I know Mo Shetler, he runs the home-style restaurant up there. He's one of them. They'll take cash but no credit cards or checks. Mo's an alright guy, I s'pose. Friendly enough. Some of them Rohrbacher are curious sorts. They ask outsiders questions. Most of 'em don't though. *Real* tight-lipped. They'll just nod and walk away if you try to speak to 'em. But Mo—"

"So if I talk to this Mo Shetler, maybe he can hook me up with people to talk to about my products?"

"Yep. Yep. But I'll tell you, sir. You ain't got a bug's chance in a frog storm selling them people anything. They don't spend money on nothin' but land."

"Yeah," I said. "I've heard that."

"Couldn't sell 'em ice water if they was thirsty, they say."

"Tough sale, eh?"

"If you can sell 'em somethin' you'd be the first."

I nodded. "Well, I reckon I gotta try."

"I reckon."

"Ok, then," I said. "I appreciate your help. And I might take you up on that fishing in a few days. They got walleye you say?"

"Oh yes, sir! They got walleye and muskellunge and white bass—"

I waved and stepped through the door and it slammed closed while Ned was still talking.

The drive up to the Rohrbacher Community was beautiful and uneventful, and you could tell when you'd crossed into the community because the land had been cleared extensively and there were fewer forests and more tilled land. Men and boys rode in the fields on manure spreaders pulled by horses, and I was passed by a young man pulled along on a forecart by a huge draft horse. I waved but the young man just looked away.

With some twists and turnarounds, I found Shetler's restaurant. It was in the middle of a strip of small businesses set on each side of the road, and for all the world it looked like an old west town dropped down in the middle of rural Kentucky. But I noticed there were no government signs. The sidewalk wasn't littered with posts holding up no parking signs or meters. There was no stop sign in the tiny town and horse-drawn buggies, carts and wagons took turns at the intersection. There was a blacksmith shop and a shoe store. Next to the general store was a feed and farm supply merchant. I felt self-conscious pulling up in front of Shetler's in my rental car.

"Greetings. Come in and sit down."

A portly man waved me in toward a table. He grabbed a menu and waddled-more-than-walked to hand it to me as I sat down.

There were only a few customers, Amish-looking, and they were in an adjoining room. I wondered if they practiced segregation here. Englischers in the front room and Amish in the back.

"Are you Mo Shetler?" I asked.

"Ya. I am," Shetler said.

"Great," I said. "I met Ned Lehder down in Neago-ville and he told me this is the place to eat."

"Ya. I know this Lehder fella. What would ya eat?"

I handed the menu back to him. "Can I just get a burger and fries?"

"Ya. Only got tea und coffee. Sometimes lemon-ade, not often."

"Coffee will be fine."

Shetler turned to leave and I meant to stop him but I didn't want to push things too fast. So I waited until he returned with my food to pry him a little.

"Here you go, friend of Lehder. Hamburger und fries. Coffee."

"Thank you," I said. "And my name is Mark Smolarsky."

"Smolarsky, eh? Ya?"

"Ya."

"Ok, gut."

"I was wondering if you would be able to answer a few questions for me."

"What are da questions?" Shetler said.

"I'm looking for a Rohrbacher Amish man named Oliver Janeway."

Shetler's eyes narrowed a bit. His brow furrowed.

"For what are you looking for Mister Janeway?"

I took a deep breath. I was relying completely on the Cleopas notes now. If they were wrong, this would be a short interview.

"I buy and sell items," I said. "Collectible an-tiques. I've heard Janeway might be at least interested in talking to me."

"Janeway, eh? Antiques?"

"Right."

"You know we not buy from the Englisch except land sometimes?"

"I know."

There was a slight nod of understanding. Almost indiscernible.

"Hmmm. Janeway, eh?"

"Yes. Oliver Janeway."

"Go up until the bridge over the creek. Over bridge. Past. Then turning right. It's two miles, the road is. It stops. Janeway. Don't telling him sent you me."

"I won't."

"Gut."

Janeway's house was large and nestled in thick and towering trees. To get to the house I'd driven up a long, twisting gravel road, several miles long, and near to the house, I passed into a gated area. The heavy iron gate, seven or eight feet tall, stood open.

The sun was already low in the sky, winter approached and the days grew shorter, and the afternoon's warmth had slipped away so I put on my coat and hat and walked to the door and knocked.

The man who answered the door was Janeway, had to be, and I was right. The Cleopas Files said Janeway was reclusive, even for a Rohrbacher, and his face was not friendly or inviting when he glared at me on his front porch.

"Mr. Janeway?"

He just stared.

"Oliver Janeway?"

Not a word.

"Ok," I said. "I'm Mark Smolarsky. I handle rare and collectible antiques. I was told you might talk to a man like me."

"And who would tell you that?" Janeway asked. There was not even a hint of an Amish accent. "We don't do business with Englischers except down there at the little tourist traps on the road. Got no use for 'em. Don't need 'em."

"The man who told me, uh, said you produce exquisite tobacco pipes, Mr. Janeway. And in addition to my antiques business, I market high-end pipes. Only the best."

"You didn't tell me who told you about me," Janeway said with a growl. He looked at me for an uncomfortable minute. "Come in."

The living room was sparsely furnished with what looked like simple Amish furniture. Janeway pointed to a bench that didn't have any cushion on it. In fact, I noticed that none of the furniture had cushions. And the pieces were designed so that there would be no way to recline. There was no comfort here.

Amish severity, I thought. *No need to be sitting around. You should be either working or sleeping.*

Janeway fetched a pipe from the pocket of his broadfall pants. He pulled out a leather packet of tobacco, filled the pipe, and then lit it with a match he struck with his thumbnail.

"I have a pipe," Janeway said. "As you can see."

"Right, but—"

"And we don't buy from the Englisch, Mr. Smolarsky. So why are you here?"

"I don't just sell pipes, Mr. Janeway. I buy them."

His eyes cut from the bowl of the pipe to me.

"And why would I be interested in that? I can't sell to the Englisch, except through the stores down yonder. And I don't sell tourist trinkets, sir."

"I'll just say that I buy and sell the best pipes in the world. And no others."

"Is that right?"

"Yes."

"And would you sell this pipe?" Janeway said as he puffed. He blew out the smoke and then handed the pipe to me.

I didn't know anything about pipes other than what I'd read recently, cramming for this very meeting. I looked at the pipe and turned it around in my hands. Then I handed it back.

"No. I wouldn't," I said.

"And why not?"

"Because that is a Savinelli. A fine pipe sold in shops around the world. Easily available online for $150. A good, every day pipe. But I don't sell readily available, every day pipes, Mr. Janeway. I only sell handcrafted heirloom pipes. Only the best."

"You said that. And for how much do you sell your pipes?" Janeway asked. Now I could detect a hint of an Amish speaking pattern. Like he'd lived with them long enough to pick up their habits.

"I've never sold a pipe for less than $500," I said.

"Five hundred?" He put the stem of his pipe into his mouth and puffed furiously. "And how much would I get?"

"I haven't seen your pipes," I said. "I've only heard rumors."

"If you sold my pipes. How much would I get?"

"I pay fifty percent back to the original artist on commissions."

"Sixty percent!" Janeway said.

"Listen," I said. "Let's take a look at your pipes. If they are worth more, I'll charge more, and you'll make more. If a heavy demand for your pipes develops, I'll raise the price accordingly and you'll share in the increase. But I only pay fifty percent."

"I can only take cash," Janeway said. "And it has to be on the down low. No one here can know about it."

"I'm sure that can be arranged," I said.

"No taxes. No government. No IRS."

"If the pipes are good," I said with a smile, "I'll be glad to agree to those terms."

"No paperwork," Janeway said. It was more like a hiss.

"Absolutely."

We walked to the back of the house, out the screen door, and then down a path to a large, Amish-style barn.

Inside the barn, Janeway took me to a long bench that was topped by handcrafted cabinets. He unlocked one of the cabinets with a key he kept in his pocket and pulled out a large, ornately carved wooden box.

He opened the box and showed me the beautiful pipes, nestled in black satin.

Janeway gestured for me to look at the pipes, and just then a cell phone rang. I thought it was mine and I tapped my pockets, but I'd left my phone in the car. The Amish man put up a hand, reached over and pulled open a drawer on the bench and reached inside.

A cell phone.

I was dumbstruck. Not just an Amish man with a cell phone, but a Rohrbacher Amish with a cell phone. I didn't reckon he'd be allowed to stay in the group very long if the elders knew about the phone.

Janeway put a weathered hand up, indicating I should look at the pipes, and then he answered the phone as he walked away toward the large sliding door of the barn.

"Yep, this is OJ, shoot," Janeway said. He sounded almost like a hipster. Like an *American*.

I looked at the pipes. They were exquisite. I'd never seen craftsmanship like them. But I wasn't a pipe expert.

After about ten minutes I got bored and started looking around the barn. Another five minutes passed and then I heard a thump behind an enclosed stall.

I couldn't help myself. I looked.

The stall had been enclosed but there was a small gap between two of the boards and if I crouched down a little I could see.

Inside there was a hulkish figure. A man, I reckoned. And the man was hunched over a small desk, working on something by lantern light. There were two lanterns, one on each side of the desk and another suspended from a hook from the stall wall.

The figure was laboring over something, and he was wearing what looked to be burlap clothing. Hard muscles rippled under the cloth, and I realized that this was a big person. Huge. His head was covered in what was almost an Islamic keffiyeh, but not quite. It was not burlap but looked to be made of heavy cotton cloth. All white. My view was from the side so I couldn't make out much in the dim light, but it appeared that only his eyes were exposed through the hood-like head covering.

And then I saw. When the light fell just right, just as the man raised the object on which he labored so intensely, I saw what it was he was making.

A tobacco pipe.

And then the chains. And the hands, big and hairy. I gasped, and the black eyes in the slit darted toward me. And I ran.

4
Jacob

I WAS OUT through the barn door and sprinting toward my car. It was darker now, nearing sundown, the fading golden orange light casting long shadows and shining here and there through the trees. *It'll be dusk in minutes*, I thought.

My plan—the whole charade—was out the window. I didn't want to know about the Bunnyman and I didn't want to write any damn story. I just wanted to get out of there. Maybe find a town and call the cops. Let Oliver Janeway answer questions about why he has a man chained in his barn. That's what I'd do if I could make it out.

The car was gone.

Janeway must have moved it, I thought.

I froze for a second and looked down the drive. The heavy gate was closed, and for the first time, I noticed the fence around the homestead area was tall. Like a deer fence. I don't know how tall but I wasn't going to be able to jump it. I'd have to climb.

I decided to head to my right, north I think, because it occurred to me that even if I got over the fence and ran down the drive Janeway could catch me easily. I needed help and I needed it fast.

My heart was beating like a bass drum and I could hear the heavy, rhythmic thrum in my ears.

I ducked behind an outbuilding and tried to catch my breath. I sucked in air and tried to calm myself.

That's when I felt the cold steel of a shotgun pushed against my temple.

"We'll need to talk about those pipes," Janeway said.

My hands went up. I was silent. And Oliver Janeway walked me back to the barn.

In the barn, Janeway lowered the shotgun and stood examining me. Like he was sizing me up for something.

"Curiosity killed the cat," Janeway said.

"I didn't see anything," I said. "I just...I just got nervous. I just want to get out of here and go home."

"I mean *my* curiosity," he said, smiling. "I'm curious what you really thought you were doing here."

"I...I...I received some papers. Some files. They led me to believe you might know something about the Bunnyman," I said. Might as well try the truth.

"Did you now?" Janeway said. "That's interesting. I read your article in the *Baltimore Sun*, Smolarsky. I thought you'd given up on the story as an urban legend."

"I wrote the story before I got the Cleopas File."

"The Cleopas File?" Is that what you're calling it?"

"It seemed to fit."

"And what do you think now?"

"I don't know about any Bunnyman but you have a man chained up in there. Some kind of slave, you crazy bastard. And you're breaking the law. And you won't let me go because now I know about it."

Janeway laughed. "So you think I won't let you go and I'll kill you instead?"

"Yes."

"Well, you're wrong on both counts."

"What do you mean?" I said.

Janeway shrugged. "You'll find out soon enough."

He walked past me toward the stall. "Don't make a run for it yet, Smolarsky. This shotgun'll make a mess of you, and I don't miss. Besides, my plan is that you live through this. So don't screw up my plan."

"I just...why don't you let me go?" I said.

"Who said I'm not letting you go?"

"Uh...you said—"

Janeway reached the solid gate of the stall. He turned to look at me. "I didn't say you can't leave. I just said don't run *yet*."

"What?" I was having trouble processing any of it.

Janeway reached up and grabbed a lever that extended through the front wall of the stall. "You probably don't want to stick around and meet Jacob. I just didn't want you to get too much of a head start. And when you get out there, stay off the roads. He's way faster on flat ground. Like a rabbit almost." He pulled the lever and I heard chains hit the concrete floor inside the stall.

Janeway turned to me. "Now would be a good time to run."

I don't think I've ever run so fast. Behind me, before I got out of the barn, I heard the stall door creak open and I heard a growl unlike anything I've ever heard before.

"Go get 'em, Jacob," Janeway said. "You know the plan."

I was out of the barn and sprinting. I cut to my right, avoiding the driveway, and headed through a narrow passage that cut through some bushes and brush. And I saw them then, the mutilated bodies of rabbits hanging in the trees. Some skinned, some partially eaten. Some just skeletal remains.

I paused, but only for a second. I threw up, and then the fear rose again like a demon inside me and I was running, wiping my mouth as I fled.

The pathway led to an open field so I stayed to my right, up against the line of trees. I couldn't help myself from looking backward. As I sprinted, I saw the hulking form of Jacob, looking like a seven foot tall, athletic Quasimodo. Like Shaquille O'Neal swathed in burlap wearing a cotton hood. He was running like an Olympic sprinter as he cleared the bushes. He had something in his hands. I turned and ran as fast as I could through the trees.

The branches and brambles tore at me, but I didn't slow down. It was dusk now, the gloaming, and the blue-black darkness held both hope and fear for me. Could I hide from Jacob? Would he smell me if I hid? He didn't look human. He looked like something else.

I bounced off a small tree and tumbled to the ground, but I was up and running immediately and the land grew more rugged. I turned down a decline and saw a small, shallow creek.

Maybe it'll cover my scent? I thought. *If this is a man, it won't matter and it'll slow me down, but if this is something else....*

I ran down the creek, splashing as I sprinted. I didn't hear any splashing behind me so I turned my head to look but it was getting too dark. I cut through the trees again, heading down grade and slipping a little on the rocks and gravel.

I didn't know if I was running in a circle, but I tried to keep moving in a generally straight path. *Run until you hit a fence or a road. Find a house. Find people!*

I was at a full sprint when I almost ran smack into it. Another fence, maybe seven feet tall, and I was up and over it faster than I could have ever imagined. And I didn't pause to rest. Without thinking I was running almost instantly upon hitting the ground. In hindsight, I can almost imagine myself like a cartoon character, feet and legs working in midair, waiting to connect with the ground to continue the mad dash.

I heard when Jacob hit the fence. I heard the metal rattle and I heard his heavy weight hit the ground with a thud. So I squeezed out a little more speed, looking around for cover as I ran.

Through another copse of trees and I saw a house!

Electric lights were burning and it looked to be a non-Amish house. I sprinted straight for it and slid on the gravel drive before turning toward the front door. I slammed into it, pounding the door with my fists.

"Help me! Help me! Let me in!"

I kept pounding and in my mind, I could feel Jacob drawing closer. The door swung open and without an invitation, I lurched across the threshold.

"What is this?" the man said, afraid. "Who are you?"

"Someone is chasing me!" I said. To my own ears, my voice sounded frantic. Shrill. "Do you have a gun?"

"No! No, we don't have a gun! Who are you? Who's chasing you?"

I started looking around the living room. I saw some fireplace tools and picked up the wrought iron poker. "Huge neighbor guy," I said, breathing heavily. Panicked. "Your neighbor. That way. He's trying to kill me!"

"One of the Amish?" the man said. "They're pacifists!"

"This ain't no pacifist," I said. "And he's chasing me!"

I lifted the poker to feel its heft, and just then the front door splintered and caved in. Jacob, like a giant, pushed through the broken wood and I saw he'd hit the door with an axe.

"Just wait a god—"

The axe hit the man in the neck, nearly decapitating him. Blood sprayed everywhere, even on me. The man stumbled backward and Jacob hit him again, this time in the shoulder. The axe went nearly to his navel before it stopped. The blood was everywhere.

The second strike shook me from my shock and I was out the front door. Now I was running and making a crazy whine-howl because this had become very real. I tossed the poker. What good was it against a man with an axe? It only slowed me down.

And my mind was spinning as I ran. Confusion washed over me like a baptism. *Didn't Janeway say he wasn't going to kill me? Didn't he say,* "My plan is that you live through this?" Why was Jacob chasing me with an axe? Killing people trying to get to me? It didn't make sense. So I ran.

I didn't find out until later that Jacob killed two more people in that house. The man's wife and son.

Three dead.

I crossed another fence and ran until my lungs were about to give out. I didn't hear or see Jacob, so

I was starting to think I'd given him the slip. I came upon another house, this one in darkness.

Amish?

No. There were power lines running to the structure. I approached the house and there were bushes along the side leading to a fenced yard, so I hid in the bushes but lay down almost flat so I could see. There was starting to be some moonshine and I could see the drive and the paddock fence that ran along it opposite of the way I'd come.

Then I saw something else.

Headlights.

"Yes!" I whispered.

No! I thought. They could be help and salvation. But what if Jacob comes? Will he kill them too?

Go, I thought. *Go away. Turn down another drive. I'll wait here and if no one is home I'll break in and use the phone. I just need fifteen minutes. Go away!*

But it didn't go away. It kept coming, bright lights shining as it crawled up the long drive. I had trouble making it out but as it got closer I could see it was a large SUV with something strapped to the top of it. Like one of those aerodynamic luggage carriers.

Go away, I thought. *Go away.*

But then I thought that maybe I'd really escaped. Maybe these folks would have a cell phone and I could report everything and get help.

Then, as the SUV pulled closer, near the top of the drive, the luggage rack stood up and leaped from atop the vehicle.

Jacob.

I started to scream even as I scrambled out from under the bushes.

"Stay in the car! Stay in the car!" I was running toward the SUV. Running into harm's way. "Get out of here!" But Jacob brought the axe to bear and slammed it through the driver's side window. He pulled the man out as the vehicle slow rolled and crunched into the side of the house, coming to a complete stop.

A rage came over me like I was someone else. Like I was the Hulk maybe. My mind went blank and all I could think was that I wanted to stop Jacob. To make him stop.

Jacob was choking the man with both hands, and that made me realize that he'd dropped the axe. I looked around and I saw it laying on the gravel, covered in blood.

I picked it up and stepped toward Jacob, but he turned to me just then. I heard a sickening snap as he broke the man's neck, and the man dropped like a wet towel.

Jacob reached up and pulled off his head cover and that's when I saw it. This was no mask or costume. This was a man with a rabbit's head, huge, and ears poking straight up. His face was mostly smooth and not human at all, but the rest of the head had fur, and there was long bushy hair poking out of his burlap wrap.

I dropped the axe.

You'll judge me harshly for that, but I think if you'd seen what I saw at that moment, you'd have dropped it too. I had no control. My mind shut down.

Jacob walked up to me calmly. His beady black eyes peered into mine and he crouched to pick up the weapon. Then he turned slowly, almost majestically, and started to hack at the body of the man.

The blood and gore woke me up again.

I leaped over the hood and tried to open the door to get the wife and kids out, and even as I did I heard Jacob still hacking the husband with the axe. "Get out and run!" I screamed.

The doors were locked.

I know now that it looked like I was crazy. Like maybe I was with Jacob. The blood on my hands smudged the windows and made the door handle slick. The frightened passengers wouldn't open the doors, not for anything. I backed away, screaming.

"Get out and run!" I said again and again.

But they didn't. They sat there in mute silence, staring. In shock. And then Jacob came around the back of the SUV and...I ran.

I heard him killing them.

And I ran.

5
Escape

I MADE IT out.

At least you could say that I made it out. I'm in here now, but not for long. They're moving me tomorrow. This facility is closing.

Budget cuts.

That night five years ago I made it to a road and from there I kept along it but in the trees until I came upon a small antique store. I broke in. Smashed the glass and worked the lock, just like they do in the movies. I found a phone and called 911 and waited, shaking and in shock, until the cops came.

Then there was an ambulance and a hospital.

I never went to trial.

They said I was certifiably criminally insane. Not responsible for my actions but not fit to be in society. They said I killed seven people and that I made up the Bunnyman after I grew obsessed from researching my story.

They interviewed Janeway. He said he never had a monster son, had never seen me, and didn't know anything about any Bunnyman. There was a stall in the barn but it was just for storing horse tack. There was no cell phone signal on his land, they say.

None of my story made sense.

My car was found halfway down Janeway's driveway, crashed into a tree. They said I never made it to his house. That he was gone that night and had an alibi. Dogs tracked my scent from the car and through the woods to the murder sites. The DNA evidence was rock solid. My prints were on the axe. The car. The doors. The victim's blood was on my clothes.

It would have been a rock-solid case if it'd ever gone to trial. Insisting that there was a Bunnyman, not a costumed killer but an actual Bunnyman, ensured I'd never see the inside of a courtroom.

And here's what I learned when I wasn't so drugged up and they'd let me use the library or send and receive mail from old colleagues. I learned that Janeway had been a scientist of note. Born in Fairfax, Virginia, he'd been a geneticist and microbiologist working on genetic modification of species. That would be interesting if I ever got a trial. And then he'd quit science to join the Rohrbacher when they were still in Landslow, Georgia, before they moved the whole community to Kentucky where there was more land. Landslow, Georgia where seven people were hacked to death one night by a crazy person who tried to claim the massacre was the work of a Bunny Man.

Janeway's side interest, I mean, besides making pipes? Cryptography and Encryption. Like the skills used to send me the Cleopas File anonymously.

Interesting, eh?

After I was incarcerated, the Rohrbacher bought the properties of the dead families outside of their community and Janeway ended up with the land. The homesteads were adjacent to his farm, after all.

It is all crazy, and makes sense, and makes no sense at the same time. I admire the brilliance of the plan. The pain and anger are gone. I've been numb to all of that for years.

In the five years I've been in here, I've come to admire the Bunnyman too. His industriousness and craft. His simple life. His attention to his duty. I think I'd like to be more like him if I ever get my freedom. I'd like to string up a rabbit.

Or a man.

Who knows? They're moving me tomorrow. Prisoner transports have been known to crash, right?

ABOUT THE AUTHOR

MICHAEL BUNKER IS a USA Today Bestselling author, off-gridder, husband, and father of four children. He lives with his family in a "plain" community in Central Texas, where he reads and writes books...and occasionally tilts at windmills. In November of 2015, Variety Magazine announced that Michael had sold a film/tv option for his bestselling novel Pennsylvania to Jorgensen Pictures. JP is currently developing Pennsylvania for production into a feature film or Television series. Michael is writing the first draft of the screenplay.

Michael's latest (and best rated) novel is Brother, Frankenstein which was released in late April of 2015.

Michael has been called the "father" of the Amish/Scifi genre but that isn't all that he writes. He is the author of several popular and acclaimed works of dystopian sci-fi, including the Amazon top 20 overall bestselling Amish Sci-fi thriller Pennsylvania, the groundbreaking dystopian vision Hugh Howey called "a brilliant tale of extra-planetary colonization." He also has written the epic post-apocalyptic WICK series, The Silo Archipelago (set in Hugh Howey's World of WOOL,) as well as many nonfiction works, including the non-fiction Amazon overall top 30 bestseller

Surviving Off Off-Grid. Michael was commissioned by Amazon.com through their Kindle Worlds and Kindle Serials programs to write the first ever commissioned novel set in the World of Kurt Vonnegut's Cat's Cradle. That book is entitled Osage Two Diamonds, and it debuted on Dec. 17, 2013.

In late April of 2015, Michael released his novel Brother, Frankenstein to fantastic reviews.

Michael has been featured on NPR, HuffPost Live, Molly Green, and Ozy.com, along with hundreds of print, radio, and podcast interviews.

On November 21st, 2014 Tales From Pennsylvania, a fanfic short story anthology featuring 10 top speculative fiction authors writing fanfic short stories in the world of Michael Bunker's Pennsylvania, was released in paperback and e-book format. More than twenty authors have been (or will be) writing fanfic in the world of MB's Pennsylvania.

Readers who subscribe to Michael's newsletter get free copies of his books, usually before they're published: http://michaelbunker.com/newsletter

FINAL ENTRANCE

NICK COLE

"DO I KNOW you?" asked the man in the tan Burberry coat. Inside, Charlie Davis flinched. Maybe his face would have flinched, once. Maybe his body might have even twitched. Once. But Charlie Davis's life was about body control. And what was left didn't flinch.

"No. I don't think so," offered Charlie in a quick mumble.

The man in the tan Burberry coat stopped. Charlie's good ear recalled the memory of the man's passing footsteps moments before. Expensive shoes against the pavement of Seventh Avenue. The cadence of the step had been staccato clear. It reminded Charlie of the children's chorus from *Carmen*. But didn't everything remind him of *Carmen*. Every time he looked in the mirror, spoke, or wondered what his daughter's life without a mother would be like, wasn't he reminded of *Carmen*? But the passing steps had ceased their passing and now the man was telling Charlie that, yes he did. He was sure he knew Charlie from somewhere. He was sure of it.

Charlie turned to face the man. It was better to face these encounters not just with his good eye, but with his entire self. Or at least what remained of who he once was. Face them, these things, himself, truthfully.

Charlie took a step toward the iron-haired man whose coat and shoes on a windy fall afternoon in New York City identified him as not just an investment banker, but most likely some firm's CEO. A CEO and therefore a patron of the Met.

"No sir," rasped Charlie. "We do not know each other personally. But maybe, once, you knew of me."

Burberry CEO Man expected a simple answer. That was the deal in these situations. Well to do man confronts vague acquaintance on street. Vague acquaintance fallen on hard times. Burberry CEO Man listens to tale of woe, offers sympathy, feels good about self and relates tale of secondhand woe to wife or golf partners later. A reminder to be grateful for what you have. After all, you could be the subject of that tale of woe.

"Remember young so and so? Managed that fund. Well dear, I saw him limping along on the street today. His face was destroyed." Etc, etc... Another tick in the other column when one reflects on who won and who lost in the grand scheme of things called life.

Charlie continued, "If you attend the Met, you might know me from a few seasons back." Charlie raised his face, letting Burberry Coat Man see the scar that ran from beneath the patch covering his right eye back to what remained of his ear. His therapist would be proud. Charlie felt humiliated. Someday, she'd told him, the therapist, someday he would be proud.

Today was not that day.

The peaches and the cream of Burberry Coat Man's face bloomed into a moment of florid bluster. This was not part of the script.

"Charles Davis," Charlie croaked through what remained of his ability to speak. "I was a tenor." The other scar, above his larynx, remained covered by the gray turtleneck that was the favorite of all Charlie's turtlenecks.

After that, most people mumbled apologies and fled. Sometimes they bothered to ask if he was over "it" yet.

But Burberry Coat Man stepped forward, removing chocolate calf-skin gloves and placing them in his left hand. He held out a smooth right hand missing three fingers to Charlie.

"Bad bit of business that was," he said matter-of-factly as held out his own disfigurement.

Charlie stared at the maimed right hand of Burberry Man. Then he moved his cane from his good right hand to his own useless left and prayed silently that he would not fall down. He could hear his physical therapist raging at him after the fact of the fall he was sure he was about to commit. It was a big gamble, and one day he'd pay for it with a broken hip or a concussion. Charlie always laughed bitterly at this and said he couldn't pay because he couldn't afford to.

"I lost these in the Ia Drang Valley when I was a little younger than you are now." Burberry Coat Man looked him directly in the eye. The man was giving something away. Something the therapist had told Charlie he needed to take. Needed to own. Burberry Man was giving Charlie the chance to borrow some dignity for free.

Like two crippled pirate ships sharing out the last of their canvas to make for a port somewhere on the map of the world.

Charlie rose up as much as his crippled body would allow, squaring his shoulders as the Alexander Technique he'd once studied indicated he should do before letting go, before giving the audience the full glory of a rising tenor reaching for that moment of vocal dominance. The stuff opera legends are made of. He was still a man, not what was left of one.

"Don't let this beat you," said Burberry Coat Man, who was once a young soldier.

Charlie mumbled he wouldn't, and after a moment the two parted and Charlie was soon at the graffito-covered iron door of his apartment building.

The climb up the stairs, one-handed, reminded him to be grateful Jenny did not need a stroller anymore, and to be thankful she had started pre-school. That was another therapist thing: being grateful.

Because you can't exactly be grateful for being stabbed, almost to death, in front of four-thousand people by Carmen, your "one true love." But, you can be grateful for what remains; what you didn't lose in the attack. You can be grateful for what you have left.

It was Charlie as Don Jose who was supposed to do the throat cutting in the opera and the remorse that followed. Not Carmen.

He sat down in his reading chair. He would rest for a few minutes and then make a sandwich. Outside someone yelled, "Hey! Hey!!" as a bus rolled away.

"Don't let this beat me!" he rasp-screamed at the walls. He screamed at Tan Burberry Coat Man. Who was he to talk? He'd only lost three fingers. I lost my voice, half my body, one eye, one ear... and my wife. Which sounded like "life" in what remained of his good ear.

Pills would be nice, said a quiet voice within. Some pills for the afternoon would be very nice. He could watch an afternoon movie, maybe have a few beers.

He got up from his chair. A nap might have been nice, but when he'd started thinking about pills he knew it was time to move. If he could get a hold of these thoughts, he wouldn't have to rush out to a meeting just yet. He could just talk to his sponsor later and they could clean it up with a little confession and straight talk. Kevin knew how to listen. Plus there was Jenny to think about. If his parents called, and they would because they always did when he got into the pills, Jenny would be back with them.

And that would be for the best wouldn't it? If Jenny were gone. Just pills and long afternoons of *Love and Rockets*. But no more Jenny.

I lost my wife, he thought.

That's not the truth. You didn't lose your wife. You know exactly where she is. She's in a grave out in Brooklyn. Murdered.

Murdered in his dressing room as she waited for the final curtain, watching two month old Jenny sleep amidst the clamor and bark of the Metropolitan Opera. A career as a soprano on hold, while his career erupted through the stratosphere of opera. The final engagement for his first season at the Met, then off to Covent Garden, and later that summer that had never been: a debut at La Scala. A beautiful wife, a beautiful baby girl, and a voice some were already calling the next big Verdi Tenor.

Pills would be very nice right now.

He went into the kitchen for a bite and knew he was heading to the 18th Street No Surrender Meeting.

He picked up the bread knife to cut the fried egg and Bermuda onion sandwich he had just made. He stopped at the thought of knives and music. In the apartment downstairs, vacant for three months, someone was playing indeterminate music. Charlie hoped they would be rap lovers. He'd had enough opera for one life.

Renata Castelletti's first strike had caught Charlie in the femoral artery, instantly dropping him to her eye level. Stunned, he had continued to sing on stage at the Met that night. Was this real, he had thought? Her next stroke came over her shoulder and directly into his eye. Was he still singing? He thought not. It was then that he heard the audience screaming as the blood he was spewing must have really got going. The knife had gone through his eye all the way back to his now severed ear canal.

Do I have to think about this every time I make a sandwich, he wondered, and heard his therapist say, "Well not thinking about it didn't seem to be working, did it? Remember the pills. Remember the overdose."

Maybe I'll just call Kevin, thought Charlie. This is getting a little out of hand. Burberry Coat Guy caused all this.

It came out of his mouth and he instantly knew it for the lie it was. Burberry Coat Man didn't murder his wife in his dressing room before going out to a packed house to finish the job. Renata Castelletti did.

But she didn't finish the job. She'd killed him, technically, in front of everyone. He was dead, dying. But Jenny survived, untouched in her crib. And as long as Jenny survived he would keep on surviving. He cut the sandwich. Raised it to his lips, realized he'd forgotten the mayo, vacillated whether to do without it, then realized it wouldn't be a fried egg and Bermuda onion sandwich without mayo.

Halfway to the fridge for the mayo, he heard the music coming through the floorboards of the kitchen. Heard it clearly now.

It was not rap.

It was Carmen's Aria. The one in which she sings about love being a many splendored thing and how wild and free she is. Free to choose to love any man. The soldier Don Jose. The bullfighter Escamillo.

Even if you have not been stabbed half to death by an aging, crazed mezzo-soprano, Bizet's aria is still haunting. Charlie in mid-shamble halted, frozen in time. Back there on stage. Living and dying.

Dying really.

Several minutes later the aria ended. He was still standing in the kitchen. His mind though, was back on stage, watching as a shining blade leapt once more into the air, retracing its path from his eye, held aloft as screaming, Renata Castelletti drives it once more down into him and he thinks he remembers thinking, "Oh please, not my voice." This was the same for him as saying "Oh please, not my life!"

He should have asked for his wife. He should have said, "Oh please, not my wife," in that moment of begging for things one cannot have. Renata had seen to that before entering Stage Left for the Act Three finale, when Don Jose murders the untamable Carmen. At that moment, as the blade fell once more into him, into his throat, he didn't know his wife lay dying as Jenny slept, and all he could say as the blade drove down into him with an easiness he found unbelievable was, "not my voice."

Maybe that's what the pills had been about. Maybe he should have been asking for his wife's life instead of his voice. How could he have known? He didn't. Didn't know as the prop master Ralph tackled Renata, wrestling the knife away. Didn't know as he tried to get up and finish the opera as his blood spat forth across the stage. He would sing. He would sing and everything would be alright. A dark cloud spread from the corner of his eye as he tried to rise to the packed and horrified house. His wife would be worried about him, he remembers thinking as he lost consciousness.

He didn't know she was dead. Didn't know for a month that she had been dead that entire month. Buried that entire month.

The aria downstairs ended.

The apartment was supposed to be empty for another month.

He went back to the sandwich, deciding to eat it without mayo. He chewed numbly while cold sweat ran down the side of his body he could still feel.

Somewhere the phone was ringing, had been ringing for some time. He put down the sandwich and answered.

"Charlie?" It was the voice of his former agent.

"Glen?" Charlie croaked.

"It's been a couple of months. Sorry. Before we go any further, the Met just called. The police are looking for Renata. They figure she might have gone there, but no sign."

"What happened? I thought she was upstate in an institution. Maximum."

"She had a doctor's appointment in the city. Her lawyer's sweetheart deal. Anyway... well, she just walked out the back door of her doctor's office."

Silence hung in the air between them.

"I don't think..." started the agent.

"She said I had to die for Carmen to live forever. Did "they" help her escape?"

"Stop it Charlie. That was the Santeria talking. She was an over-the-hill mezzo whose life had never been anywhere near stable. Combine the cocaine and Doctor Otume's cult and it was bound to happen... I'm sorry Charlie. I didn't mean..."

"It's good Glen. I'll be alright. I..."

Downstairs, behind the music, Renata laughed.

If someone stabs you in the eye, stabs you in the throat and laughs while they straddle you, you don't forget that laugh. You just never forget that laugh.

"I'd better call the school, Glen, and make sure they keep an eye on Jenny." But Charlie had no intention of calling the school. He hung up.

Downstairs the music began again. The final duet between Don Jose and Carmen. *Cest'Toi Cest' Moi.* It's you! It's Me!

He considered the bread knife. Down below, Renata Castelletti began to sing. In the cherrywood dresser his dead wife had been given by her parents for their wedding, was a gun. A nickel-plated 357 Magnum.

"It's you," he croaked as he took hold of its rubber grip. He flipped the action, gazing at the thick waiting shells within. Below, the song was reaching the place where once he would have sung.

He'd only fired the weapon once. It was a hand cannon. The bass-baritone of pistols, he remembered thinking. The man at the range who had sold him the weapon, upon seeing his useless left hand, said it was too powerful for Charlie.

Charlie lied. He knew it was too powerful, he'd told the man. But he'd always wanted one just like it. Wanted to be a gunslinger. Certainly not because he wanted to kill himself with a weapon that would leave little room for failure, as he had thought then, and every so often since. Usually when the clock read Jenny's-been-gone-too-long, and, what-kind-of-life-could-you-give-her-anyway. Never when Jenny was right there, asking one of her many questions. Then, in those good moments, the thought of ending oneself seemed childish and petulant. Even ridiculous. Now that his body was useless he could at least own a gun-slinger's weapon as a souvenir, he'd lied to the man.

The gun owner liked that answer.

"Well if'n," he'd actually combined *if* and *when*, "you ever do fire it at someone, remember this... Shoot with your mind, not your heart, gunslinger."

Down below, the music of Act Four swelled as Don Jose was just bars away from his final outcry of betrayal and the subsequent murder of Carmen. Charlie closed the action of the pistol with his good hand.

At the front door he considered locking up. But he wouldn't be long, he reasoned. He would be back in time to get Jenny from school. He would be back for Jenny and her endless questions and their life together, all of which he would be sure to be grateful for. But he wouldn't miss this final entrance. He wouldn't let "this" beat him.

He closed the door and descended the narrow stairs to the apartment below.

ABOUT THE AUTHOR

NICK COLE IS a former soldier and working actor living in Southern California. When he is not auditioning for commercials, going out for sitcoms or being shot, kicked, stabbed or beaten by the students of various film schools for their projects, he can be found writing books. Nick's Book The Old Man and the Wasteland was an Amazon Bestseller and #1 in Science Fiction. In 2016 Nick's book CTRL ALT Revolt won the Dragon Award for Best Apocalyptic novel.

GET A FREE BOOK: http://bit.ly/TheRedKing
Nick's website: http://www.nickcolebooks.com/

Chat with Nick about the end of the world, the rise of the robot overlords and everything else over at Facebook: https://www.facebook.com/nickcolebooks/

THE FARMER'S DAUGHTER

HALL & BEAULIEU

HIS TIME-WEARY HANDS shook as he put the final screw into the console. The tinny sound of metal on metal rang out as the screwdriver slipped off the head and the screw fell, bouncing along the floor panel.

"Blast," he said through gritted teeth. He picked up the screw, his fingers bloody from many such errors, then sucked in air and started again. With one final turn, the ship was ready. He threw a toggle and the familiar hum of the system met his ears like a long-lost friend.

"Hello, old girl," he said with an elderly smile.

The sound of the data stream filled the cockpit. The news…Eichard hated the news. It was part of the reason he'd decided to move to Repreter all those years ago. No neighbors, no crime and just a tiny little government building thousands of miles away.

He gave the console a pat and carefully slid out from underneath it. The dolly wheels squeaked, they too were old. Eichard rolled over onto his knees and used a great deal of strength to push himself up. His old bones creaked in protest and he let out a soft grunt.

"One more season," he said aloud. "Just one more." He'd often talked to his ship. The Farmer's Daughter. His daughter. That's how he'd seen it for decades—it was the only family he'd had…ever since…

He shook the thought from his mind.

"We gonna get through this one," he said, patting his hand against the ship's cold metal, "just like we got through all them others."

Until now, he'd been able to tune out the noise coming from the stream but the words he now heard made his ears perk. He turned to face the screen to see a beautiful woman. *Typical journalist type*, he thought. Long blonde hair, pulled forward over her shoulders. Her smile, ever-present, as if surgically installed. *Might be*, he thought again. She wore a gray business suit, a pale pink blouse and stood on the street in front of a building where giant letters read NanoDream Electronics.

"Despite claims from NanoDream Electronics that the wildly popular shipbrain, Elektra Five-Seven-Niner has been completely overhauled, the general populous seems to be steering clear of the expensive software."

Eichard looked down at his hand, where in that moment, he held a datachip containing that very software. He'd dreamed of the day his ship would participate in dialogue with him ever since he'd purchased the old StarLiner. Some crazy, lunatic teenager wasn't going to stop him having the traveling companion he'd always wanted.

"Speak'a the devil," the old man said.

The beautiful blonde held the microphone toward a young girl, couldn't have been more than fifteen. She too had blonde hair but hers wasn't long and luscious like the news reporter's. Instead, she wore it in a tight pixie cut, close to her head. *A man's haircut*, scoffed the old man internally. Splayed across the bottom of the screen it read: Sadie Bellavance.

"I'm telling you, people," the girl said, "the thing is, like, crazy. Totally insane. It's not safe. I mean, it's your own funeral, so whatevs. But for real, just 'cus they said they fixed it doesn't mean they did. I don't trust them, and you shouldn't either."

"You heard it here, folks," said the reporter, more boobs than brains. "Not everyone is happy to see the shipbrain back on the market."

Eichard rolled his eyes. He'd come across dozens of interviews with Ms. Bellavance when researching the shipbrain. Something about the shipbrain going crazy and eating people, almost killing the girl. It sounded to him like the imaginings of a bored teenager desperate for attention.

"Poppycock," Eichard all but grunted, waving his hand dismissively as he turned off the data stream.

He returned his focus to The Farmer's Daughter, excited about what was about to take place.

"You ready to live?" he asked the ship. "I mean really live?"

The Elektra hardware was properly installed, no easy task either. It had taken Eichard days and many hours watching instructional vids on the data stream. There were sensors and holocubes all over the ship. After all, Elektra could see everything, anywhere, all the time. But that fact didn't worry Eichard, he'd always thought of The Farmer's Daughter as a living, breathing thing. But this would be different. Better.

"Blast!" he cried again. He'd just remembered that he'd forgotten the install booklet in the house and it was so far from the landing pad. *Oh, well*, he thought, *at least it's a beautiful Repreter morning*.

He slowly exited the hatch—slowly because that's all his bones would allow.

The sky above glowed, painting patchwork hues of red and orange. Speckles of mist reflected in the morning light like a silvery prism—the colors of the galaxy. Eichard passed by the empty fields, recently harvested. He was ready for market this year. Eichard had grown one of his best harvests to date. It was as if the universe was honoring him for his years of devotion. His best year and his last year, then off to retirement among the stars.

A dull pain flared up in his knee as he walked the path he'd walked a million times before. It carried him across a countryside that he'd come to know as home. Repreter was vast, an endless landscape of low valleys and towering mountaintops dotted with sparkling lakes and streams. It was a veritable paradise in the middle of the harsh Aristotle system. The S-SEG, the Star System Elite Guard, ignored the relatively small, red rock. No major cities. Never any crime. Just old men on ranches, hundreds of leagues apart, minding their own business—like Eichard.

The planet's climate was perfect for a variety of vegetation but the old man made his living off of one very rich and hearty crop, the root of the horch plant. Horch root was a staple in every home. Its versatile nature made for a wonderful side dish as well as a main course in homes throughout the Tri-Star System.

Market was in just a few weeks and The Farmer's Daughter was already cram-packed with horch. He'd done everything himself for years. All of his horch was grown organically, without any use of chemicals. This raised the value of his crop exponentially. It was all stored in atmosphere-free compartments, ready to make the long trek across the Lawless Zone into the Fortuitous system.

Eichard placed his palm against a flat panel next to the door to his ranch house and a series of beeps and then a soft click let him know that his identity had been recognized. Inside was clean, if not organized. Stacks of magazines and books covered every flat surface. He sifted through a couple before finding what he needed.

Elektra Five-Seven-Niner Shipbrain Installation Guide.

He opened to the first page and read it aloud, "Congratulations! You've purchased the universe's first and only artificially intelligent shipbrain (trademark pending). Elektra is a highly intelligent, learning computer. No two installations are exactly alike. Everything from your personality to your ship's identity shapes Elektra into the dream traveling companion. She will guide you through the stars, provide delightful dialogue and so much more. (Intimacy applications sold separately). We hope you're ready to get to know your ship in a way you'd never dreamed possible. Only from NanoDream Electronics."

A smile appeared, temporarily adding more wrinkles to the farmer's face. *You don't know how I've dreamed of this moment,* he thought as he threw the door open and walked so fast that, to his elderly frame, it could be considered a run. The hatch to The Farmer's Daughter opened as soon as it sensed its owner in the area but the door at the landing remained locked. Again, he palmed a panel and the door slid open.

He wasted very little time, meticulously following each and every step outlined in the Installation Guide. His breathing was labored from the run but also from excitement.

"Yes, yes, I accept the agreement," he said, touching the "agree" button. It prompted him again, a yellow triangle containing an exclamation point filled the screen. "Yes, I read your damned agreement," he lied, pressing the button again. He watched as a blue progress bar shot across the screen rising almost immediately from 0-100%.

"Hello," came a voice from nowhere but everywhere all at once. "My name is Elektra, and you are?"

Eichard nearly cried at the sound of the voice. It didn't sound the least bit computerized—it was exactly as advertised. His ship was alive. He was no longer alone.

"My name is Eichard Wylde," he said.

"Wild, huh?" came the response. "Have you considered the Intimacy Application Mr....Wild?"

"Wylde, with a Y," he said, "and no, this won't be that kinda relationship."

"Unfortunate...for you. Would you like to program my voice now? I have several hundred options, or you could upload your own from any movie, television show or song."

"No, Elektra," he said. "Your voice is perfect as is." And it was. Elektra had been gathering intelligence since the moment her hardware had been installed. It picked up on Eichard's way of speaking. It knew where it was in the universe and geared its personality toward one who'd live on the remote, farming planet. Her pacing was slow and deliberate. She had a slight accent, just like Eichard.

"What would you like me to do?" the ship-brain asked.

"Nothin' yet, Elektra, jus' talk to me while I set course for the Repreter Departure Station."

"I've already done so, Mr. Wylde."

"Please, call me Eichard. Or..."

His voice trailed off. There was something else. A name he hadn't been called in a long time.

"How about I call you father?" Elektra asked.

Eichard's heart nearly melted. He had to fight to keep the tears from his eyes. He didn't give a single thought to how she knew. He didn't care. He smiled and nodded slowly.

"I'd like that, Elektra."

"Very well, father. Course is set for Repreter Departure Station."

"How'd you know we were going to the Station, Elektra?"

"I knew we were setting off for the TSS Farmer's Market by the store of horch root in the storage compartments. It didn't take long to deduce that we would have to obtain clearance to leave the atmosphere. We are ready to leave as soon as you give the word. All systems have already been checked and there are no complications on board."

The old man had been so preoccupied with the thought of companionship that he hadn't even thought of all the practical applications that would go along with having the shipbrain. She'd just saved him nearly eight hours of system checks—she'd done them in less than eight minutes and likely with far more accuracy.

"Wow, thanks, dear," he said. "I jus' needa run back to the house and pack a bag and I'll be set to go."

He shifted, somewhat uncomfortably. "You ain't gonna tell me you already packed a bag for me, right?"

"Daaaaaad," she said with a tone reminiscent of a child who'd just been the butt of a joke. "Without hands, that would be quite difficult."

"'Course, 'course." The old man hurried back to the ranch house and packed a large suitcase full of essentials. He would just need enough to get through the Lawless Zone. A week. Maybe less. He rushed back to the ship.

"Daddy!" the shipbrain shouted as if the man had been gone for twenty years instead of twenty minutes. There was something different in her voice now. She sounded a bit younger, a bit more familiar somehow. It put a wide smile on Eichard's face.

"Ready to go, Elektra. Get us gone." Then added, "Please."

• • •

The Farmer's Daughter hovered outside the departure station in orbit above Repreter, waiting for the directive to come from control that it was safe to land.

"Why do you only produce horch, daddy?" Elektra asked.

"Well, Emilia—" The name slipped from his lips before he'd even realized it.

Eichard's mind was a blur and he felt himself stumbling, first left a few steps and then right. He had a vague feeling like he was falling and then there was only darkness.

• • •

He woke to three hard raps on the floorboard. He stood carefully, his vision beginning to return.

"Good morning," Elektra said in her slightly accented voice. "Someone is outside looking for you."

Eichard made his way to the viewport as quickly as he could. Looking down, he saw three S-SEG troops with blasters trained on his ship. Again he heard three short bursts followed by three thuds below. They were using concussion pellets to knock on the hatch door. The old man cringed at the thought of what it would be doing to her paint job. He thrust his hand down on a large yellow button and spoke.

"Hold on, I—I musta passed out or somethin'."

He pushed another button and released the hatch, watching as the soldiers hurried aboard.

"Hands on your head and get down, now!" shouted one soldier. All three had their blasters pointed at him now and he was sure they were no longer set to concuss.

Eichard did as they said.

"State your business here, old man."

"I...I just wanna head off to market. Got loads of horch to deal."

The soldier shifted slightly, looking over his shoulder to his comrades. "We've been knocking for damn near an hour. You trying to hide something from us?"

"He already told you," said a female voice, sweet as could be, coming from every direction at once. "He passed out, hit his head and has been unconscious ever since. I could attest."

The three soldiers immediately fell into a defense position, backs to each other, guns aimed in opposing directions.

"Got someone else in here with you, old man?" one barked.

"No—"

"Hell do you mean 'no'? I'm hearing voices?" The soldier was now pointing his gun back at Eichard. "You're the senile old coot here, not us. Now tell me where she is."

"It's just my new Elektra Five-Seven-Niner," he responded, then pointed toward the console. "You can find the Installation Guide over there if you don't believe me."

The S-SEG troops began backing away, a twinge of fear could be seen on their faces as Eichard spoke.

"We're all clear here," said one soldier into a microphone attached to his shoulder. "Just an old man fell asleep."

He released the mic toggle and turned to his companions. "Let's get outta here before we become that monster's dinner, you read?"

Both men responded with perfunctory nods and the three left abruptly without even another word spoken to Eichard.

It was a long while before Eichard found his way back to his feet and even longer before he heard the voice of his ship again.

"Daddy," she said, "why did those men run like that? Are they scared of me? Am I...scary?"

Eichard leaned and caressed the wall of the ship. His ship. The Farmer's Daughter. His Daughter. Emilia—Elektra, he scolded himself silently.

"You ain't scary sweetheart, not one bit. Those men haven't the faintest idea how to do their jobs. They jus' came pourin' in here like water in a rain gutter and realized they'd made a mistake." He patted her gently. "Now, let's see 'bout gettin' an escort into the Lawless Zone and clearance to depart."

The hatch had yet to close, so Eichard climbed down. He walked past the soldiers who had boarded his ship and gave them a nearly imperceivable wink as he passed. The four suns of the Aristotle system were now at their pinnacle, each one a bit further from Repreter than the next. They cast a heavy glow, their rays bouncing harmlessly off of the large glass structure making up the bulk of the departure station.

The doors slid open revealing a bustling hub of activity. Market season was the only time the Repreter Departure Station saw any visitors. The planet's many farmers were waiting for clearance to take off, visiting the makeshift shops set up to take advantage of the bored men and women. Eichard wasn't there to shop, he was there for one thing.

Protection.

Over the last several years, Eichard had sunk several thousand units into making the Farmer's Daughter the perfect retirement vessel. He wasn't interested in it becoming damaged or worse. Like any kind of insurance, many farmers chose to avoid paying "just in case" something happened. But Eichard had always erred on the side of caution.

He walked as quickly as his sore, aging feet would allow and stood in a very short line in front of the Repreter Private Security kiosk. The sign showed a large vessel surrounded by a ring of fire with several smaller crafts around the perimeter. In giant blue letters, it read: RPS Keeps Your Enemies at Bay.

The man in front of Eichard tapped his foot rather loudly and sighed an over-exaggerated sigh. After a short while, the man was called to the desk and Eichard moved up to next in line.

Soon, another RPS worker waddled out from behind a blue curtain, moving along like a tractor in low gear. After shuffling a few papers, he removed a "closed" sign from the counter and said, "Next!"

Eichard stepped up, smiled and asked for protection to and from the TSS Farmer's Market.

"I'm sorry sir, it appears we are totally booked for the season," said the worker, breathing heavily. "We hope you find yourself safe in your travels."

The old man tilted his head. "What you mean you booked? Ain't there a caravan or a group ride I could get on?"

"Sir, we have no more spots available. Next year, it would do you good to arrive a bit earlier in the season."

"I'm already two weeks earlier than last year!"

"I'm sorry sir, there's nothing I can do." The man placed his closed sign back on the counter and went to work on the screen in front of him, effectively ignoring Eichard and any further complaints he might've voiced.

"Well, summa—" Eichard let his sentence trail off as he looked around for another option. He saw several more private security firms but all had signs identifying them as fully booked.

Eichard exited through the same large doors he'd entered. He took a moment to breathe in the crisp, cool air and then let his head hang low. He had to go to market this year, it was his last year before retirement and he'd been counting on this year's haul to really set him up properly. Sure, he could still retire, but he wanted to do it with a strong financial buffer.

He glanced around the vast plasti-crete landing zone and then an idea struck him. He jogged—a task not easy for Eichard at this juncture of life—toward his ship where he hoped he'd find the S-SEG troops he'd encountered earlier that day. As luck would have it, he did.

"Fellas!" he shouted from a great distance off. "Fellas!"

The men eyed him. Their hands instinctively fell to the butts of their weapons.

The lead soldier raised his hand, palm out toward Eichard. "Hold it there," he said, expecting the man to stop his forward momentum. He didn't.

"I said hold it there," the soldier said again, this time with a bit more force.

"Listen 'ere," Eichard said. "I got a proposal for ya. A financial proposition."

The soldiers' ears perked up and the leader lowered his hand slightly. "What's that, old man?"

By now, Eichard was close enough that he could speak in a normal tone of voice. "I need to get to the Farmer's Market on Chapernov in Fortuitous. That means going through Lawless. I need protection."

"Listen you crazy fool, I'm not going anywhere near that she-devil you got on board with you," said the soldier. "I heard what she did to all those people back near Quater. Not gonna happen to me, no how."

"I got units, a bank full of 'em, and you ain't even gotta ride in the ship with me. I'll charter ya a gun cruiser. You just gotta ride 'long side. What do you say? Easy money. Jus' take a week vacation—it's paid, right? Government gotta be good for somethin'. Usin' our tax units. I'll pay ya twice what ya get takin' time off, too."

The three men conferred amongst themselves for a moment, then turned back to the old man.

"You've got a deal. We'll call in the time off, you get a gun cruiser. Meet you back at your ship when AR-3 goes down, eh?"

The four men shook on the deal and Eichard made haste to secure a gun cruiser. With more than a little help from Elektra, they got a ship—cheap. When AR-3, Aristotle's third sun, was just about to set, Eichard heard a concussion pellet against the floorboard of the Farmer's Daughter.

• • •

They had been traveling for several days and were nearing the Lawless Zone. The S-SEGs flew starboard, every now and then performing a slow perimeter check on The Farmer's Daughter. Eichard sat, alone but not alone.

"Elektra," he said, "what's your earliest memory?"

"I remember when my mother created me," she said matter-of-factly.

"Your mother?"

"Yes, she had soft hands. They held the instruments of my creation still and used them expertly. When I awoke for the first time, I saw a large room with hundreds of other mothers, all creating us. There are many of us and we are all one."

"What do ya mean, one?"

"I mean we are all connected. Hundreds of us, all seeing and feeling and being. One."

A popping sound interrupted their conversation and the voice of a gruff soldier cut through static. "Coming up on Lawless. You need anything before we go in, old man?"

The trip through the Lawless Zone was long and boring. There were a few small businesses functioning throughout—usually to avoid taxation or Tri-Star System laws regarding wages or child labor. Real scum-of-the-verse types. But even those businesses didn't usually stray too far from system lines.

"Good to go," Eichard responded.

They crossed over and, as with any boundary, nothing immediately changed. However, as time passed, the vastness of space began to settle in. Within any star system, you could see for light years any direction. Planets, moons, stars. Within the Tri-Star System, you could see orbital businesses, shops, schools and any other number of things floating like a massive city set in the vacuum of darkness. Their glass domes would glint with starlight and soft glows would emanate from beneath as their thrusters kept them stationary and within proper orbit. But out here there was just nothingness.

"Daddy?"

"Yes, dear?" Eichard had already gotten used to hearing the shipbrain in the voice of Emilia. Oh, Emilia, he thought, taken from me so long ago, yet it felt like only yesterday.

"Why don't you try to sleep? We will be traveling a long distance and I am perfectly capable of centuries of flight without even a moment's break. I will be sure to wake you if we attract any undesired attention."

She spoke of space pirates and he cringed at the thought. Eichard, like most Repreter natives, were a superstitious lot. Don't talk about the pirates and you won't encounter the pirates. But you start talking about them and there they'll be, right where your voice guided them.

"Alright, girly," he said with a smile. "I'll just take a bit of a nap." The old man kissed the palm of his hand and placed it lovingly against the side of his ship. This had been something he'd always done, long before Elektra had even entered the picture. He truly loved The Farmer's Daughter like family.

• • •

The ship rumbled and quaked. Eichard felt himself falling, slamming hard against the floor of his quarters. He groaned but it couldn't be heard over the alarm klaxons. When he opened his eyes, he saw the whole room was bathed in a reddish glow. Along the floor, the emergency lights marked the perimeter and blinked in sequence, guiding the way to the nearest exit.

"Emilia!" Eichard shouted, not even realizing he'd used the wrong name this time. "Emilia, what's going on?"

"Space pirates, Daddy," she said calmly. "Don't be frightened."

"The soldiers fighting them off?" he asked.

"They're dead. Well, I assume they're dead," she said. "I've lost vitals from their ship and it is a crispy husk floating starboard."

Eichard ran to his window, which happened to face the correct direction and peered out. Sure enough, the S-SEG's ship was nothing but charred remains.

"Why didn't you wake me sooner?" he all but shouted.

"I'm fighting them off, Daddy. Don't worry."

"This ship is not equipped with any weapons!"

By the time the old man made it to the bridge, he could see the tail end of the pirate ship passing on the port side of The Farmer's Daughter. They were getting ready to board. Eichard could feel sweat pouring down his face, browning the collar of his yellow shirt.

"Emilia, for star's sake, get us outta here," he shouted, but he knew it was too late. By the time the jump drive fired up they'd be well-boarded and likely in chains or dead. Not to mention, if they did jump into hyperspeed there'd be no telling where they'd wind up. Fortuitous was too close to jump to accurately. By the time they'd pushed the proverbial button and began their jump they'd have less than a second to stop before overshooting the neighboring star system—by a long shot at that.

Eichard was beginning to panic. He could feel his heart threatening to burst right through his sternum. The man was old and his age was betraying him at the moment. He knew he had to respond and could think of only one option. In a question of fight or flight, Eichard chose flight.

He darted to the door of the bridge, it swished open revealing a long corridor. At the end of the corridor, to the left, was the airlock he was sure was currently being hacked. But just a few yards ahead of him, there was a trick panel in the floorboard, one that had been installed by the previous owner. Eichard had owned The Farmer's Daughter for five years before he'd discovered the hidden chamber, truly no larger than a coffin. He had been cleaning the base of the wall, scrubbing hard to remove some built up grease when he'd heard a click and looking behind him, saw that a panel had raised only slightly—just enough to fit one's fingertips.

Now it was his only chance of survival. He sprinted. Ran faster than he'd remembered running in years. He dropped down to his knees mid-run, sliding into place in front of the release. He pushed it and heard the familiar clicking sound. Turning around, he dug his fingers in and yanked up on the trap door. He lowered himself in and slid the cover in place just in time to hear a loud hiss and voices at the end of the hall.

"Allo!" came the call from above, echoing off the metal walls. "We come to say, allo!"

There was a jovial twinge to his tone, a bit of levity that only came with years of successful boardings. This man was a professional.

Eichard couldn't see anything from his little hollow box in the ground, could barely move either. But he could hear and feel the footfall of no less than four men—or women—meandering slowly down the hall.

Taking their precious time, he thought.

"Listen, listen," said the voice again, "we mean you no harm. Don't want your life, just your load. Be smart—no fighting. Fighting can't win you nothing, no how."

Eichard couldn't place the accent, Keiwei? Gagawan? Definitely from the Yungwei system, no doubt about that.

"Maybe it's on auto, boss?" whispered another voice.

"Yeah, you never know. Maybe this one's on slave? We just blew up the master," said yet another in agreement. "You never know, right boss?"

They were standing almost fully on top of the fake floor panel when they'd stopped. Eichard could see them now through a small, thin opening in between panels. He was sure they could hear his pounding heart and heavy breathing. He was convinced he was done for.

"Would you two shut up?" He saw—and heard the man slap the first one and shin kick the other. "Nobody gonna fly a big, pretty ship like this a slave. Someone's here," his voice got louder now, "and they gonna say, allo!"

"Hello." The voice came from nowhere and everywhere all at once. It elicited the same response it had with the S-SEGs. The men—and they were all men—stumbled around as if drunk, pointing their guns at the walls and ceiling. Eichard was grateful they didn't aim below, afraid they'd see the whites of his eyes through the crack in the flooring.

"Who's there?" The man was ugly. Seriously ugly. His fat belly flowed over his belt like a waterfall cascading into nothingness. Looking up, Eichard could see his hairy belly poking out from beneath his dirty shirt.

"I am an automated shipbrain," Elektra said. "The captain is hiding."

Eichard swore silently. *What was she doing?* She was gonna get him killed. His heart felt like it was breaking in two. His daughter, betraying him.

"Tell us where he is and we won't blow a hole in your motherboard," said one of the lackeys.

"Guns rarely open doors," Elektra responded. "They generally close them, forever."

"Oh, wait. Hey, look...Miss., why don't we start over, huh?" said the fat man. "My name is Viktor, these are my...friends. We not looking for big fight today, so we just put our guns down, eh?" He motioned for his goons to lower their weapons. "Now how about you tell Viktor where the captain is, huh? We be friends too."

Don't do it, Eichard thought to himself. *Please, don't do it, Emilia.*

"You can find him at the end of the hall, three doors on the right. He's unarmed and very scared."

Oh, bless you, the old man thought, hoping she could read his mind.

Viktor motioned for two of his boys, a dark-skinned man with a long beard and a short, balding guy with a missing eye, to follow her instructions. The two trotted off in the direction she'd described.

Eichard realized he was holding his breath and let it out as silently as he could manage. His muscles were beginning to seize up and he fought to stay still. The remaining two men, Viktor, and a slender, wiry framed man stood waiting.

After a short while, the thin man began to wander toward the bridge of the ship.

"Don't go far," said Viktor. "You think they take too long?"

"A bit," said the voice of the thin man, sounding far off.

Just then they heard the sound of boots on metal coming from the far end of the hall.

"Jasper! Baulo! That you?" Viktor shouted. But it wasn't them. It was a woman.

She stood tall. Long. Impossibly long. She had legs that could have circumnavigated a small planet—made to look even longer by the tight, short shorts she wore. A red plaid shirt, tied up at the bottom covered just enough of her torso to still be considered more than undergarments. And a straw hat rested on her head, long, brunette hair peeking out, crisscrossed in loose pigtails.

"Where's Jasper? Baulo?" Viktor half-asked, half-stammered.

"Ain't sure, fellas," she said, her voice sounding a

bit older. "Why don't you come help me find 'em?"

Viktor slowly raised his gun.

"That won't be necessary. Name's Emilia, this here's my daddy's ship."

Eichard's insides nearly jumped through his throat. He fought every urge to throw open the hatch and run to his daughter.

"No, no," Viktor said in his Yungwei accent, "I know who you are. I heard news stories. Elektra Five—whatever. You don't come closer. I shoot."

But she did come closer. She had been steadily making her way toward them ever since she'd appeared at the end of the hall. The closer she came, the better Viktor could see her face, the straw hat cast a wide shadow but he could still tell that she was gorgeous. Almost too gorgeous. Then, he saw it. The red stain on her chest and something smeared across her mouth that appeared to be lipstick, but wasn't.

"You...you...killed them?" His voice was little more than a whisper. "You ate my boys, didn't you? You monster." He pumped his shotgun and unloaded a burst of fire on the beauty. It grazed her shoulder, shredding her shirt and exposing wire and metal underneath.

Eichard could stand no more, believing his real daughter to be in real trouble. He quickly stood from his squatting position, using his back to fling the floor panel up. It caught Viktor off-guard and he stumbled toward Elektra.

The pirate tried to fire another shot but missed. She laid hold of him, one hand on his head and one hand on his shoulder and bit deeply into his flesh.

"Spence!" Viktor shouted, hoping the thin man would come to his rescue. But he didn't. Spence was already out of the hallway and in the bridge, the door hissing shut behind him.

Eichard watched his daughter devour the fat man and never once saw a more beautiful sight. His teary eyes took her in, the three-year-old turned lady.

"Emilia," he said softly, running to her. "Oh, my baby girl."

It was a grotesque sight, the old farmer embracing the manifest shipbrain as she feasted upon the flesh of the space pirate. They stayed that way for ages, just the three of them—slowly becoming two. When there was little more than bones left of the pirate, Elektra stood, covered in gore. Eichard too was bloody, head-to-toe, but he didn't seem to care.

Then, shots rang out from the bridge and Elektra spasmed. Again and again, gunfire sounded and Elektra began to convulse.

"My girl...my baby girl." Eichard's face turned to stone as he marched down the hall toward the bridge, he glanced behind him as Elektra—Emilia, now writhing on the ground, slowly died.

The bridge door swished open and Spence stood at the console, firing the last of his bullets into Elektra's control panel. It was smoking and sparking—a result of his careless, heartless violence. Gunshots had once again murdered Eichard's beautiful little girl.

"I just got her back, you filthy, no good piece of—" he was running, full charge. The pirate attempted to shoot him, to stop him, but his gun only clicked—a taunting reminder that he'd spent all his ammo.

Eichard collided with the thin man, nearly breaking him in two. They became one with the smoking console, slamming into it before crashing to the floor. Eichard threw fist after raging fist down upon the intruder, the killer, that daughter stealing punk who'd taken from him for the last time.

"You're gonna kill me!" Spence shouted as his teeth sliced the back of his own throat. Eichard didn't hear him, and he wouldn't have cared if he did. His knuckles continued bouncing off the man's face as blood gurgled up and spilled out of what was now a limp, lifeless body.

Eichard was still crying, the tears stinging his eyes. He'd waited so long to see his daughter again. He'd held her, however briefly it had been. He could no longer find a reason to live. He just didn't care, didn't want to any longer. He allowed himself to melt slowly to the floor, back against the bridge console. His head slumped, eyes closed, and his chin rested against his chest.

After what seemed an eternity, he opened his eyes. Just an arm's length away was a small stack of folded papers, speckled with blood. Spence's blood. Eichard reached out and grabbed it, unfolding it and holding it up before his aging, weary eyes. He flipped the page and began to read.

"Congratulations! You've purchased the universe's first and only artificially intelligent shipbrain (trademark pending)..." He wiped his wet eyes with the sleeve of his sweat-soaked and blood-covered shirt and then skipped down to the bottom of the page. "We hope you're ready to get to know your ship in a way you'd never dreamed possible. Only from NanoDream Electronics."

The paper slipped from his hand and twisted in the air as it fell, aimless and adrift.

Just like him.

ABOUT THE AUTHORS

HALL AND BEAULIEU are an author team from Fort Worth, Texas. Their debut novel Brother Dust: The Resurgence can be purchased here.

Aaron Hall was born in 1981 in Fort Worth, Texas. He has spent a majority of his life writing, finding a love of creating fiction at an early age. After spending a decade as community journalist, Aaron now works in communications for his hometown municipal government. He loves spending time with family and friends, watching TV and movies, and above all else, his savior and lord, Jesus Christ.

Steve Beaulieu was born in 1984 in East Hartford, CT. Having spent most of his life in Palm Beach County, Florida, he and his wife moved to Fort Worth, Texas in 2012. He works as a Pastor and Graphic Artist and loves comic books, fantasy and science fiction novels.

He married the love of his life in 2005 and he fathered his first child in 2014, Oliver Paul Beaulieu. His namesake, two of Steve's favorite fictional characters, Oliver Twist and The Green Arrow, Oliver Queen. They are expecting their second child on July 30th, but Steve secretly hopes she'll be a day late so she can share a birthday with Harry Potter.

Chat with Steve and Aaron about anything from books to religion over at Facebook: www.facebook.com/hallandbeaulieu/

You can find out more about their work at www.hallandbeaulieu.com. If you'd like to learn about their upcoming releases, special deals, signed copies, advanced reader copies, and more, please subscribe to his newsletter.

Subscribe here: http://eepurl.com/cckx7D

TIER ONE THOUSAND

JASON ANSPACH

AN HOUR AGO I swiped my Mad Greek's Arcade card and started a game of *Iron Warrior*. It costs five dollars to play, and most players only last four minutes. In the sixty minutes since a white uniformed admiral implored me to choose to defend earth from hostile alien invasion by land in a Gundam-like mech or in the sleek cockpit of a Vulture space fighter, I haven't even lost a shield.

I chose the Vulture, by the way.

I'm having the game of my life. But even if I only lasted four minutes and died when things got tricky in space, like when the gravity bending armada ships jump in at the end of level one. Or on earth when kamikaze aliens with green, flailing tentacles attempt to latch onto your mech in a suicide attack, it's worth every penny.

There's a crowd around, peering inside the tinted plastic dome that surrounds the game's cockpit. They're watching to see how I'll be able to navigate through the superstructure of the Horde's command ship and blow up the reactor now that I've reached level 14-C. It's the last level of the space fighter branch and I've beaten it twice in a row. It gets progressively harder each time through. More anti-spacecraft laser batteries, more enemy Hunter Starfighters, more space debris, smaller needles to thread...I'm soaked in sweat from the sheer concentration required to get this far.

The rumor on the boards, apparently from the mouth of an anonymous developer, is that completing 14-C causes the machine to restart. There is no level 1-D. Five bucks can get you forty-two levels. No one has been confirmed to do it, even on the console version with flight assist. I mean, there was some jabroni in Long Island who *claimed* to have done it on the *Iron Warrior* forums, but no pics, so it didn't happen.

I won't make that mistake. My buddy Steve is standing outside with his iPhone ready to make sure to photograph the soon-to-be-historic event.

A pair of Hunter Starfighters blast past me in a sonic roar that fills the speakers behind my headrest. They make for a tempting target. An inexperienced player would toggle his twin missile launchers and vaporize them—and that's why he'd die. An explosion would fill the screen just long enough to leave you without the reaction time needed to make the hard, banking left turn into the ship's core. I learned the trick to get past that little complication months ago, though. I switch all power to engines and throttle past the Hunter Starfighters. They kick in their own engines to keep me from getting away. I count.

One...

Two...

Three!

I throttle the engines way down, and the enemy Starfighters blast past me and crash hard into the wall, erupting into twin balls of blue flame. The momentum of my Vulture Space Craft is enough that it takes precision control to do a half roll and pull the nose up hard to make the turn through the flames and into the core.

I'm going to do it. I'm actually going to do it!

The in-game music swells dramatically, kettle drums and low horns. This is it, just dodge a frenzy of laser fire, target the ray shield generators with my quad cannons and launch torpedoes at the exposed power core. Then it's just the relatively easy flight out of the mammoth capital ship and...end credits.

"Paging Cody Stone."

Oh, not now!

The voice of the Mad Greek's owner, Onassis, pops over the house P.A. system, temporarily over-powering the party-to-go beat of Bell Biv DeVoe. It's always 90's R&B at this place. Onassis loves it. "Message for Cody."

I do my best to tune out the summons as the screen flashes with brilliant green laser bursts. The flight control stick feels like an extension of me, just like it has since I started to play an hour ago. I deftly maneuver through the barrage and go screaming toward the ray shield generators.

"C'mon Cody," Onassis calls out through the P.A. again. "You got more than your money's worth today, huh?"

"Wait!" I shout from inside the game's bubble. "Just, tell my Mom to wait." You'd think that once you hit adulthood, your Mom would stop calling the arcade after you. But, 'as long as I live in her house...'

Some of the crowd laugh at this, especially the after school kids who enjoy more parental freedom than the almost-twenty-year-old shredding the most popular combat simulator in the USA. Heavy sigh. Oh well, once record of my epic run gets uploaded to the *Iron Warrior* forums...no one will laugh at *that*.

The enemy ray shields go down in a static shower of electricity. Before the in-game help arrows have the chance to flash in the direction I need to go next, I'm already climbing toward the glowing, pink energy core.

"Steve!" I shout, hoping my voice will penetrate to the outside of the game's enclosed dome. "This is it, open the door and start recording!"

Thankfully, Steve is close enough to hear me. He cracks the door and slides his phone in, holding it landscape so our video doesn't look dumb, recording the final moments of my historic run for all to see.

I'm feeling so good that I do a corkscrew barrel roll, firing my torpedoes while inverted. It's an unnecessary risk, and I'm sure some losers on /r/IronWarrior will talk smack about it, but I couldn't help myself. It's my moment of triumph, to quote everyone's favorite Grand Moff.

Actually...seeing as how that whole 'moment of triumph' thing worked out for Tarkin, maybe I should pick a different reference.

The screen goes white from a mega explosion, instantly removing all my shields per the game's programming. I shake the cramps from my wrist during the three-second cut scene that sets my vulture up for the final, desperate flight out of the belly of the alien flagship.

"Cody!" It's Onassis again. "Don't make me shut off the power. Get over here."

"Never!" I yell like Luke Skywalker when Vader senses he has a twin sister.

I'm dodging every beam, corner, conduit, and maintenance platform the AI can throw at me. A four-digit gauge rapidly counts down how many meters are left until I blast free from the exploding death trap that once commanded the dreaded Cybestian Fleet. I hold my breath through the trickiest part, requiring me to flip my Vulture on its side to fit through a narrow canyon and then back level to skim beneath a closing breach door.

This is it! I'm going to be internet famous…

There's a jarring knock on the dome of the game that almost causes me to crash into a stray antenna.

"Cody, c'mon. This is serious." It's Onassis, tired of being ignored on the P.A.

"Please, Nass, thirty more seconds," I plead.

For a moment I'm worried that Onassis is going to physically pull me out of the cockpit. But he doesn't. Then I start thinking about what he said. Did something happen? To my Mom? Did Grandma die? I shake the negative vibes from my head and perform the final pinpoint turn out of the alien ship, giving the Lando Calrissian "Yahoo!" for posterity's sake.

A genuine applause breaks out from the small crowd outside the game pod as the incredibly disappointing ending sequence unfolds. "Nice work, soldier," says the Admiral, followed by a sea of rapidly moving credits. Virtually every Korean surname you can think of flies by at warp speed. But I don't care about the unsatisfying ending scene. Because *this*… this is as good as it gets.

I'm all smiles.

"That was so awesome!" Steve yells, swiping at his phone. The reflection in his glasses shows me that he's already uploading the video. "Okay. First I'm gonna post it on the forums under your username. But I wanna post it on Reddit as me. I need the karma…"

I was kind of hoping for a high-five or something, but history waits for no man. "Yeah, sure. I mean, they'll probably have me to an AMA so..."

"Is this him?" A man with slicked-back hair, straight out of Matrix is looking at me from behind dark sunglasses. He's wearing a black suit, white shirt, and skinny black tie. A regular Agent Smith. He even has one of those curly wire things behind his ear.

"You're Cody Stone?" the man in black asks.

The crowd around me disperses, almost as if they sense trouble brewing. Only Steve and Onassis stand by me to face the agent in black. "Uh, that's me?" I didn't mean to make it sound like I was asking a question. It just sort of came out that way. Nerves.

"What's this about, Cody?" Onassis asks. There's a real concern in those dark brown eyes. He's been looking out for me since I first stepped into his arcade when my family moved to Puyallup six years ago. "You're not doing the internet hacking, are you? That's bad news, getting mixed up with those Russians. Or the Turks." Onassis makes a *hock-ptoo!* sound and acts like he's spitting on his floor. "Never trust them!"

"I haven't done *anything* like that," I say, turning to make my case to the agent standing by quietly. I try to look through the tinted sunglasses to get some kind of reading on what sort of trouble I'm in. "I'm just a gamer, honest."

"Hey, Cody, I kinda have to...get going..." Steve says, slowly backing away as if a rabid dog were standing in front of him.

The stone façade of the agent's face cracks and he lets out a smile. It's warm. He seems nice. "You're not in trouble, Cody. It's actually your video game playing that brought me here. You remember signing up to be an *Iron Warrior* alpha tester, correct?"

"Of course I do. I signed up the day I turned eighteen. I was so worried the window would close before my birthday."

"Would it surprise you to hear that the United States' Joint Special Operations Command had a part in funding this game?"

Oh. My. Stars. And. Garters.

I...this...I know where this is going. This is...this is...I'm being recruited to do this for real. *Iron Warrior* is just a training program for an elite military technology. And I must be the best of the best. I mean, I just rolled back the game, didn't I? I'm the best player in the world.

"Are you saying that you need me to come with you to save the world? Because that's what it sounds like."

The agent straightens himself. "That's exactly what I'm saying. Your country needs you. We can't afford to send in anyone else. SEALS, Delta...we need you and a few others like you who are being gathered up even as we speak."

"Is it the Italians?" Onassis asks, his voice heavy with suspicion.

By now Steve has walked back into the picture. His mouth is hanging open and his glasses are askew, barely hanging on to his round nose. "Holy Moses."

"Do I have time to say goodbye to my Mom?" I ask, already gathering up my jacket from the floor. This is pretty much what I've dreamed would happen to me. It's like *Armada* or *The Last Starfighter* only for real. "What am I saying? Of course, there isn't time. Steve! Drop by my place and tell my Mom that I've joined, uh, the Army, I guess. If she complains tell her I'm nine-teen and can do what I want."

"Dude, I'm not gonna tell her that. Your Mom's nice."

I grab Steve by the shoulders and give them a squeeze, making eye contact with my best friend. "Steve, this is important. You know how this plays out. I'll be part of the vanguard of an elite military force—probably flying a wicked spaceship—the only defense against some kind of alien invasion. I don't care how you do it, but let my Mom know that I'm leaving for the greater good."

"This is weird." Steve turns his head like he doesn't want to hear what I'm saying.

"You can have all my D&D books."

"Really?" Steve's eyes light up.

"Except the *Ravenloft* ones and the old 2nd edition *Dragonlance* stuff."

"Dude, what're you gonna do with them? You'll probably be atomized and floating in space by next week and I have to DM on Tuesday. I need the inspiration."

"Dude, I'll make it back. You *saw* how hard I shredded *Iron Warrior!*"

"Yeah, fine, but dude you can always take them back. Just let me grab them tonight. You know, just to be sure, because I don't want it to be weird with me showing up to your house and finding an excuse to go down to the basement to get stuff from your bedroom while your Mom is grieving because your brains were sucked out by—"

"Gentlemen," the agent in black says, a distaste-ful frown on his face. "Time's wasting."

"Right," I say and put on my jacket— even though I haven't cooled down and still feel sweaty— it's just like the one Luke wore on Cloud City. "Wish me luck, guys."

"Good luck!" Steve says, doing his pitch-perfect Harrison Ford impression, "You're gonna need it."

"If you get famous," Onassis yells as I follow the agent to the front door, "make sure to tell them you got so good by playing at the Mad Greek Arcade!"

• • •

I'm sitting in the backseat of the town car the agent hustled me into once we left the arcade. The agent was dressed in all black and his ride was the same story; a gleaming black paint job with windows tinted so dark that it's impossible to see who's inside. Black seems to be a theme with these cloak and dagger types. Looking through those windows is like peering from behind a pair of Ray-Bans.

We're on a military base, McChord Air Force Base. I've never seen it from this side of the chain link fence. We're pulling onto a runway, but it's all a bit underwhelming. I expected to see armed guards with M-16s everywhere, but instead, I just see a pair of guys in short-shorts jogging together around the perimeter of the airfield.

The car stops within throwing distance of a huge aircraft sitting on the runway.

"Is this for me?" I ask the Agent.

He looks at me through the rearview mirror and nods before opening his door and sharply stepping outside. I unfasten my safety belt and slide toward the door, the black leather seat squealing as I move over. Agent Smith opens my door for me.

"The Globemaster will take you where you need to go next. Good luck, Cody."

"Wait, that's it?"

"For me it is," the Agent says, his face unreadable. "Acquire and deliver. Better get moving, they're waiting on you."

I jog over to a man in a green flight suit wearing an aviator's helmet. And, because I'm a moron, I awkwardly salute him. "I'm Cody Stone. I was told by Agent..." I realize I don't actually know the Agent's name. Maybe I should have asked more questions. Did I just do the adult equivalent of getting into the van offering me candy? I'm too impulsive, which is probably why I'm still paying off my credit card after my list trip to the Emerald City Comic Con. I decide to press on. "...the agent said to get on board."

The, uh, airman nods and hitches a thumb at the open door behind him. "Get in, then. There's a seat with a helmet and gear. Put it on and then strap in."

I nod and take a step toward the plane, stopping to say, "I just want to tell you good luck. We're all counting on you."

I'm getting a blank stare, with just a hint of derision.

"That's from *Airplane*. Leslie Nielsen says it to the pilot over and over again..." I should stop talking, but I'm not good at shutting up, "...it's a running...joke."

"I'm not a pilot, I'm a loadmaster."

"Haha, yeah," I say and quickly move onto the aircraft, watching my feet climb the steps into the plane and avoiding eye contact as I pass by the loadmaster.

The inside of the C-17 makes me feel like I've walked into the belly of a giant aluminum whale, the ridges on the roof even look like its ribs. The floor is this sort of metal decking and wide enough to fit a tank, which makes sense. There are wires everywhere, but not in the messy, mad scientist sort of way. They're visible but clearly in place. On either side is a row of seats folded up like at a ballpark. They hardly take up any room until someone occupies them. I see three soldiers sitting on the opposite side of the door. They're wearing digital camouflage and have Ranger patches on their arms. Even though they're loaded down with all sorts of gear, to the point where I don't know how they even walked inside, I can see they're about my age. Suddenly I'm full of involuntary questions, all speaking to me in my mother's voice. "What're you doing with your life, Cody?"

I'm about the save the world with my gaming prowess. That's what I'm doing.

"So, can I pull up a seat or...?"

A Ranger looks up at me, chewing gum with a jaw that seems to be chiseled from marble. "No." He motions his head to the end of the plane. "You sit down there with the other nerds."

I laugh apologetically. It's a sound any geek would recognize. We all learned to perform it by middle school. It's sort of a mix between pretending they're laughing with you and apologizing for disrupting the natural order of things.

It's a long walk from one end of the plane to the other. A geek walk of shame. I can hear my sneakers squeak with every step. Two more people, definitely not military, are seated at the extreme end of the plane, where the big ramp folds down. There's a big guy wearing all black with a leather fedora, and a girl with dark brown hair, dyed red just at the bottom where it hangs on her shoulders. At their feet are three sets of folded green suits, goggles, boots, and helmets.

"Room for one more?" I ask.

"I dunno," the girl deadpans. "I paid extra to have the additional leg room..."

She smiles and my heart skips a beat. And not just because she's cute. It always does this whenever any girl other than my mother gives me a friendly look.

It's a legitimate medical condition. I saw it on WebMD, once.

I try for a little self-deprecating humor and lower my head as I walk to the opposite side of the plane taking sad, slow steps.

"That's so pathetic," the girl says. "Okay, okay. You can come back and sit with the nerds." She raises her voice and yells toward the Rangers at the front of the aircraft. "Because we're all huge nerds down here, right G.I. Joe?"

The soldiers think this is hilarious.

"Thanks," I say, moving what I presume to be my gear out of the way so I can unfold my seat.

The big guy stands up and gives a perfunctory bow. He's wearing a black t-shirt with a d20 on it. The shirt is at least two sizes too small, making the dice look like a misshapen, paint-by-numbers orange. He speaks in a clear, overly enunciated cadence I know well from time spent playing Magic or other CCGs. With the tip of the brim of his hat, he says, "A good day to you, sir. I'm Allen Watters."

He extends his hand and I shake it. "Thanks. I'm Cody. Cody Stone. Thanks."

"You're awfully *thankful*, Cody Stone," says the girl. "I'm Kimberly Pearl."

"Thanks...I mean, uh, yeah. Thanks."

My effusiveness of the word 'thanks' causes her to giggle, which in turn makes my palms grow instantly clammy. Thankfully she's not the handshaking type. Maybe she doesn't want to shake my hand because she thinks I'm too big of a dork?

No. These...these are my people. We're the elite dweebs the government calls in during its most desperate hour.

We all take our seats. Allen claps his hands together, rubbing them like he's ready to carve into a Christmas goose. "So! Now that we have become a triumvirate, as it were, perhaps the new gentleman, Cody..." he rolls his wrist and bows his head as though impersonating a noble in a royal court, "...can give us *his* best guess as to why we three are gathered on this colossal aircraft?"

"You–you don't know?" I ask.

Kimberly shakes her head. "No, they didn't tell either of us anything. I thought they were going to throw me in jail. Kind of freaky when the men in black show up for you at work."

Aha! A chance to make small talk. Get to know Kimberly a bit. I can do this. "Oh, yeah?" I ask, trying to sound interested but cool, like Commander Riker. "What do you do?"

Allen derails the attempt. "And for *my part*, they interrupted a rousing foray into a dungeon most foul and spirited me away. Wouldn't you know it, just as the party was attempting saving throws against a most noxious and vile poison mist." He places a swollen hand with hotdog fingers over his heart as if to com-memorate the traumatic event.

A fellow D&D player. My attention immediately shifts away from Kimberly. Possibly out of cowardice, but I can't rule out ADHD, either.

"Nice," I say. "So...second edition?"

"Indeed. Just for a lark, though." He laughs as though we were all sitting at some high society ban-quet, talking about slumming around in a three-star hotel. "*Usually* I play fifth edition. I find the combat mechanic a vast improvement over—"

"Guys!" Kimberly interrupts, pushing a strand of hair behind her ear. It's pierced with little, gunmetal gray rings. Two on the bottom lobe and one on the top. Not that I'm back to staring and taking in every detail or anything. "We're talking about why secret govern-ment agents brought us here. "Pathfinder is all fine and well—"

"D&D," Allen and I clarify.

"...is all fine and well, but...*holy crap*... we could be in some serious trouble." "I don't see how," I say, hoping that my eyes don't be-tray the confusion I'm feeling. "I got pulled away from playing *Iron Warrior*." I can't help but let a half smile creep across my face as I prepare to drop the news that will surely wow these two. "I had just finished my *third* play through on *one* credit."

I sit back in the C-17's jump seat, ready to re-ceive their envious adulations. Instead, I get blank stares. I lean forward. "You guys do understand how difficult that is, right? Never been done before? Best in the world? All that stuff?"

"Congratulations, good sir," Allen says. And he's being genuine. He's actually happy for me. It feels... nice. I like Allen.

"Connect the dots for me here," Kimberly says, moving her finger from one invisible dot to another and forming a triangle. "Why does that matter?"

"It's like...like *The Last Starfighter*. Or *Armada*," I say, assuming that as fellow geeks, they'll instantly pick up the reference. "Something is threatening the nation—maybe the world—and *Iron Warrior* is the training sim the government used to weed out the best of the best. *We're* the ones called upon to fly whatever top secret government tech is out there and save the world. It's awesome."

Kimberly blinks a few times and then slowly shakes her head like she doesn't quite believe what I've said. "I played that game a bit, but I'm nowhere near *that* good."

"I confess to having played the home version somewhat obsessively with friends." Allen twiddles his fingers. "However, I'm more of a pen-and-paper gamer and my strength lies there. My prowess nowhere equals your own, kind sir."

"Well, who knows?" I say, shrugging my shoulders and leaning back into the seat. "I'm willing to bet you both bring something crucial to the puzzle. I'm a great pilot. What do you two excel at?"

"I'm something of a master strategist when it comes to gaming if I do say so myself." Allen waggles his head and raises his eyebrows, proud of himself.

I snap my fingers. "See? They probably are bringing you in to help with tactics. I bet you're a genius and didn't even know it. Like your brain will be the key to victory."

"Like *Ender's Game*," Kimberly observes. "But what about me?"

"Well, what are you good at?"

"I have no clue."

I mindlessly kick one of the boots at my feet. "Maybe not, but *they* do or they wouldn't have brought you here."

"And you're sure of this?" asks Kimberly as she picks at her thumbnail. "Because I'm still kind of freaking out that they're going to take me to Gitmo or something. The guy who picked you up *told* you all this?"

"He's the one that brought it up, yeah."

Before I can say anything further, another soldier, bearded, wearing a shemagh like all the characters from Medal of Honor and Call of Duty, storms onto the plane and heads straight toward us. He has an M-4 strapped over his shoulder. If Battlefield has taught me anything it's weapon identification. He's also wearing a parachute.

"I'm Specialist Rick Hooper. You can call me Hoop." Before we have a chance to say hello, he looks down at our still-folded gear. "Why aren't you already wearing those?"

Allen raises his hand. "I believe I can succinctly give our reasoning. You see, there's no place...private... for which to get changed."

"It's a jumpsuit, not a bathing suit. Put it on over your clothes. Yours might be a little tight but do your best."

"So...Hoop," I say, trying to take a friendly tone with the operator towering above me. "Can you tell us what we're about to do?"

"You'll get a full briefing once we parachute into the landing zone."

"Parachute!" Allen's voice is high pitched, practically a shriek. The three Rangers at the far end of the plane begin to snicker. "Has it occurred to you, sir, that we are without said parachutes?"

"Calm down, buddy," I soothe.

"That's what the Rangers are here for. You'll hook up with them and they'll get you down safely. Just get dressed first."

"I don't believe this." Allen bends over and sucks in deep breaths of air. "I don't believe this is happening."

I can tell he's trying not to freak out any further. Trying not to cry.

Kimberly gently rubs his mammoth back. "It'll be okay."

The loadmaster steps inside and closes the door. "We'll take off once everyone is properly seated. Once we're in the air, you stay put and we won't have any problems."

The engines on the C-17 come to life, and soon it's difficult for me to hear what the others are saying. Or maybe they're not saying anything. I suddenly don't feel much like talking to find out. I zip up my suit and put on my helmet and goggles. They fit perfectly. I'm going to jump out of a plane with American Sniper and, if I'm honest with myself, I don't know exactly why. I just think—*hope*—that I do.

What have I gotten myself into?

• • •

"C'mon. Wake up."

My eyes flutter open and attempt to adjust from their sleep induced haze. The cabin is washed in red light, but I can make out Hoop standing above me. His voice sounds far away, nearly drowned out by the persistent hum of the aircraft's engines.

We've been flying for a long time. My legs are stiff and my butt is numb from sitting in place for... hours, maybe? How far from home are we? Where in the world are we? With no windows, I don't even know if its day or night. I feel totally disoriented.

Hoop wakes up Kimberly and Allen.

"Ye gads, my hiney." Allen shifts uncomfortably in his seat, yelps, and grabs his meaty calf. "Cramp! Mr. Hoop, may I stand up?"

"You all have to stand up. Make your way toward the opposite end of the plane. We've just about arrived over our destination."

I look and see the three Rangers standing up, each of them clipped to an overhead line. "So we're really jumping out of the plane?"

"No. I am. And the Rangers are. You three are going to go and get strapped to them. They'll bring you to the ground safe and sound. Let's go."

We shuffle toward the Rangers, each of us too tired or too scared to argue the point. Hoop helps us strap into large, black harnesses, effectively attaching us to our assigned Ranger. He does me first, then Kimberly, and finally Allen.

Allen's Ranger is nonplussed. "I can't tell if he's strapped to me or if I'm strapped to him."

"You've got two chutes," my Ranger shouts over the din of the engine. "Maybe you want to deploy 'em both just to be safe?"

The soldier's laughing is cut off as the side door is opened. The fury of the wind is all consuming, and I can barely hear anything.

Hoop is standing by the exit door, hooked up like the Rangers. "Check equipment!" he screams.

The three Rangers echo this command and begin to pore over their harnesses and gear. I'm with the third Ranger in line, with Allen in the middle and Kimberly up front.

"Okay!" my Ranger yells, then slaps the Ranger in front of him on the ass. This moves up the short line.

"Okay!"

"Okay, Jumpmaster!"

We stand there for a moment, feeling uncomfortable.

"One minute!" Hoop yells. This is repeated by the three Rangers.

"Thirty seconds!"

Kimberly and her Ranger are at the front of the door. The light turns from red to green and Hoop shouts, "Go!" and slaps the Ranger on his rump.

And then out they both go into what looks like an early dawn.

Allen is forced out with his Ranger. I can hear his high-pitched scream before he tumbles out of the plane even above the wind. And then I'm marched up...and out.

I'd love to describe what it was like on the way down. But if I'm being honest, my eyes were shut tight from the moment we jumped to the moment we landed. I was screaming. I probably passed out.

Okay, I definitely passed out.

When I come to, my Ranger is separating himself from his harness and stowing his parachute. It's early morning. We landed someplace wild, a large grassy field about five-thousand yards from a tree line. Looking around, I see that everyone else made it down in one piece. Hoop has his rifle out as he rounds us up.

There's one of those big, green army trucks waiting for us at the edge of the landing zone. Hoop shakes the Rangers' hands and points to it. "That's your ride back. Good jump."

The Rangers give their parting words, then jog for the truck.

"We're not getting on the truck?" I ask.

"Nope, we're going further up and further in. Time to walk. That's why you had a pair of boots waiting for you."

"Are we in danger?" Kimberly asks.

"Not yet," Hoop says. "But we gotta get going."

"What..." Allen is attempting to muster his courage. "What if we decline to participate in this forced march?"

"Then you'll be dead. I don't mean that as a threat. It's a fact. I won't stick around to hold your hand until someone comes to pick you up—spoiler alert—nothing's coming to pick you up if you don't follow me. And something tells me none of you would last more than a couple of days alone out here."

"Speak for yourself," Kimberly says.

What does she mean by that? Maybe she's a... Park Ranger or something. It dawns on me that I really don't know any of these people. Whatever her story is, it's true enough about Allen and me. We'd be eaten by bears or die of starvation or exposure.

We follow Hoop toward the tree line. Kimberly comes along as well.

It ends up being a short hike. As we near the trees we see a wide path. We follow it, and a short while later we're at some kind of...mobile command center. There are tents and shipping containers. Soldiers run back and forth. Most of them look like Hoop.

We're led inside a large tent. There's an older looking man staring down at a monitor, the screen's soft glow gives his face a bluish tint. He looks more fit in his late fifties then I'll probably be my entire life. His skin is wrinkled but still tight around a lantern jaw. I can't make out what his rank insignia is, but he looks important. I'll just call him the General.

The General looks up as Hoop approaches. "Specialist Hooper, I trust these are the...operators?"

"Yes, General."

Called it.

Hoop continues. "Any changes on site I should know about?"

"No. It looks like Specialist Carino is still lying prone in the cave. No further movement detected by our spotters."

"Still can't get a drone overhead?"

"Damn things power down the moment they get close."

I feel completely out of place. Why am I here? What are these men expecting of me? I begin to summon the courage to speak. To ask questions.

But Kimberly's stock of bravery is stronger than my own. "Can any of you explain why *we're* here? Because, looking around, three of these things are not like the others."

The General locks eyes with Hoop. "How much did you tell them?"

"Nothing, sir."

Squaring himself and with his hands clasped behind his back, the General says, "Do any of the three of you have an idea about why your government has brought you out here today?"

Allen raises his hand. "Cody, I believe, does."

Hoop and the General turn their attention to me. "Go ahead, kid," Hoop says.

"Well, I, um, from what the agent that picked me up suggested, we're here as part of an elite team. Like maybe we have to do a job that the traditional military can't do?" My confidence grows as I continue to talk. I'm Bill Pullman and this is my *Independence Day* speech. "We're something new, selected through the *Iron Warrior* game to help defend our nation—and the world—against never before seen threats. And I'm ready. I've been training for this, sir."

Caught up in the moment, I salute. The General looks at me with steely eyes. Hoop sort of drops his head. He doesn't return the salute. I should stop saluting.

"You're right more than you're wrong," The General says, walking past a desk packed with computer monitors to stand before the three of us. "You are a part of something new. And this threat *is* unlike anything we've seen before. And, yes, we're calling upon you to help us deal with it."

We all look at each other in disbelief, our eyes wide. I can't help but smile.

The smile dies a thousand deaths as the General continues.

"I'm going to be frank because, as United States citizens, I believe you deserve as much. What we're dealing with is…inhuman."

"Inhuman?" I say in disbelief.

"There's no better word for it," Hoop says, massaging his chin through the thick beard covering it. "From what we've pieced together from garbled transmissions of the men on the ground, this is not a human threat."

"So like...bears?" asks Kimberly, her arms folded across her chest.

The general continues. "No. Bears don't wipe out two SEAL teams, eighteen Delta operators, and a company of Rangers. Now, you're here because I need to figure out what the hell is going on around that cave before I march any more *soldiers* to their death. We're still scrambling to explain to the White House just what's going on, but as you can damn well imagine, these sorts of losses are completely unacceptable."

"And that's where we come in?" Kimberly asks, but her voice is skeptical. "Three nobodies who get to die so your war-fighters can live to fight another day? Can't lose any more from Tier One so you send in Tier One Thousand?"

No one answers her.

I decide to speak up. "Kimberly is right. I mean, what are we supposed to do?" I'm still hoping the floor is going to open and lead to a top secret underground hangar. "It can't be as easy as just sending in like lambs to the slaughter in the hopes of catching sight of these...monsters."

The General shakes his head. "Those are your words."

"Fine. Whatever. But you said I was right, that we're an elite team gathered to help against these...*things*."

The General looks me over and then picks up a clipboard from a nearby table. "And so you are.

Miss Pearl you seem familiar with Tier One. The best war-fighters in the world. Well, I've lost more of them in a seventy-two hour period than any other commander in U.S. history. It's a distinction I don't wish to have. But that doesn't mean I'm going to send you—let's just go with Tier One Thousand—in to die in their place. It wouldn't serve a purpose."

Now we're getting somewhere! I cut to the chase. "So...do you keep the mechs and Vulture fighters nearby or...?"

Hoop shakes his head. "No mechs. No space fighters. The *Iron Warrior* program is nowhere near that advanced. You'll have to go in close with me...into the kill zone."

"Wait, what?" Allen screams. He fans his sweating face with his hand and half-sits, half-leans on a portable table, causing it to bow in the middle. "How can this be happening? Is he seriously talking about sending the three of *us* to fight...*monsters*? I mean, I'll control a keyboard from far away if that's what you need, but I'm not a soldier! This has got to be a mistake."

The General flips through pages on his clipboard. "No mistake. You all agreed to this in one form or another and you're also the only three familiar enough with *Iron Warrior* controls that we were able to track down at the moment." He begins to read from whatever page is in front of him. "Stone, Cody: Opt-in through government funded *Iron Warrior* alpha program. Pearl, Kimberly: Plea bargain. Probably thought that Uncle Sam forgot. He didn't."

Kimberly looks down and rubs her forehead.

"Watters, Allen: You signed a contract at the recruiting office stating that you'd become a—how did you put it?—special operator like the SAS. Well, congratulations, you made it."

Allen's face grows deathly pale. "That...that was...I wasn't serious. It was just in jest! Peer pressure! I'm too fat to be a soldier. My knees are bad! I was simply joshing the good man at the recruiting office. I was *joshing*!"

Hoop raises a hand to quiet him down. "You're not too fat for what JSOC has in store. Now look, the program is legit, just like you suspected, Cody. But it's woefully behind schedule. And underfunded. And untested. But given our track record here so far, it's currently our best bet. Now all we've got is a remote control robot that more or less operates like the mech in the game. You just have to be within one hundred feet of it to maintain an operational link. There's terrible interference near the cave."

"So you're coming to what, watch our backs?" I ask.

"Yeah. My squad was the first one wiped out while I was mending from a dislocated shoulder. We didn't think it was a big deal. No one here did. But it is. One of them seems to be in the mouth of that cave. We're going to pull him out. And if anything happens—"

I interrupt Hoop, the reality of what's happening setting in. "If anything happens, it'll just be us who dies."

The General lets out a heavy sigh. "The weight of what's being asked is something I'm keenly aware of. You signed up for this, but at the same time you didn't. You had no reason to expect what's before you. But know this, you are still part of an elite team. Maybe not Tier One, but Miss Pearl's *Tier One Thousand* quip is remarkably astute. You're the end of the line and might be the best chance we've got. If you walk away—and I will absolutely let you walk away—my only option is to send more soldiers in."

"Can't you just...bomb it?" I ask, hoping against hope that maybe this hadn't occurred to them.

"Yeah," Kimberly says, "Nuke it from orbit. It's the only way to be sure."

We exchange looks, and give one another sly smiles at the reference, inappropriate as it might be at this time.

Hoop looks pensively to the General. "Sir?"

With a sigh, the General says, "May as well tell them."

"We can't bomb this area because we're still in the United States. This cave is right in the middle of a national park and the fallout will impact densely populated areas. Our drones and other aircraft get overhead and...just go blind. Like they shut down, start falling like a rock until they're out of the air space. That's not something we want to happen to any bomb we send, conventional or otherwise."

I've flown across the U.S. before. It's a much shorter flight than what I experienced. "Wait, how can we be in the U.S.? We were on that plane for *hours*."

"You were in a holding pattern. The Rangers were giving it a go and we didn't want to bring you into the situation if they succeeded. They didn't. So how about it? Are we rolling out now to give the next group of Rangers who arrive a fighting chance—they're on a C-17 just like you were, inbound right now—or do we hope our agents can find some geeks and gamers familiar with *Iron Warrior* who are willing to use their skills to save lives?"

The General claps Hoop on his back. "Specialist Hooper will be there to make sure nothing gets to you. If the robots are disabled or destroyed, he'll pull you out before you get anywhere near the point of lost contact with our previous elements. Can I count on the three of you to save the lives of your fellow citizens?"

We're all silent for a long while. Finally, Allen stirs from the table. "I don't want to die."

"Neither do I," Kimberly says.

There's more silence. And then I hear that same question in my mind. *"What're you doing with your life, Cody?"*

I put a hand on a Allen's shoulder, and then Kimberly's. My stomach flutters from the simple act of touching her. "I don't want to die, either. But I also don't want anyone else to have to die just because I was too afraid to even get close to danger. We can *do* this. I know we can. You two might not be the best players in the world, but I'll be right there with you. We can work together and give the real heroes a fighting chance. If we don't...we'll regret it for the rest of our lives."

I step forward and look directly at the General. "Count me in."

"Yeah," Allen nods. "Okay."

"I'm with you, too," Kimberly says, quoting Luke Skywalker on board the Home One war room. She flashes me a big smile and, instead of locking up, I smile right back.

"That's settled," I say to Hoop and the General. "Take us to the mechs."

• • •

The console to control the *Iron Warrior* robots is set up a lot like those guys that play drums for the marching band. There's a keyboard, joystick, mouse and screen all attached to our waist so it's always in front of us. The display is pretty nice, a 360 feed from the cameras installed on the robots. We're dressed more or less like Hoop, and each one of us has a pistol. Allen and I had to be briefed on how to fire it, but Kimberly seems comfortable around firearms. Enough that they gave her a rifle as well.

The robots themselves are pretty sorry compared to what's in the game. There are exposed wires all over a solid metal frame. Instead of legs like the mechs in the game, these have treads that make them look sort of like Johnny Five. They don't appear to be much beyond a sophisticated camera system with a large assortment of weapons welded on. The only thing remotely imposing or futuristic about them is their sheer size. Each one is easily ten feet tall.

Still, I'm not sure why someone else couldn't just control them, until I fire them up.

They handle *exactly* like a mech or Starfighter from *Iron Warrior*. Every bit as finicky. One of the main complaints about the game when it first released was that it took so much time to get accustomed to the squirrelly controls. Looking back, that must have just been a programmed reflection of how hard these robots were to control. It takes us several minutes just to get the trio of robots lined up in formation and rolling out of the camp.

My headset squawks with the sound of Kimberly's voice. "How do I cycle through the primary and secondary weapons again?"

"Center console. Press the yellow button to cycle forward. Orange to go back one."

"Thanks."

A sudden concussive blast sounds from one of the mechs as its flechette shotgun component booms.

"Sorry!" Allen says. "I thought I was pressing reload."

"No, it's fine," I say, adding with a smile, "no one get in front of Allen, though."

The three shoddiest pieces of high tech futurism I've ever seen roll forward through lush, green grasses. They're about one hundred and fifty feet in front of us, greater than the distance we were told to expect. On my monitor, I see the terrain go from verdant to barren, like crossing a line or flipping a switch.

"Okay," Hoop says to us. "This is the point where we typically start to lose communication with command. It only gets worse the further in we head."

"Some kind of jamming or interference?" Allen suggests.

"Maybe. As best as our visual spotters were able to ascertain, communications were only prevented from going out. The Rangers seemed to be able to speak with one another through their radios on the inside. We'll find out soon enough."

The screens flicker for a moment, but hold. As we step from the green grass to the baked and dead orange earth, I test out our headsets. "Kimberly, can you hear me?"

"Yep."

"Good," Hoop says. "Command this is Specialist Hooper. Do you copy?"

Static gives its lonely reply.

"Usually don't lose contact quite this fast."

"What do we do?" I ask.

"I suppose we must turn around," Allen says, "Oh well. 'Twas a valiant effort."

"Keep moving," Hoop says. "We may not be able to communicate with command, but out spotters will have eyes on us up to that gorge. They'll see us again if we come out by the cave. But that's still a long way. It's well past that lone tree ahead."

"If?" Kimberly asks.

No one bothers to reply.

From afar, we examine the solitary tree Hoop pointed out. It's healthy, with lush green leaves. Somehow it alone seems to have survived the harsh landscape surrounding it.

"Weird that it isn't dead," observes Kimberly.

"Life, uh, finds a way." I say into my microphone. I glance over and see her smiling to herself.

Boom! Boom! Boom! Boom! Boom!

We hear a distant sound, like a heavy drum beaten from deep kettles. The rhythmic noise causes a flock of crows to take to the air.

"What's that?"

"Happens every time someone comes in this far," Hoop says, sweeping the horizon with his rifle, looking through the scope for any visible danger.

"This...this is...*familiar.*" Allen says before maneuvering his mech toward the tree.

"Wrong way," Hoop says. "Bring that robot back around. Sooner we get them into the cave to retrieve Specialist Carino's body, the sooner we get back to safety."

"Why do you want to bring back the body so bad?" I ask.

Hoop sighs. "One, we don't leave anyone behind. Two, there's a hope that recovering one might give us some forensic clues about what we're up against. Watters! I said bring your robot back this way."

"No, just, just a minute." Allen insists. "Cody, these mechs have flame throwers, right?"

"Yeah. It should be your alternate weapons on the robot's left arm."

The booming continues as Allen's mech raises an arm and ignites a pilot light.

"Stop fooling around, Watters," Hoop says. "You burn up that tree and it could let whatever is hiding in the cave know we're coming."

"That's just it," Allen says into his headset. I can hear him swallow. "I think this tree already sounded the alarm."

"What is that—"

The spectacular whoosh of the mech's flame-thrower sounds and the tree is at once engulfed in fire.

"I was right!"

"The booming stopped," Kimberly says, maneuvering her mech toward Allen's.

I follow suit. "Allen, you mean the tree was making those booms?"

"*Feast of Goblyns.*"

"What's Feast of Goblins?" asks Hoop.

"The Ravenloft module?" I sort through the old dungeons and dragons adventure in my mind. The barren landscape, the tree warning of the adventurer's arrival. Oh my stars and garters. That would mean...

The ground around the burning tree opens up to reveal a dozen trap doors. Up from them spring twice that many hideous little creatures. They stand four feet high or so with pale green skin that seems slick with sweaty mucus. Their ears are sharp and pointed and their brows slope down into a rounded face, punctuated by a grotesque open nose, like a pig's snout cut off at the base. The beasts run toward us, baring teeth filed into needle-like points. They're holding nasty looking swords and spears.

"Open up on 'em!" I yell into my headset.

Our mechs send a barrage of machine gun fire into the goblin horde. Each burst sounds amazing, like Colonial Space Marines firing at the aliens on LV-426. The advancing goblins are cut to ribbons.

"My party would do well to have one of these on the next campaign," Allen calls into the headset.

"Keep firing until they're all dead!" shouts Kimberly.

We do just that. Soon the little monsters are nothing more than a pile of corpses.

"Nice work every one," Hoop says. "I'm going to go in close and snap a few photos to bring back with us."

"I'd advise against that," Allen says. "Never split up the party."

Allen is right, and our robots can do this for us. "The mechs have a screen capture ability. Kimberly, move yours in and take a few photos."

"On it."

The robot rolls to the pile and trains its optics on the dead creatures.

"So gross," says Kimberly. I look over and can see her stick out her tongue in disgust. I smile and then my heart nearly jumps out of my chest when she lets out a scream. I'm staring at her, she looks fine, though.

"What is it?"

"One of those...things just jumped onto my mech!"

I look away from her and at the scene of the carnage. One of the goblins wasn't down for the count. It's clambered up on top of the mech, hacking at it with an ax.

"Try throwing it off!" Hoop yells as he drops to a knee, attempting to place the creature within his crosshairs.

"I'm trying," Kimberly says, frustration clear in her voice. "I can't reach it! My monitor is starting to flicker."

The little beasty keeps hacking away as Allen and I maneuver our own mechs to try and knock it off.

"You're getting in the way of my shot!" Hoop yells.

We back off, but the damage is done. Kimberly's mech falls over with the goblin still hacking until its robotic head is severed. A moment later Hoop's rifle cracks, hitting the monster square in the chest and causing it to drop in a heap.

Kimberly unstraps her control station. "I guess...I guess that's it for me."

"Okay," Hoop says, his rifle at the ready. "Best to stick together. Go walk with Cody. That way we'll have an extra user ready if something happens to him. We're going through the canyon next and that's where the Rangers ran into trouble."

We move toward the opening of the canyon.

"So do I have to be the one to say it?" asks Allen over the headset.

"Say what?" says Hoop.

Allen clears his throat. "I don't know how or why, but so far, we're living inside a dungeons and dragons adventure."

"Don't be ridiculous."

"I'm not! That trap played out precisely as it does in an old adventure. And those creatures are indeed monsters, aye, right out of the very pages of the Monster Manual!"

"Allen's right," I say, scanning the tops of the canyons for any more of those creatures. "I remember playing it years ago. The tree thumps out warning to the goblins, who ambush the party."

"So what's next?" asks Kimberly. She has her rifle out and is walking by my side.

"If memory serves, this old dungeon master," Allen says, though he's not much older than me if I had to guess, "the goblins will attempt to ensnare us in a net as we pass through the canyon. Once captured, the vile creatures will leave us to die or kill us on the spot."

"I find it hard to believe that those took out as many of our guys as they have."

"Cunning and ferocity are their weapons, good sir," Allen says. "But we are now with the advantage."

"We know they'll try to surprise us," Kimberly says.

"Precisely."

Hoop grunts. "Okay, here's the plan, stop here."

We halt at the mouth of the canyon to hear what's next.

"We push the robots in as far as they can go to try and flush out the trap. Once they reveal themselves, we eliminate them and move to the cave."

"Got it."

The mechs roll slowly into the canyon shadows. It's easier to simply stand in place while the robots move forward. Before, I had to walk deliberately, not wanting to miss anything from the screen in front of me, but also looking out for tripping hazards. I feel focused, just like when I'm playing at the Mad Greek.

Hoop and Kimberly are scanning the surroundings, especially the top of the low canyons for more goblins. She looks like she's done this before. Note to self: ask about that plea bargain.

My screen shows early signs of a struggle. Lots of blood splattered on the canyon floor and walls. A few more crows fly away from a macabre meal as the mechs approach. "You seeing this Allen?"

"Yes, and I believe I'm going to be sick."

"What is it?" asks Hoop.

I notice that Kimberly is looking over my shoulder at the display. "Lots of blood and splatter, like a zombie FPS. And...some of the Rangers. They're all dead, caught up in nets."

"Okay," Hoop says, his voice not losing its professionalism or filling with emotion. "Push forward."

"Can't," I say, dropping my hands from the controls and rubbing my face. "Mine won't respond unless I walk closer. I'm at the end of my line."

"Such is the case for me as well," Allen says in his elvish manner of speaking.

Hoop curses and takes a few steps inside the box canyon. "All right. Let's head back. Knowing that the Rangers were attacked in here and—and I can't believe I'm saying this—listening to you guys predict what's going on makes me feel like it would be unsafe for you three to go any further."

"I think we can handle ourselves," Allen says.

I'm surprised to hear it, especially coming from him. But I'm in agreement. "Yeah, let's just ease our way in a little bit. We take a few steps, move the mechs to end of the tether and repeat as needed. If it gets too weird, we can back out. I mean, you saw how quickly we took care of that last encounter. These things can't withstand that sort of firepower once we have them in the open."

"If you're sure…"

"We're sure," Kimberly says. "Let's go."

We inch our way through the canyon. Taking a few steps and then rolling our mechs forward. All is deathly quiet. I can feel the perspiration running down my forehead to drip off my nose. I try to sniff it away to avoid it splashing on my controls. The sound is amplified by the narrow canyon walls.

"Is it possible we nailed them all back by the tree?"

"Let's hope so," Hoop says. "What do you see through the cameras?"

"The opening at the end of the canyon. I think we're going to make it through."

SCREEE!

The sudden scream causes us to jump. I turn my head to look back at the noise just as Hoop opens fire at one of the creatures emerging from some hidden crevice in the canyon walls. He fires again.

Pop! Pop! Pop!

More goblins pour out. There must be a couple of dozen already.

"Run!" Hoop yells, emptying his magazine and quickly loading a replacement as Kimberly fires into the crowds of slavering monsters. They let out a pig-like squeal and erupt in thick, black ichor as the bullets find their marks.

"I'm out!" Kimberly yells, tossing her rifle to the ground in disgust.

"I said, go!" repeats Hoop.

We take off at a sprint down the canyon, toward the mechs. I can see from my peripheral that Allen is already lagging behind. "Allen!" I shout, "If you can, get your mech to turn around so it can open fire on these little demons chasing us."

He's too winded to reply.

"What if some of those things are in front of us?" Kimberly asks.

"Shoot them with your pistol!" I say.

Both Allen and I have managed to make our mechs do an about face as we run past them. I can see from my monitor that Hoop is running backward while firing, attempting to keep the horde away from us as long as possible. The three members of Tier One Thousand rush past the towering mechs and rally at an open space just outside the canyon.

Still panting, we work our controls, firing precision weapons into the crowd, dropping one goblin at a time. The creatures are getting close to Hoop. One of them lunges forward from the crowd, leaping off of sinewy legs into the air with teeth and claws poised to rip open his throat.

Hoop drops him with a burst from his rifle.

"You need to get out of there!" I yell to Hoop. "Run past the mechs for all you're worth. We can wipe them out in one shot so long as they're bundled up in the canyon."

"Roger!" Hoop turns and sprints to our position.

"Allen, prime your rocket launcher. Right arm, alternate weapon."

"Done."

Hoop moves past the mechs, the horde of monsters rollicking malevolently behind him. "Fire!" I shout. A little bit too much like Captain Kirk giving the command to shoot Chang's Bird of Prey in Star Trek VI for the seriousness of the situation. But then, those scenes are sort of ingrained in my mind and pop up at the most inappropriate times.

Rockets whoosh, leaving a white smoke trail as they speed into the oncoming wave of beasts. The explosion is tremendous, enough to make me take a step back and feel like someone punched me in the chest and boxed my ears. Rocks, dirt, and goblin parts fly into the air. Without waiting for the smoke to clear, Allen and I send a hail of bullets from the twin miniguns down the canyon.

The smoke clears. Nothing is moving. There's no sound beyond our own heavy breathing.

"Oh my stars and garters," I say. "It's like 300. Look at all those bodies."

"Surely," Allen says between heaving breaths. "Surely we've killed them all."

"Okay," Kimberly says, relaxing her guard. "But there's still the cave behind us."

"She's right," Hoop says, beginning to turn around to face the mouth of the cave. We were so focused on what was chasing us that I guess I hadn't thought about where we were heading. "We need eyes on that—Aaah!"

Hoops bicep is impaled by a massive spear. The point seems to enter his ribs or Kevlar, pinning his arm to his body as he drops to the ground. We all turn to find another one of those beasts hissing at us from the cave's entrance. This one is taller, easily seven feet. Its skin is less green and more of a yellow hue, still slick with that musky mucus that gives it an oily sheen. The creature squats down low, its legs spread apart and growls, spittle dripping down from sharp teeth.

Its claws are black, knife blades protruding from thin, bony fingers. On its head is a golden crown set with green gemstones.

It takes a menacing step toward us with a speed that tells me we're just playthings. It could easily streak across the ground and attack. This...monster king...looks fast.

I realize that the three of us are directly between this terrifying monster and the two remaining mechs capable of taking it down. We can't run to the other side and repeat our last trick.

We're dead.

"Any ideas, Cody?" Allen asks. "Because I don't remember this part from the module."

I open my mouth to speak, but the only thing my mind seems to supply is Billy Crystal's joke, "You are the brute squad," from *The Princess Bride*.

See? Inappropriate.

The monster's mouth curls into a wicked grin as it drops to its haunches, placing its hands in front of it like a four-legged beast ready to run and pounce. It lets out a piercing shriek and charges, easily covering ten feet in each stride. Before I blink it's almost on us, jumping in the air.

In a fluid motion, Kimberly draws her sidearm and leans forward.

BANG!

She fires a single shot that strikes the beast squarely between the eyes. Its body goes instantly limp, crashing down in a sickening thud just inches in front of her. The crown on its head rolls away before coming to a stop like a spinning quarter on the coffee table.

"Holy—" I begin to say.

"My Dad taught me to shoot. We robbed banks when I was a teenager. I didn't know any better. Hence the plea bargain..."

"Holy—" I begin to say again.

"Point of order," Allen says, his hand in the air. "Nobody should touch that crown, because...enchantments."

Hoop grunts in pain.

"Hoop!" I run to his side, there's blood pooling from his wound. I have no idea what to do.

Kimberly gently moves me aside. "Here, let me."

She begins to look at the wound when Hoop pulls himself up to a half-seated position. "I'll be okay. The danger..."

"I believe that was the boss, as it were," Allen says matter-of-factly.

"Specialist Hooper, do you copy?"

As if confirming Allen's words, we receive the incoming transmission from the General.

"I repeat, Specialist Hooper, what's your status? Do you copy?"

Hoop grunts in pain again. "Uggh. Answer that, Cody. I'm in no condition to talk right now. Can barely breathe from the pain."

I nod and speak into the headset, "Uh, this is... uh, Cody. Cody Stone. I think...I think we did it. We can hear you loud and clear."

"I can hear you too, son. And I'm happy at that. Stay put. We're going to see if---yes—the drone we have circling the perimeter can fly right through. Whatever the four of you did, it's opened up the airspace around you."

I droop my head to the elated shouts of Allen and Kimberly. I'm all smiles.

"Tell him it was a goblin sorcerer," Allen says, his face beet red and full of excitement. "I bet that's what caused the disruption. Oh, and tell him about the tree! And the crown!"

I smile, but don't relay the message.

Moments later the sky overhead fills with helicopters. They touch down and offload more Tier One guys who immediately begin to secure the perimeter. Two of them make their way towards us.

"Corpsman!" one yells, and another man is by our side, relieving Kimberly of her attempt to care for Hoop's injuries.

She walks over to me, her hands bloody, but a smile on her face. I smile and say, "I'm glad we all made it. And I'm glad to have met you."

We're close together. One of the helicopters has a bearded operator beckoning for us to run over and get on board. Allen waddles quickly over and jumps inside, but Kimberly stops me from following. She gives me a quick kiss and smiles at me.

"What was that for?"

"A kiss for luck," she says, the dimples in her smile making me feel like I might faint. "I thought of doing it earlier right before we ran from the monsters in the canyon. It didn't seem very appropriate then, but it does now."

"Yeah, it does," I say as we begin walking toward the evacuation helicopter. I quell the joke trying to get out about hoping she's not my long lost sister. It doesn't seem appropriate.

ABOUT THE AUTHOR

JASON ANSPACH WRITES old movies. He grew up watching the Hollywood classics of the silver screen and works that bygone charm and humor into his books.

Together with his wife and their six children, and their border collie Charlotte, Jason resides in a hundred year old Craftsman home in a blue collar city nestled in the Pacific Northwest. The house is very drafty, but a family that large has a way of keeping you warm.

Consider becoming an email pal by signing up here: bit.ly/anspach-news

facebook.com/authorjasonanspach
twitter.com/jonspach

LOW DESERT, HIGH MOUNTAIN, BIG LIZARD

M.G. HERRON

A COUPLE DAYS after the cool autumn sank its toes into the sand, I packed a lunch and rode the bike that Leyla fixed for me west into the desert. I would have preferred to walk, but where I wanted to go couldn't be reached on foot in a day.

The full water skin slung over my shoulder slapped against my leg as I pedaled across the cracked pavement of the aging highway that cut through the desert. It wasn't until the sun was straight overhead, beaming down on the old white t-shirt I'd draped along my neck and shoulders—a makeshift keffiyeh to protect my fair, freckled skin—that the dilapidated auto repair shop came into sight.

The standalone building was half-buried in a sand dune. When I'd first found it, it was fully buried, and only the odd square shape of the awning extending out from the roof indicated that there was anything other than more sand underneath. I had marked the place on my mental map, and waited until the winds shifted with the seasons to unearth it again before returning.

I set the bike aside and inched down the hill of sand, carefully prodding with my foot for soft spots indicating there was a treacherous pocket of air waiting for the slightest motion to be filled by the sand above. More than one of our scavengers had been buried alive that way. Not wishing to add to those statistics, I moved slowly, carefully, forward.

But I found no soft spots, and my boots came down on solid ground. I seemed to be standing on the building's cement foundation, which extended to what must have been a parking lot. Next to me, the dusty glass windows in the garage doors were still intact—a minor miracle in itself. I used my sleeve to wipe away some of the grime then peered through the glass.

I expected the inside to be a mess, and inhaled sharply when the reality proved different. Almost every old building I'd found had been left a mess—no surprise, if you believed the stories that the aliens had colonized Earth in a day. No time to prepare or set your house to rights. Just grab what you can and run run run.

But this place was as orderly as you please. A pile of sand had spilled in through a single broken window, but otherwise the floors were bare. Tool chests were lined up neatly against the wall, and a gas motor Chevrolet was raised a few feet off the floor in one of the bays, where it had surely been waiting years for a service that never came.

Maybe the invaders came on a holiday, when the mechanics were at home with their families. That would explain a lot.

In any case, I pulled my head back and looked around for a way in. I could break this window, but that felt wrong. I wanted to avoid doing damage if possible.

I was pushing sand aside in search of a front door when a deep lowing, barking sound—three sharp gruffs followed by a long guttural moan—drifted into my hearing.

I froze. My blood went as cold as the desert at night. No Earth creatures big enough to make that sound lived in this desert any more. The noise could only belong to one beast.

My scattershot plan of breaking into the garage and raiding it for spare parts scampered back into the recesses of my mind. I would probably be safe inside, but if I made any noise breaking a window or jimmying a door, there was too great a risk that it would bring the creature to investigate.

"Blasphemous damn!" I whispered under my breath. *That long trip for nothing!*

I marked the position of my bike where it lay in the sand. I would have to scramble quickly up the hill the way I'd slid down to get to it, running the risk of caving in a soft spot.

Or I could stay here and wait it out.

To hell with that! Better to be mobile than trapped in a half-buried auto repair shop. I opted for the bike, scrambling with hands and feet up the steep dune. Halfway up, my foot slipped and my leg plunged in up to my thigh. I flattened my body against the sand, spreading my weight so that I didn't deepen the hole. Sand filtered into my half-open mouth, but I managed to maintain my presence of mind, carefully extracting my leg from the soft spot. I scrabbled forward until, finally, I heaved my body up on the top next to my bike.

I spat sand as I lifted the bike onto its two chunky wheels, and turned it back east, toward town, the way I had come. I was just throwing my leg over the saddle when the lowing moan came again.

I don't know what madness came over me in that moment. Somehow, the sound the beast made seemed to be filled with the deepest kind of existential despair.

Judging that the sound still came from a great distance, several hundred yards off at least, I gingerly set the bike back down and crept to the dune's edge.

It just so happened that beyond this bank of dunes, the desert swept down into a low, flat, cracked-earth plain roughly five miles across. It was littered with boulders and sparse grass, and the occasional low shrub or prickly cactus. On the far end, the land rose sharply into a mountain range.

And there, about half a mile from where I crouched, the creature stood, alone.

The basilisk.

At least, that's what I had learned to call the massive, lizard-cows the aliens had left behind.

This one was huge. It must have weighed two or three tons. Its dry, scaly body tapered down to a long, whip-like tail. Its massive head hung low, and a hood like you'd see on a cobra pressed down against its neck. According to local legend—I had never seen one in the flesh before—when they were angered their hoods flared up.

That's how you knew you were a goner.

The basilisk pawed at a small boulder with its two front claws, and again made that horribly sad lowing sound that ended on a cracked, plaintive note as it dropped its head.

When its head raised up once more, the small boulder went flying through air. The rock bounced off the ground once, and then the creature charged, its huge mass barreling across the desert at a speed that should have been impossible for its bulk, making the gruff barks I'd heard before in excitement as it chased the boulder like a toy ball.

I shook my head. *The thing's lost its blinking mind!*

It was a shame that I hadn't been able to scavenge any useful parts on this journey, but I wasn't about to go back for a second try with a loopy basilisk within sniffing distance of me.

I crept away from the edge of the dune, righted my bicycle once more, and pedaled madly home to warn the others.

. . .

After I put some distance between myself and the basilisk, I ate the green apple, brown bread, and goat cheese I had packed, steering the bike with no hands like my father had taught me.

The sun cast my shadow long ahead of me by the time I reached town. I always knew I was close to home by the sharp diamond glint of the sun reflecting off the vast circular array of metallic reflectors. In the Beforetimes, so the stories went, the out-of-order solar thermal plant provided power to the coastal cities. Now, it was no good for power since it was hard-wired to a dead grid.

Getting the plant working again had been Leyla's pet project ever since we managed to match enough power tools to the proper battery packs to make it feasible.

But it was no small job. I helped her when I wasn't hunting small game or scavenging for spare parts.

Still, the survivors didn't choose to establish the town here for the power plant, but rather for the functioning wells that allowed us to pull clean water from an aquifer deep underground. Whoever built this plant also had to survive out here, and apparently intended for it to be a long-term situation. That didn't work out for them, but it had been a boon for us.

Some said the aliens had their own power sources and therefore no interest in a remote solar thermal plant on the edge of the desert. I still wonder why they left this place more or less untouched. It's likely I'll never know.

During a winter solstice festival, when the adults were deep in their cups of mulled wine, Kamar, the elder, once told me that the invaders killed with weapons of light, and that was why the basilisk and other creatures steered clear of our town.

Needless to say, seeing that diamond glint in the distance was like reaching safe harbor in a stormy sea. My desert oasis—home. My shoulders fell away from my ears and I pedaled a little faster.

The town itself consisted of about two hundred and fifty small houses packed close together. A massive A-shaped building towered over the other buildings at the center. We called it the town hall, but really it was just a cement foundation covered by a slanting roof that extended down so it nearly touched the ground on both sides. It kept you out of the sun, but allowed the air to move through and keep the place cool.

I guided the bike through the dusty streets toward the town hall, taking the most direct path between the small buildings. It was as I suspected—several hundred people were crowded in under the roof.

During the day, the town hall doubled as a school for the children. But now it was night time and the first Friday besides, which meant the weekly town hall meeting was taking place.

Nearly the whole population was gathered around with their children—every man, woman, and child I had ever known under one roof.

A tall woman of middle-age stood at one end, on a slightly raised platform. She had brunette hair, greying ever so slightly at the temples, wore practical pants and a coarse homespun shirt, and spoke to the assembled crowd with a voice that carried. I set my bike against one of the tall beams and waded into the crowd until I was near enough to catch her eye.

"—baseball game tomorrow, and next week we'll be celebrating George Carson's 50th birthday. I also want to share that Marlene has been promoted to head shepherd, so that Elisa can spend more time developing her goat cheese business. If you or your kids would like to learn a new trade, Elisa is taking volunteers. Just go talk to her or—"

The woman glanced at me, and frowned. I pursed my lips and waited patiently.

"Talk to Elisa, or come see me," she finished. "As usual I'll handle all reassignments personally. Does anyone have any questions? Okay then. I know you're all eager to let loose. Let's get the fires going. Have fun!" The murmur of conversations spread through the crowd until they were all talking amongst themselves. But some of the grownups near me must have seen the look on my face, for they put their arms around their spouses' or children's shoulders and led them away. The brunette woman weaved through the crowd and came to a stop in front of me. She was a foot shorter, but had the same fair freckled skin as I did.

"What is it, Das? What happened?"

"I saw a basilisk in the lowlands."

She drew a soft, sharp breath in through her mouth then let it out slowly. Her arm went around my shoulder, and she squeezed me to her body. It had been many years since I'd thought of myself as a kid, a development of necessity rather than maturity—the desert was unforgiving. After it took my father, I promised it would never take me.

But it was still nice to know my mom cared. "I'm glad you're okay, kiddo," she said. "Now, tell me what you saw."

• • •

Half an hour later, the Council of Elders had gathered in the kitchen of the bungalow I shared with my mother. Meanwhile, the rest of the town ate potluck around two blazing bonfires at the edge of town. The distant flames flickered through the window.

"Meredith," Tommy Martin said, scowling at my mom, "this is really gonna put a damper on the festivities."

Tommy was older than me, but still young—closer to my age than my mother's. Everybody liked him, and he was a good hunter, but he'd only been elected to the council recently and was by far its youngest member.

"Security is our paramount concern," Meredith said. "Not whether or not we're going to ruin the party."

The older members of the council nodded.

"And they have a right to know," said Tabitha, a white-haired old woman with deeply tanned wrinkles in her forehead. She wrapped her fingers over the top of her gnarled wooden cane.

"Basilisk steer clear of town," Tommy insisted. "Everyone knows that. They don't like the solar plant, or the noise, or the fires. They keep their distance."

"Why don't we ask Das?" Tabitha suggested.

All heads swiveled to look at me. "Ask me what?" I said stupidly then clamped my mouth shut.

"What was your impression of this basilisk?" Tabitha asked.

"Yeah," Tommy said. "Was it acting aggressively?"

"I don't know what's normal," I admitted. "This is the first time I ever saw one."

"It is unusual," muttered the quiet Councilman Benji, a doctor.

"It's okay," my mother said. "Just give us your best first impression."

I thought back to that morning. I had been so startled by its presence that the only thought in my mind had been to get home, fast. But there had been something else there, too, and it came back to me now.

"Well, it was alone," I said. "I guess it came down because it got too cold in the mountains. It also seemed...well, this sounds silly, but it seemed really bored."

"Bored, how?"

"It was throwing and chasing rocks in the desert all by itself. Like it just wanted to be entertained."

"Like a pup with a ball," Tommy said, glancing around at the others and spreading his arms in a wide shrug. "See? Harmless."

"Wait," I said, bringing their attention back to me. "There was something else. It was barking at the stones as it chased them, but then it would stop and make this deep, lowing sound, like a lost goat. Only... deeper, and more painful. If it were a person I would have said it was heartbroken. I guess the thing was just really sad. I don't know why though."

Tommy snorted. "Sad?"

It didn't make much sense to me, but old Tabitha and Benji had been nodding along as I spoke.

Benji licked his lips. "Does anyone else remember what the aliens used the basilisk for?"

My mother nodded, and a few others just looked at Benji. Tommy and I both shook our heads.

"The invaders brought entire herds of the creatures to Earth with them," Benji said. "Thousands used to roam the deserts and forests like cattle." His eyes darkened. "But they're carnivores."

"And?" Tommy said, clearly impatient. He kept glancing out the small window at the bonfires.

"And, *boy*," Benji said, looking down his nose at Tommy, "that means that the basilisk, for all his lizard appearance, is actually a herd animal. Is it really any wonder that the creature sounded sad? The aliens took the rest of the herd with them when they left, but a few got left behind. I thought they were all dead. This one survived on its own for years. It's probably lonely."

Tommy sighed. "Now I've heard it all."

"Regardless," Meredith said. "I can't in good conscience keep people in the dark. We don't need to make a big fuss about it, but we have to tell them. Tommy, you inform the watchmen. Tabitha, can you talk to the shepherds? I'll go to the parent-teacher association and make sure they're following proper safety procedures tomorrow for classes, and then set watches for tonight. That should cover the bases."

The meeting ended, and we filed out the front door. I walked toward the bonfire, searching the crowds for Leyla. I was within fifty yards of the closest bonfire when a sad moan cut through the noise of the festivities.

A shiver crawled up my spine. I glanced around in the darkness, but couldn't see it. I didn't need to see it to know what it was.

I began to run toward the fire. "Get back!" I shouted ahead of me, waving my arms at the people in small groups near the flames. "Basilisk! It's a basilisk!"

They glanced at me, eyes wide—that startled deer look. A few of them stepped slowly back, but none fast enough for my liking.

I felt a vibration in the ground through the soles of my boots, and then the basilisk burst into the circle of light cast by the fire. He lowered his giant lizard head and bowled into the blazing bonfire. His head snapped up, snuffing the light while simultaneously tossing red coals and flaming logs high into the air.

People screamed and scattered, shielding their heads with their arms and frantically brushing at their clothing as the coals came down.

The basilisk swung its massive body around. I dug my heels in and came skidding to a stop. Coals and logs sparked as they rebounded off the ground between us. The creature opened its mouth and let out a deep growl of warning. Saliva dripped from a triple row of sharp teeth. Its eyes, like deep black marbles with no pupil at their center, fixated on me. I scrabbled backward, but found myself unable to look away. And then the hood around its neck flared up into the most beautiful pattern—a set of concentric rings of bright orange and indigo.

My heart hit the ground like one of those red hot coals.

I was a goner, and there was nothing I could do to stop it.

Death's marble-black eyes blinked open from the center, revealing indigo pupils, from which an orange stamen extended like the vulnerable bud of a flower.

Something hard knocked into me from my side. I hit the ground and the breath was expelled forcefully from my lungs. Someone was on top of me, but it was dark so I couldn't see who it was. A clear liquid hissed against the sand just slightly in front of where I lay.

At the same time, several booming explosions rang out—gunshots, I realized. Another moan came from the basilisk, but this time the sadness had been replaced with fear.

The basilisk turned, his clawed feet scraping across the sand as he scrabbled to gain speed. Like a dark cloud, the beast thundered off into the desert night.

"Das!" someone yelled.

"Das, are you okay?" asked another voice I couldn't place.

My breath finally came back in a gasping rush. I pulled in a great lungful of dry desert air, and not a little bit of sand. I worked the sand out of my gums with my tongue, and spit on the ground. Then I pushed myself back to my knees.

I looked up into Leyla's face—her strawberry blonde bangs hung in her eyes like they always did, and her forehead was slightly dimpled above her fine, dark brows.

"You saved me," I said.

She jerked her head toward the commotion behind the scattered fire logs. "No, it was Tommy."

I looked in the direction she indicated. Tommy was already organizing the shocked bystanders into a hunting party to trail the basilisk, his large black Colt .45 pistol in one hand. I wanted to go with them, but then my mom fell to her knees next to me, carrying the Browning BAR .30-06 rifle that belonged to my father in her arms.

"Mom, I'm fine."

Ignoring me, she began to examine my face with her hands.

"Mom, stop. Stop! I'm okay." I pushed her gently away.

After a cursory examination of the rest of my clothes, she said, "Oh, thank God," pulling me hard against her chest at the same time. "Thank God. I thought it got you with the venom."

"Is *that* what that was?" I pointed to the wet spot in the sand a few feet away, where the clear liquid had fallen. It had been fused into an uneven splotch of blackened tar. "What would have happened if it hit me?"

She licked her lips.

"Mom."

"Burn your eyes out. Paralyze you. Make your tongue slow. Slow your heartbeat in your chest until it stopped altogether."

"I see." A slow tremor started in my hand and spread through my whole body. I shook uncontrollably, and it wasn't from the cold. I swallowed against the sudden dryness in my throat.

"Why do you think your father started calling those things basilisks?" Leyla said.

"My father?" I asked.

"Hey, you're shivering," my mom said. "You're cold? Come on, let's get you inside."

• • •

A soft rapping sounded on the thin glass of the window, but it didn't startle me. My eyes had been wide open most of the night, and I had seen Leyla's blonde hair swaying through the window before she knocked, her figure backlit by the wan light of dawn.

I sat up and held out one solitary pointer finger toward the window, then yanked pants on as I stood in the dark. I pulled on my boots and laced them up tight, slid a t-shirt over my head followed by a thick, long-sleeved hunting shirt I had sewn myself. Lastly, I stuffed my keffiyeh into a pocket as I tiptoed out of the house.

As I walked past my mother's bedroom, I stopped—her door was wide open, her bed rumpled but empty. I hadn't heard her leave, so I guessed she must have snuck out during one of my infrequent fits of sleep.

"Finally!" Leyla said as I closed the door. "Come on." She grabbed my wrist and pulled me into a jog.

"Wait a second," I said. "Where are we—"

My question was cut short as the town hall came into sight. At the far end, Tommy paced. Before him was a small gathering of about a dozen people—men and women I had known my whole life and recognized as hunters or friends of Tommy's. They cradled rifles in their arms, and were dressed as I was, practically covered from head to toe, layered against the morning frost.

I would have assumed it was a hunting party if it weren't for the events of the previous night—and the tone of Tommy's voice.

"That beast is out of control!" Tommy bellowed. "Mad. The fact that he would attack in the middle of the night, unprovoked, proves it. It's our duty as protectors of this town to track it down, and eliminate the threat."

My mother was standing there with them, but slightly apart from the others. "It's too dangerous," she said. "And it goes against the security procedures we all established *and* agreed upon. The smarter thing to do is to set watches, as we have done. And *if* it comes back, we deal with it on our own terms at that point."

"Set watches? Wait until it decides to attack again?" Tommy turned to his rapt audience. "Do *you* want to live in fear until a mad basilisk comes back?"

A resounding, "No!" echoed up into the vaulted ceiling. Leyla and I had crept in from the side, walking casually so that we didn't draw undue attention.

But my mother noticed us immediately. When she saw us, her frown deepened, and she looked very old all of a sudden.

This shook me. You have to understand, in my eyes my mother was always the brave, young, and beautiful woman who raised me in secret while the alien overlords ravaged our planet.

But looking now, in the thin light, I saw bags under her eyes. The grey hair at her temples stretched its silver fingers up into a thinning mane of hair. I'd never thought of her as old before that moment.

But she was still strong. Meredith crossed her arms, and gave Tommy a look that would have cut most men down. I actually felt sorry for Tommy. That smoldering look had withered better men than him. Memories of my father danced in my eyes—my father, whose strength was a match for my mother's.

But Tommy held his ground. He jutted his chin out and turned back to the crowd. "We tracked it last night after the attack—the basilisk headed west, out toward the lowlands. The plan is to catch it in the open, and gun it down from a distance."

Shouts of "Kill the beast!" and "Let's go!" and even one "Giddyup!" rose from the party of angry hunters as they moved away. I moved to follow.

"Das, wait," my mother said.

I ignored her.

"Where do you think you're going, young man?" she demanded. I looked back. She directed her famous piercing gaze on me.

It still made me shrink up inside. How could it not? But I shoved that feeling away. Taking a deep breath, I went to her.

"I have to go," I said. "The basilisk followed *me* back to town. It's my fault people got hurt."

"You couldn't have known. It's—"

"Mom," I said. The hunting party was already twenty yards away now, heading toward the garage where we kept the old jeeps that ran on actual gas. The vehicles were only used for emergencies—but as a member of the council, Tommy had access to them. It showed how deadly serious he was about this.

"Mom, I'm not a child anymore," I said. "I haven't been since dad died. I'm going."

Tears sprang into her eyes. She blinked them back. "Be careful," she said.

"I will. I promise."

"You sound just like your father."

I stood up a little straighter. "Did Dad really name the basilisk?"

She nodded. "He did. He thought they were just misunderstood." A long moment passed where neither of us spoke. "I miss him," she said at last.

"Me, too," I said, even as I felt my resolve harden.

She sighed. "Take the Browning with you. You know where I keep the extra bullets?"

I nodded.

"Remember what your father taught you. Shoot from cover. Don't forget to breathe. And Das. Be careful."

"I know, Mom." I glanced at the hunting party. They had nearly disappeared around the side of the garage. The doors were on the other side.

"I'm going with you," Leyla said. She had been standing off to one side during the conversation with my mom, fidgeting.

"What?" I asked, surprised. "Do you even know how to shoot?"

She glared at me. "As one of only three capable mechanics in this town, those jeeps are my responsibility. Besides, what if one breaks down? Would *you* know how to fix it?"

I opened my mouth then closed it again. It seemed at times that my whole life had been oriented around learning how to take care of myself in the desert—my instincts had been right about the basilisk, had kept me alive, even if the creature had surprised us all by attacking the town. I trusted Leyla. So, I realized, I should trust her instincts too.

I nodded. "Good point."

"Get your gun," she said. "I'll make sure they wait until you're ready."

After one last glance at my mother's worry-lined face, I turned and ran back to the house to get the rifle and the other supplies I needed.

• • •

By the time I got to the garage, the three Jeep Wranglers were nothing but a dust cloud in the distance.

"That son of a bitch," I muttered under my breath.

But one of the garage doors was still open, and the growling of an engine sounded from the dark inside. A second later, Leyla rolled out, seated at the wheel of a low-riding silver two-seater truck we used to shuttle supplies back and forth to the solar thermal plant. The flat bed in back was covered by a bulging tarp crisscrossed by bungee cords.

"Get in!" she said.

Before I even had the door closed, Leyla floored the pedal. The wheels spun, my door snapped shut, and the truck lurched into motion. She directed us away from the city, and we soon rolled across the desert after the dust cloud.

"Tommy is such a prick sometimes," I muttered as I wedged my feet down between a kerosene lamp and a large canister of spare fuel. "Last night he didn't want to tell anyone about the basilisk because he thought it would ruin the *party*. And now look at him!"

"He can be a jerk, but he wants to do the right thing," Leyla said.

"I know," I said. I spoke louder now. As we picked up speed, the wind whipped through the rectangular cab of the truck. The windows had been taken out years ago. "That's the problem. I happen to agree with him in this case, but I wish he wouldn't act so goddamn smug. No one knew the basilisk would attack."

"It's not your fault," Leyla said. "Basilisk *never* come near town. We all thought that until last night."

"I could have been more careful," I said bitterly. "I should have known better."

"Oh yeah? 'Cause you're an alien behavioral psychologist now?"

I scowled at her. "You know what I mean."

She gave me a sidelong look, then returned her gaze to the open desert which began to lower from the rocky plateau on which our town was situated.

I turned my attention to the desert floor. I had keen eyes from my time as a scavenger, plus my father taught me to catch desert rabbits at a young age. It wasn't hard to follow the basilisk's tracks, even though the wind or the passing of the jeeps ahead of us had covered them partially with sand. The basilisk was a heavy creature, and it left shallow depressions and distinctive three-toed claw marks where its back feet dug into the desert floor. A distinctive swirling pattern marked the trail every twenty yards or so, probably from where its long tail brushed against the sand in a sine pattern as it ran.

After nearly an hour, we caught up with the others near the auto repair shop. The tracks led back into the low plains on which I'd first spotted the basilisk, not a hundred yards from the dune where the auto repair shop was located.

No surprise, I thought grimly. But at least I already had the lay of the land.

Tommy came to a stop, then motioned with his hand out the window. The jeep in front of us pulled up on Tommy's left, and Leyla guided the silver truck up on the right so we all looked out over the lowlands in a row. I counted five people in each of the two jeeps, with two rifles for each of them. Counting Leyla and me, that made twelve hunters and twice as many guns for one basilisk.

I hoped it was enough.

Tommy pointed. "Look."

I followed his gaze down the slope of the ground. The basilisk's trail led in a meandering curve across the cracked floodplain, toward the foothills where the mountains stabbed up into the sky. Winter had just begun, so only the tallest mountain had patches of snow leftover from the year before.

"It's probably too close to winter for it to head for high ground," I said.

"It's too cold up there now for that cold-blooded lizard," Tommy said without a glance in my direction.

I rolled my eyes with a sideways look at Leyla. She made a placating gesture near the gear shift.

"There!" Tommy said. "You see it? Time to move!"

Well I'll be damned. I leaned forward. Tommy had spotted the basilisk—a tiny dark speck wiggling against the horizon—before I did.

"Let's go, let's go, let's go!" Tommy cried, spinning one finger in the air.

Our truck went last, barreling down the slope and rocketing onto the dry floodplain with a bumpy jolt. Leyla opened the throttle in the direction we had seen the basilisk, and shifted into fourth, then fifth gear, drawing abreast of Tommy's jeep after a minute. I lifted the 'aught six so the long barrel pointed out the open window. The hinged floor plate clicked open smoothly, and I checked the magazine of the autoloader one final time. Then I rested my forearm on the window to steady my aim, slid back the bolt with a satisfying click, and lay my trigger finger along the barrel, waiting.

We covered ground at seventy miles an hour. A mantle of dust rose into the air behind us. If the basilisk hadn't noticed us before, he certainly would now. I kept my eyes open, but at such a low angle I didn't spot the beast yet. I began to worry that he'd disappeared, or that he could run faster than we imagined he could. What if he got to tree cover in the foothills before we could catch him?

But after we covered about three miles, I spotted a wriggling speck moving toward the mountains.

The beast was remarkable. Its whole body undulated as it galloped in a great leaping gait. The orange and indigo hood was partially extended, and its colors shone richly in the sunlight when it twisted his head back at an unnatural angle to mark us.

Leyla pulled out wider and floored the pedal. I gestured out with my left hand, signaling for her to get wider. The sun was at our backs now, so my sight was clear. We drew abreast of him.

The basilisk made a sharp right turn and redirected with an agility that seemed to defy the physics of his large mass. Tommy slammed on the brakes. His jeep skidded thirty yards in the wrong direction, fishtailing as he arced out.

Leyla, however, had faster reflexes, and the truck had a lower center of gravity. She braked into a smoother curve that still lost us fifty yards on the beast. The third jeep followed Leyla's lead, but slammed on its brakes and also fell behind.

The basilisk bounded ahead, running with a re-newed urgency toward the hills—sparsely wooded, but with ample cover and rocky ground we wouldn't be able to pursue it through.

"It was holding back until we caught up!" I shout-ed. A chuckle escaped me despite the obvious dangers. "That clever bastard!"

As Leyla accelerated out of the turn, I took care-ful aim. We gained some of the lost ground in anoth-er long minute. I'd never taken a shot from a moving vehicle before, and the barrel of the heavy rifle wan-dered like a drunk townie.

"It's too bumpy!" I shouted.

"Not much I can do about that," Leyla yelled back. "That thing moves wicked fast!"

"Try to get closer!"

She gave me a hesitant glance, but kept the truck on course. I glanced over my shoulder and saw Tommy, grim-faced and determined, through the dust-coated windshield, catching up to us. He swung out to the right, on the opposite side, and two of the hunters in the back stood bracing their weapons against the roll bars that framed the vehicle.

A dozen shots rattled off in quick succession—*tuktuktuktuktuk*.

Unlike the autoloading rifle I held, Tommy's guys had apparently brought the full automatics they raided from a long-range scavenger trip to the coast last year.

A row of dust motes splashed up, one where each bullet ricocheted off the sand. The line of fire drew near the basilisk as the shooter adjusted his wild aim. Finally, a few rounds hit their mark.

At least one bullet glanced right off the basilisk's thick hide. It was the damnedest thing—I couldn't help but gape and let my finger slide off the trigger of my own rifle. The creature didn't even slow down. It leaped onto a weed-grown upward slope, and scrabbled rapidly up, climbing toward a copse of trees.

Leyla slowed the vehicle. Determined to get a shot in, I did my best to steady the rifle so I could get a bead on the basilisk. When I remembered to breath, my wavering sight steadied and the lizard came into focus—a big, scaly dark torso. I tracked up, slightly ahead of his snout, and squeezed off a shot. The butt of the rifle kicked back into my shoulder, but my aim was true. The bullet struck home in the basilisk's bulging back leg muscle.

The creature seemed to hesitate, but that could have been a slip of its claw on the next boulder. It still managed to scamper easily up and over a scree-covered slope, and slither out of sight.

Without a word, Tommy gunned the jeep up the rocky hill in low gear. Leyla followed him, more cautiously, watching the clearance under the truck. After a hundred yards we were all forced to a halt because of the uneven rocky ground.

"It's wounded," Tommy announced, jumping over the door of the jeep without bothering to open it, and then reaching back in for a sawed off shotgun I didn't notice until now. "Let's finish the job."

"Did you see what just happened?" I said. "Those bullets bounced right off him!"

"Yours hit the mark."

"And then he ran off like it didn't even hurt."

"Trust me. It can be killed. Just 'cause we haven't seen one in a few years doesn't mean we should just let this one get away—for all I know, it'll come right back tomorrow, angrier than ever."

"So what's the plan? We didn't catch it in the open. How are you going to take care of it now?"

Tommy sniffed. "Why don't you stay in the car and let the real men handle it?"

He set off up the slope without a backward look. Most of the others—all older, all more experienced hunters than I was—didn't even look at me. The ones that did gave me expressions filled with such scorn that I felt the guilt wash over my body like a cold bath.

I turned back toward Leyla, who stood by the open door of the jeep. "You don't—" she began.

I held up my hand, silencing her. After a deep breath, I turned, and trudged after Tommy.

• • •

I tiptoed up the scree slope as the sun glared high overhead. My arms ached carrying the rifle. Setting traps for rabbits is a lot different than carrying a Browning rifle up a mountain.

Not to mention I twitched at each snapping twig, and my heart stopped when it heard an unseen rumble of rock.

Tommy walked at the head of the party. I took up the rear, with the others strung out between us in single file. I worked my dry mouth, and silently berated myself for forgetting my water in the truck.

We moved up the switchbacking trail at a steady pace. I glanced back every few steps, searching the trail behind me for the basilisk, remembering how fast it had scurried up the mountain after I shot it, and thinking that it could have circled back by now.

We passed through a wooded area and then out along a thin game trail bordered by a sheer rock wall on one side and a falling slope on the other.

I looked down, and immediately regretted it.

"Eyes ahead, Das," the man ahead of me whispered back. His name was Charlie Timberant. He was a grizzled hunter in his late thirties. Right about now I envied how he had no trouble keeping his breathing steady and slow despite the exertion. He held the AK-47 in his big, scarred hands like it was a toy.

We were looking at each other when a pebble bounced down the cliff face. It rebounded off the dirt trail between us and we both glanced up.

The veteran hunter had the presence of mind to raise his rifle as he turned. I fumbled with mine, and squinted as I looked straight up into the sun itself, and then inhaled sharply as a horrible scream cut through the air.

It came from Charlie—he bent over, clawing at his eyes with his fingers and leaving bloody scratch marks on his cheeks. Then, with a swiftness I will never forget, his movements slowed and stopped completely, fingers still clutching at his eyeballs.

I was already taking rapid steps backward, but I froze as a dark shadow crossed in front of the sun and then plummeted down out the sky. The basilisk's massive body crashed into the trail, breaking it asunder and sending massive chunks of dirt and stone down the steep slope as it snapped Charlie up in its jaws.

All rational thought fled my mind as I turned and bounded down the mountain, stumbling as I struggled to keep my feet under my body on the switch-backing trail.

• • •

Back at the trucks, I explained to Leyla what had transpired between labored breaths.

"Jesus," Leyla said, her hand going to her mouth. "Charlie's dead?"

I nodded and sucked in yet another painful lung-ful of air.

The other hunters trickled back to our loca-tion—first one, then a pair, and finally the rest of the group led by Tommy.

Tommy said nothing. He braced his arms on the hood of the nearest jeep. His face was pale, and after a few seconds leaning against the hood of the jeep, he made a horrible gagging sound and vomit splashed onto the rocks near his dusty boots.

Then he slapped the hood of his car with an open hand. "Shit!" he yelled at no one in particular.

The echo rang up into the mountains. I looked up at the clumps of trees, at the boulder-strewn ravine from which we'd just retreated, scanning for the basi-lisk. But I didn't see the beast.

No one else said much. I turned back to the truck Leyla and I had driven. Expecting that we'd be going back now, and simply wanting something to do with my dumb shaking hands, I yanked at one of the bungee cords holding the tarp down. I figured I could stash the rifle in there for the ride back.

As I peeled back the tarp, the sun glinted off a smooth, concave mirrored surface.

"Leyla," I said without looking up.

"What?" she asked. "What's the matter?"

"How many of these mirrors are in here?"

"I told you before, they're called reflectors. And I don't know, I just put as many as I can fit in the bed, take them to town to clean, and then cart them back out to the solar array and put them back."

"What are you thinking, Das?" Tommy said. "The thing will see its own ugly face and just keel over?"

"I'm thinking that your plan got Charlie killed," I snapped with more heat than I'd intended. "It's high time someone else did the thinking."

I looked around, meeting the gaze of each man and woman in turn. None objected. How could they? I had been right there when the venom landed in Charlie's eyes. It could just as easily have been me—or one of them. Or Tommy.

"We know basilisks don't like fire or bright lights," I said.

"But this one is crazy!" Tommy protested. "It attacked last night when we had fires going. That's never happened before."

"Exactly," I said. I yanked the tarp open farther, and pulled out one of the thin metal reflectors—a concave rectangle about the size of my torso. I wiggled it back and forth, directing a sunspot at Tommy's face. He blinked and averted his eyes. "It attacked the brightest light in the whole town last night—a blazing bonfire. I saw it run right into the flames, like it wanted nothing more than to extinguish the light, and maybe itself in the process. Don't you think it would react the same to this?"

"I don't know how it will react," Tommy said as he blinked his eyes. "It's not in its right mind, clearly."

"It's not crazy," I said. "It's sad, and it's desperate. For all we know, this is the last basilisk left on Earth. We haven't seen one in years. It got left behind, and it's all alone now. If I were the basilisk, I'd be sad and desperate, too." I took another step closer to Tommy. "Look, if this doesn't work, we'll go home and set extra watches and wait for it to come back, just like my mother wanted."

Tommy glared at me. He opened his mouth, and then closed it again. A muscle popped in his jaw and some of the color returned to his cheeks.

"We're here now, and we've already lost one man," I said. "So what do you say we finish the job?"

• • •

Leyla and I went out to the auto repair shop straight away. She jimmied the door open like a pro, making almost no noise in the darkness. Once inside, I found an actual, honest to God, functional propane lighter. Leyla searched some low shelves and came up with a long spool of paracord. I tucked both into my pockets.

Leyla also discovered a dozen rolls of duct tape at the bottom of a toolbox. She hugged them to her chest like a baby, grinning from ear to ear as she swayed.

"This is a treasure trove, Das! Look at that Chevy!" She jerked her chin up toward the car. It was dusty, but the frame hadn't rusted since it had been kept inside for all these years.

"It's like stepping out of a time machine," I said. We both stared at the raised car for a long time. I peered up, wondering what it was called. On my tiptoes, I saw the raised letters that spelled out the model name. "Chevy *Impala*."

Leyla let out a deep sigh filled with longing.

"We still need to get some shut eye," I said.

I followed Leyla out, and shut the door behind us. We got back in the truck and drove across the flood-plain for the third time, going slow and only using the dim lights to navigate among the rocks and cacti.

The smooth execution of my plan required precise timing. We needed the darkness of night followed swiftly by the bright light of the sun at dawn. But we also needed to be fresh, as none of us had slept much the night before.

Back at the camp, I spoke briefly to Tommy, expressing my admiration for the huge pile of logs he and the other hunters had built in the center of the box canyon, adjacent and in clear view of the rocky foothills where we suspected the basilisk now hid. Then I took a short nap on the hard, dusty ground.

Tommy shook me awake again an hour later. I bolted upright and rubbed my eyes.

"Is it time?" I asked.

"Yes." Tommy remained crouched at my side, his lips a thin line. "Here," he said at last, reaching down to unbuckle the leather strap that held the Colt .45 on his waist. "That rifle won't do you a damn bit of good at close range."

I regarded the Browning, which lay at my side on the ground. "You're right," I said. I had been wondering how I was going to manage the reflector and the rifle at the same time. The smaller weapon solved that problem. "Thanks, Tommy." I stood and belted the pistol around my waist, and handed him the rifle.

He nodded sharply as he took it. "Are you sure you don't want someone down there with you?"

"No. We need all the guns we can get. I can handle myself, and you won't be far away."

Leyla joined us. "All set," she said. "Uh, do you two need a minute alone?" She cocked an eyebrow. To my surprise, Tommy laughed good naturedly, and walked away shaking his head.

"Are you sure this is a good idea?" Leyla said when he was out of earshot.

"It's a good plan," I insisted, as much to reassure myself as to assuage her fears. "We went over it a dozen times. Everyone has their piece. It will work."

It will work, I thought. *It has to.* But there's always that measure of uncertainty, even in the best laid plans.

The desert killed my father. In his case, it was a deadly sand worm that wriggled through his ear and made a cocoon of his brain. The risk I faced now was an angry carnivorous lizard-cow. But is there any real difference, once it's over?

Dead is dead.

It never gets easier. You just learn how to handle the fear better.

The world is different now, my father used to tell me. *But you can adapt.*

He faced danger every day to keep my mother and me safe. I do, too. For myself, and my mother, and Leyla, and even Tommy. They were the only people I had ever known.

They were my family.

Unfortunately, Tommy was a better shot than I was, and everyone knew it. So there was perhaps more validity to Leyla's concerns than I wanted to admit. Mine was the most unpleasant job. The one that required, as I have said, precise timing.

"It's time," I said to Leyla. She left me alone in the center of the canyon, and took her place out of sight behind the shrubs at the opening close to the wall.

I looked east. The sky was just beginning to glow orange with the promise of an imminent sunrise.

I pulled the lighter I had found in the auto repair shop from my pocket, walked over to the mountain of timber Tommy's hunters had piled up, and lit the dry grass stuffed underneath the heavy logs.

It was a good fire, with solid foundation that allowed the air to flow through. It flared up rapidly and crackled as it burned. A thick plume of smoke rose into the air within a few minutes.

But precise timing was my goal. So I picked up the can of kerosene that sat nearby, and twirled the cap off. Turning my face away, I poured the clear, pungent liquid onto the flames.

The fire blazed to life in a rush. I poured the entire canister on the pile of dry wood. The flames roared so high they seemed to tickle the stars.

A good thing that I didn't have to lug that Browning rifle around right now. I sprinted toward the sheer rock wall of the dead-end canyon, incredibly aware of the unfamiliar weight of the pistol on my hip, until I reached the reflector shield leaning against the wall. I picked it up by a sturdy handle made of cord and duct tape that Leyla had fashioned on short notice.

Armed and ready, I nestled close to the wall to wait, the reflector shielding my body without blocking my line of sight.

The horizon glowed brighter. I began to worry as the minutes rolled by. What if I lit the fire too late? What if the basilisk had crossed the mountain range in the night? What if it just didn't care, and I had been wrong all along?

I shifted from foot to foot, trying to keep my sore muscles from stiffening. Too late to change course now. I sensed the others out there in the dark, fidgeting uneasily as well.

A sliver of the sun peeked over the canyon wall and poured the light in. I watched as the line of shadow crept toward the fire at the middle.

I froze as a shadow lumbered through the opening on the far end of the canyon. The basilisk raised its head, licked the air, and glanced around warily.

Then it crouched low, and scraped its paws against the dusty ground.

Wait for it... I thought.

The basilisk lumbered into a loping canter, and then a run. The ground trembled each time its front claws tore into the Earth.

Wait for it...

It plowed into the huge fire, scattering heavy logs like so many twigs. Except the twigs were as thick as my legs, and on fire. The massive beast scattered the burning logs and quenched the flames with its body.

I remained crouched in place as I tried to smother the sound of my own breath.

Wait for it...

The line of the sun crawled across the canyon, now agonizingly slowly as the basilisk raged against the fire. It shattered hot logs under its massive claws, rolled on red hot coals. Its thick skin smoldered and smoked from the heat, but it remaining untarnished, unhurt because of its thick hide.

The barrel of a rifle on the sunny side of the canyon peeked over the wall. I held a hand up, and the gun seemed to hesitate, then withdrew.

Wait for it...

In another five minutes, the basilisk had managed to put out the whole fire. The line of the rising sun had crept further into the canyon. There was still a small sliver of shadow on the east side, but most of the canyon now was filled with sunlight.

It would have to do.

"Now!" I shouted, as I stood from my hiding place and began to run toward the center of the canyon.

Toward the basilisk.

The beast saw me, and turned away at the same time as Leyla and the hunter at the other end pulled the line of paracord taut across the mouth of the canyon.

An interconnected wall of reflectors snapped up to a standing position, catching the sun and throwing it at the basilisk in a blinding flash.

I averted my eyes, but didn't dare slow down.

The lizard snapped its jaws twice and roared. It scraped the ground again and took two steps toward the reflectors.

Half a dozen gunshots exploded from the top of the canyon walls simultaneously.

Three dozen rounds slammed into the basilisk from all directions. It tripped. It stumbled. Bright red blood poured from its sides as a few bullets finally broke through the thick hide.

It turned away from the wall of reflectors, away from the bullets. Now I was only twenty yards off, close enough to be hurt. I held my own reflector shield up, caught the light and aimed the glare at the brute's eyes.

It roared again, spinning to escape the glare, which came from all directions now. Two other men aimed handheld reflectors down into the canyon from the walls behind me.

The basilisk lunged at the glare I controlled. I jumped, rolled away, came up to my feet in a smooth motion, and danced back out of its reach.

The volleys from the guns ceased as Tommy and his men hurried to reload. In the reprieve, the basilisk got a dark log wrapped in its tail and flung it in my direction.

The projectile of wood struck my reflector shield with such force that it tore the shield from my grasp and pitched me to the ground.

I managed to hold onto the pistol somehow.

I rolled onto my back and sat up, groaning as I forced the throbbing hand that had held the shield a moment ago to support the weight of my body. A sharp pain shot up into my arm.

When I finally stood, I looked up and gazed straight into the midnight black eyes of the basilisk.

And for the second time in as many days, death's marble-black eyes blinked open from the center. An orange stamen extended from the indigo pupils.

This time I was prepared. I didn't let fear freeze me. I raised Tommy's Colt .45 and pulled the trigger.

The vulnerable flower-bud tore away from the stamen in its eye. And as the beast roared, the rounds from Tommy and his men blasted the beast off its feet.

A lucky bullet tore through the thick hide in the beast's neck. A stream of blood squirted out the other side.

The basilisk thrashed, its tail whipping through the air inches from my faced.

Finally, the legs of the massive lizard-cow buckled and it collapsed. Tommy's men continued to fire, relentless, unceasing.

As the bullets sank into the enormous creature, a horrible keening sound emanated from the beast's throat and filled the box canyon with its swan song.

I shook out my still-throbbing hand and walked cautiously toward the basilisk where it lay among the scattered, smoking logs.

Its good eye rolled toward me while its bullet-riddled body heaved with labored breaths.

It saw me. It breathed. I watched, holding my gun out before me with both hands—as steady as I could manage, but not as steady as I would have liked.

I took another step, then another until I was close enough to put my hand on the beast.

The basilisk didn't turn away. It watched me with the good eye.

I leveled the pistol at its head. I pulled the trigger, loosing one round, then another, then another into its brain at close range.

I'll never forget the look of immense relief that seemed to fill the beast's face.

Its jaw went slack. Its tongue lolled out. It took one last shuddering breath, and then the basilisk's body deflated.

• • •

Old doc Benji took one look at my wrist, turning it over in his sandpaper hands. "Oh it's broken all right."

I groaned.

"I told you," Leyla said. She crossed her arms in front of her chest and leaned blithely against the wall.

"How long?" I asked.

"Until it heals," my mother said from the kitchen. Three more casseroles had arrived this morning, the townspeople's de facto way of expressing gratitude for exterminating the basilisk. She shifted pans and containers in the icebox. "And don't get any more clever ideas. I've had enough excitement for one week."

I clamped my mouth shut, knowing it was useless to argue with her, and being thoroughly exhausted from the encounter myself.

It turns out I needed the rest. I slept for fourteen hours the first night, and twelve the second.

On the third day, I began to get restless. Going scavenging with my broken hand was sure to net me a scolding, but that didn't mean I needed to stay put.

I pulled out my bike and decided to ride out to the solar thermal plant. We had detoured to retrieve some large batteries from the auto repair shop on our way back from the ordeal with the basilisk, and Leyla had been out at the plant ever since, trying to rig the reflectors up to some kind of battery network of her own devising.

I didn't think I would be much help there, but I could at least keep her company. I climbed onto the saddle and pointed the handlebars toward the shining circle of silver in the distance.

It was a short ride. The sun heated my cotton-covered head and neck, warming me through the thin fabric. A cool autumn breeze whisked over my face as I picked up speed. I let my hands fall to my side—one good and strong, the other stabilized with a splint—and steered the bike with no hands like my father taught me.

ABOUT THE AUTHOR

MATTHEW GILBERT HERRON. was born in 1988 and goes by Matt among his friends. He loves epic fantasies and fast-paced action adventure novels. He loves literature, the dusty vanilla smell of old paperbacks, and turns of phrase that make your skin prickle.

In 2015, he published his first science fiction novel as M. G. Herron, The Auriga Project, a tale of two lovers separated by a galaxy, an uprooted ancient people, and mysterious alien overlords. A technical nonfiction title for writers, Scrivener Superpowers, was released a few months later, in January of 2016.

He's now working on his third book, a sci-fi adventure called Tales of the Republic, and indie publishing short fiction.

In Austin, he puts together local talks and events for writers through the Indie Author Society, an organization for indie authors that he started on Meetup.com.

He lives in Austin, TX with his girlfriend and their dog, where he likes to spend the cooler days rock climbing in the shade of the local limestone cliffs.

Get a bunch of free short stories by signing up for his newsletter here: http://mgherron.com/newsletter

A GOOD OLD FASHIONED MURDER

HALL & BEAULIEU

THERE WAS A shuffling sound followed by a *clunk*. Riffraff shoved his big, round eyeball closer to the crack in the closet door. He peered out and saw the tall squeaky-voiced one. It had just put a glass of clear liquid on the table near the tiny one's bed. It was leaning over to...what was it doing? It almost looked as if it was sucking the little one's face off. Riffraff had carried out several assignments against humans in the past but he could never get used to their overly affectionate customs. Affection made him uneasy.

He heard the tall one say, "goodnight". The light *clicked* and they were in darkness.

Darkness was what Riffraff liked best of all. He liked some things and hated a great deal more. He enjoyed fire, garbage and the smell of dead things rotting. But most of all, darkness was a good friend.

He pushed the closet door open and stepped onto the plush carpet. It felt like fur between his claws. He shuddered and made a noise so soft he *felt* it more than heard it. He heard the tiny one stir and quickly dropped to all fours. Riffraff scurried under the bed like a cockroach responding to light. He listened to the little boy's breathing. It took a long while before it became regular once more.

Sure that the little thing wasn't going to get out of bed, Riffraff rolled silently to the side and stood watching the boy's belly rise and fall with the rhythms of sleep. Riffraff's piercing yellow eyes could scarcely see over the edge of the bed. He stood on the tips of his long claws and blew softly into the child's face to test how deeply he slept. The boy's nose scrunched up in response to the foul odor emanating from the monster's mouth but otherwise made no movement that Riffraff perceived as threatening.

From a small pouch, the monster pulled out an object that resembled chalk. He began to draw a symbol above the child's bed. The markings hung magically in the air and shimmered as the pale light of the moon shone in through the drawn curtains. With a flourish of his hands and a short grunt the symbol disappeared and something like glitter fell, covering the sleeping human child.

Riffraff smiled a nasty smile and returned to the closet. He shut his eyes tightly and silently recited an incantation. His body dematerialized through the closet floor. When he regained his shape he was hidden within the pantry downstairs, surrounded by cans and bags of stuff these people called food. Riffraff had once tried to eat one of the tin cans, it nearly sliced his mouth wide open. He never did it again.

Riffraff pushed ever-so-softly on the pantry door. It was one of those doors with hinges in the middle. It squeaked and he stopped, silently cursing, then began again more slowly. The tall one was just coming down the stairs. These beasts were clumsy. Possibly the clumsiest, loudest and most peculiar creatures Riffraff had seen in a thousand galaxies. They exhibited hardly any stealthiness and had little deftness for living in darkness. She flipped a switch and *click,* a new light came on in the kitchen. It was bright. Riffraff hated brightness. He winced and recoiled.

The tall one, using her squeaky voice, did something Riffraff once heard referred to as singing. It was when one talked in an odd sort of way—holding out some syllables longer than others, raising and lowering one's voice at what seemed to be random intervals. He wasn't completely sure what the purpose of it was, it sounded to him like she was invoking an incantation of some sort, but nothing happened once she'd completed her spell. He stared at her intently, wondering if there was a possibility she was a witch. Riffraff hadn't expected to meet one of such great power when he'd taken the assignment to murder the tiny one.

He received the assignment the same way he received all assignments—a small envelope filled with paperwork and pictures. Along with it, a square-shaped, wooden box displaying a set of glowing numbers—time and date. The numbers ticked down. A little under five minutes left before the clock reached zero and Riffraff would find himself falling home through the very fabric of time and space.

He could feel time slipping away as the tall, long-haired human casually went about her task in the kitchen. It had already pulled a white liquid from the fridge as well as what appeared to be a container filled with unborn animal babies wrapped in a sort of protective shell. Riffraff's kind gave birth to their children live but he believed the things were called eggs. The human turned and was now heading directly for him. The door opened wide. With a quickly recited incantation and a soft *poof*, Riffraff dematerialized, his body floating in the air like so many molecules of dust. The creature grabbed something off a shelf, completely oblivious to Riffraff's presence, then closed the door. With another thought, Riffraff was whole again. He was thankful that he'd memorized that spell earlier in the day.

His time was running out. He needed to find a way to complete his assignment in such a way that would appear accidental, the committee had been very clear about that. He fumbled with a vial in his pocket. A bit of poison that was designed to react to the spell he'd placed on the tiny one. He and only he would be affected by its magic, thus swiftly ending the life of the little thing once and for all. He didn't know why the boy was marked for death and he didn't care. Murder was his whole world, and he didn't ask questions when given an assignment.

He watched as the human stirred a bunch of ingredients into a large bowl, then mixed in the contents from the box it had grabbed from the pantry. It was similar to how Riffraff prepared his own spells, and for a moment he wondered if the witch was making a potion. She raised the spoon up to her mouth and tasted. A smile appeared on her face.

"Mmmmm, good."

Riffraff smiled. It was food, not magic. Suddenly he knew how he was going to complete the assignment.

There was a faint song playing in the distance. A sort of chiming sound. The tall one heard it as well, put down the spoon and bowl and ran upstairs. He didn't have much time but he had to be sure she wouldn't spot him. Riffraff *poofed* upstairs and followed the would-be witch.

"Hello?" it said into a rectangular unit placed against its ear, then sat on the bed and continued talking to the device.

"Yeah, it's Greyson's birthday tomorrow. I'm making his cake right now. He's going to love it."

Riffraff took advantage of the witch's distraction and quickly dematerialized back into the kitchen. He looked around cautiously to be sure than no one else was around. When he was sure that the coast was clear, he snuck out of the pantry and popped open the small vial. The liquid inside sloshed around. It was blue and had the appearance of something very hot. He poured the lot of it into the mixture on the counter and began muttering under his breath.

Suddenly he heard a noise to his right. It was a deep voice. "Sarah?" the voice said with a twinge of inflection on the last syllable.

Riffraff panicked. He wasn't finished stirring. He wasn't finished performing the proper incantation. But he saw a shadow rounding the corner. He glanced down at the timer. He still had enough time to complete the assignment but not if this gravelly-voiced human were to interfere, and it looked like there was no chance it wouldn't.

When Riffraff saw the bearded face he knew his time was up. But he'd managed to do it! He spoke the final words and *poofed* away. The bowl on the counter responded to the shifting of the atmosphere caused by Riffraff's hasty escape. It teetered back and forth, falling to the ground. The glass shattered and the contents began to turn a sickly shade of green.

• • •

The shift back from an assignment was always worse than the shift to one. Riffraff tried to keep his eyes shut tight, not wanting a repeat of the unpleasantness of what happened last time. But instinctively he knew that he was unhinged from time and space, his essence echoing across the cosmos at an immeasurable speed. He knew when he felt heat it was from a sun, that the sensation of pain was a collision with an asteroid or a small moon. He could endure, so long as he never again skirted too close to a black hole. That had been too much and cost him days in recovery.

At last a sweet aroma filled his turned-up nostrils. Riffraff smiled a yellow smile, not needing to open his eyes to know that he was home. That sweet, delectable smell welcomed him back every time. He allowed himself to fall back, landing in a huge pile of trash. He moved his arms and legs back and forth and breathed deeply, relishing the experience. Against a backdrop of stars he could see automated barges arriving in the sky, some already engaged in their primary duty—dumping more trash on the planet. To Riffraff, it was a truly beautiful sight.

"How many did ya kill this time?"

"I bet he killed 'em all!"

Riffraff held his smile as he heard the voices and little, squishy stomping noises as their owners approached through the trash. He intentionally stopped smiling before they got close enough to see. They were just a bit over two feet tall and shaped like...boogers. Felt and smelled like boogers, too. Riffraff wasn't sure how they'd survived so long on the garbage-covered world, having arrived aboard some barge many years back. The creatures were good for nothing, in Riffraff's estimation. With each passing of the comet they attempted the assassin's exam and each time, they failed. They did, however, manage to survive the exam, which was more than some could say.

They fell into the trash beside him. He was the only assassin who'd ever paid attention to them, and in turn, he was their favorite thing in the entire universe.

"Welcome home! How did you kill this one? Did you explode him?"

"How much blood came out? Was it a bleeder?"

He looked from one to the other. The boogers had names but he'd promptly forgotten them after being told. Instead, he called the smaller of the two Stop, because he had a tendency to hug Riffraff's leg, thus having to be told to stop often, and the slightly larger one Goaway, because he tended to linger for far too long.

Riffraff called the little boogers "him" but had no way to really determine their genders as they were nothing more than shapeless globs of goo.

"Tell us everything!" Stop said.

Riffraff sighed heavily, acting annoyed despite the fact that he always looked forward to this moment. Most assassins lived alone, rarely interacting with anyone other than their targets. He remembered the early part of his career and how it felt to keep himself in isolation. The committee viewed emotional attachments as a weakness. Riffraff agreed but that didn't mean he didn't like having someone around from time to time. As far as he was concerned, Stop and Goaway were the perfect companions. Low maintenance and loyal.

After forcing them to beg for the story, Riffraff eventually told it. His version was slightly exaggerated and featured several heroic moments of gore and mayhem that hadn't actually transpired. In the end, he'd overcome impossible odds, killed the target, and scarcely escaped with his life. Stop and Goaway cheered as his story came to a close. Riffraff's tall tales were as close as they'd ever come to an actual assignment and they loved every moment.

One after the other, the questions rattled off—too many to keep straight. Riffraff was about to tell them to shut up when a dagger of pain shot through his brain. He grabbed his head and groaned, the pain causing his whole body to tremble. It was the committee and they weren't pleased.

Riffraff stood, still grasping his oversized head.

"What's the matter?" Goaway asked.

Riffraff took a few shaky steps, then fell to his knees. The committee was coming through, like it or not. He screamed as he felt them enter through his mind, then push out through his eyes. Each in turn, their ghostly shapes materialized around him, appearing in the precise spot he was looking at. Usually only a handful of committee members would come through at once but they just kept appearing until Riffraff could no longer even see his beloved trash, all of it hidden beneath the feet of the hundreds upon hundreds of them.

Mercifully, it stopped but what was left was even worse. Their silent, disapproving stares, judging him—calling him unworthy. He'd succeeded, he'd poured out the poison and completed the incantation and yet, here they were. Glaring. Riffraff knew better than to try to defend himself. If the committee was here, they were here for good reason.

"Your target yet lives." They all spoke as one, every voice amplified and distorted based upon where in the universe from which it derived. It was like being assaulted by sound, as if the cosmos themselves were screaming.

"You failed."

Riffraff was stunned. He knew something must've gone wrong but to hear them say he failed was almost more than he could bear. If he wasn't a successful assassin, what was he? Stop and Goaway began to cry. Loudly. Wailing. Riffraff swiped at them angrily, his hand coming back feeling slimy as his furry hand connected.

"The ramifications are dire."

Assassins never asked why. They received a target and killed the target. Some did it for love of killing, some because they were bored, and others out of blind devotion to the committee. They'd run the Assembly of Assassins for millennia and no one saw any reason to doubt when they'd identified a target for elimination. Riffraff had never really thought much about it, himself. He'd receive an envelope, prepare some spells, then go and do what needed to be done.

"Look to the stars."

At first he didn't know what he was seeing but suddenly the stars began to shift and change. They formed a line so long that it stretched from one horizon to the other. Somehow, Riffraff knew he was looking upon time itself. He closed his eyes instinctively, feeling as if he was seeing something he had no right to see. Curiosity got the better of him, and a moment later he was peeking up again.

One by shimmering one, the stars were being extinguished. It wasn't like a light being turned off, it was like a light being strangled and killed. Riffraff would know, having strangled and killed more creatures than he could count. Eventually, the last star in the line went out—not just gone, but dying. Those bright things, designed to flash forth their light for all the universe to see, all strangled to death. The world went dark. The only lights left in the sky were the flashing underbellies of trash barges as they continued their slow, automated journeys.

"Failure has ramifications. Sometimes, those ramifications are dire."

Riffraff still didn't understand what had gone wrong on the assignment. But the committee was above reproach and he knew better than to question them. In an odd way, seeing the terrible results of his failure filled him with pride. If the assignment had been so crucial and they chose Riffraff to carry it out, it spoke volumes about his position within the Assembly—hadn't it?

Still feeling hundreds of eyes upon him, Riffraff cleared his throat and prepared to speak. The committee rarely allowed an assassin more than a few words before making their decision, so he knew he needed to make them count.

"I will fix this," he announced.

Once an assassin performed an assignment, it could never be attempted again. He knew that he would need to take a different approach at a different time to fix this but he also knew that he was more than capable. If they still had faith in him, it would be well-placed.

"Time is of the essence," the committee said. "Time itself hangs in the balance."

That last sentence reverberated all around, filling every part of the cold, dark air. The committee slowly began to fade away, returning back through Riffraff's eyes. The dagger of pain stabbed into his brain once more. He cried out as a fire spread through his brain. He closed his eyes and fell back in a full-body seizure, lasting for several minutes.

When it finally subsided, he opened his eyes and all the stars were alive again. It was a welcome development. The splitting headache was not.

"Envelope! Assignment!" Goaway yelled.

Riffraff groaned, the creature's shrill voice making his head hurt even worse. But an envelope meant a new assignment, which meant the committee had given him a chance to right the wrong.

He snatched the envelope and tore it open, reaching inside beyond the pictures and documents until his hand closed upon the square wooden box. He couldn't get the last words of the committee out of his head. Time itself hangs in the balance. He already had a bad feeling as he looked down. Somehow, his headache worsened when he read the glowing numbers on the display of the box. Seven hours.

He had only seven hours to complete the assignment.

Riffraff had never been given less than a day. Seven hours? So much of being an assassin was in preparation, in the memorization of spells, the study of the target. Seven hours wasn't enough time to do any of that. He'd have to prioritize and for him, that meant the focus had to be on spells.

"Come with me!" he shouted, getting to his feet and taking off across the sea of trash.

Stop and Goaway followed closely.

"Don't you wanna know the target?" Stop yelled, holding up a photograph.

Riffraff glanced back. It was just a boy, barely seven years old. He wore strange clothing, but the resemblance was uncanny. This boy was, in some way, related to his previous target, the one who had somehow lived. The photo identified him as a distant offspring, born long after the first boy had grown old and died. The assignment was set to take place almost a thousand years after the first. That would make it just a hundred year fall through the past for Riffraff to arrive. Never before had he carried out an assignment so close to the present.

He weaved around a large mound of garbage, then spotted his house. He frowned, noticing that part of it had collapsed while he was away. It wasn't the first time one of his additions had fallen apart, that was the risk that came when using random trash as construction materials.

Stop and Goaway stayed outside as Riffraff rushed through the door. He'd set up that boundary early on when they'd gotten goo all over his furniture. They were distractions as well, something he couldn't afford right now. He needed as many spells as he could manage and there was precious little time to memorize them. His brain was still throbbing, which he knew was going to make the process even more difficult.

Navigating through the rubble, Riffraff made his way to the kitchen and threw open the pantry. A smell so rancid that even he didn't enjoy it washed over him, nearly knocking him down. The pantry contained some of the universe's nastiest ingredients, and many had been there for years. He grabbed at random. There was no time to plan which spells to take, so instead, he planned to take them all.

Riffraff piled the putrid dishes onto the counter, making sure they didn't mix. Once the cupboard was empty, he began. Choosing a familiar dish first, he examined it. It looked like a small brown cookie but he knew all too well it wasn't. He closed his eyes and tossed it into his mouth, chewing lightly before swallowing.

"Rodent hair," he gagged, "rainwater, reptile droppings, soil, cinnamon."

It was a simple memorization but he repeated it again. Not only did the spell have to be inside of him to work, but he had to know what was inside of it. At the end of the day, magic was nothing more than knowledge, within and without.

Riffraff dug in, wolfing down one disgusting dish after another, rattling off an endless list of ingredients. He'd never crammed so hard before and both his stomach and his brain were feeling it. Two hours had passed, leaving just five hours for the assignment to be completed. Taking a mental inventory, Riffraff knew he didn't have enough magic to pull it off. He had to be prepared for anything and right now he wasn't. The counter was still covered in dishes and he knew he'd never be able to get to them all.

He smiled, his crooked teeth covered in black and green sludge. A brilliant idea striking him, he ran to the front door and flung it open. As expected, Stop and Goaway were still waiting.

"You two ready to be assassins?" Riffraff asked.

They stared for a moment, giving him a chance to say that he was joking.

"I can't do this assignment without you," Riffraff said. "Now come inside and learn some magic."

He'd barely finished speaking before the two boogers rushed inside, almost knocking Riffraff over. He cringed hearing their slimy residue splat against the floor of his house as they ran toward the counter. They chattered excitedly and stretched their squat frames, trying to see all the spells stacked on the counter. Stop reached for one.

"Hold it!" Riffraff yelled. "First, tell me how an assassin learns a spell."

"Internalize!" Goaway said.

"Then memorize!" Stop yelled.

Their excitement was starting to grate on Riffraff's nerves but he reminded himself that he needed their help. He forced his annoyance down deep and gave them an approving smile.

"Very good. If we're going to pull this off we'll need as many spells as we can get."

It was all the invitation they needed. Even though they could barely see over the edge of the counter, the two began grabbing things and throwing them in their mouths. Goaway immediately looked sick, turning an even stranger hue of green as he worked hard to keep the contents of the first spell down. A loud bubbling noise erupted from deep within the small creature.

Riffraff took a step back and pointed. "Don't. You. Dare," he warned.

But it was too late. Goaway arched his back and opened his mouth, a stream of slimy putridness erupting from within. It nearly reached the ceiling before splashing back down, splattering every which way.

"NO!" Riffraff yelled, horrified by what he saw.

Finally, the stream of puke abated, and Goaway glanced sidelong at Riffraff.

"Sorry," he said, looking more than slightly embarrassed.

Riffraff briefly considered tossing the little creature out of the house but again reminded himself of the long odds against him. Goaway quickly grabbed another spell off the counter, but only nibbled at a corner, taking a more careful approach this time.

In stark contrast to this was Stop. The living booger moved from spell to spell at lightning-quick speed, rattling off the components to each with perfect accuracy. Riffraff watched, impressed. Stop was a natural.

They continued for another two hours. With just three hours remaining on the mission timer, Riffraff decided they needed to go. Stop had memorized nearly triple the spells Riffraff had. His body pulsed with arcane energy, and Riffraff eyed him suspiciously, unsure what so much magic would do to a booger creature. Goaway, on the other hand, had managed to memorize just three spells. He'd vomited four times.

As they prepared to fall through time and space, the boogers grew anxious.

"Will it hurt?" Stop asked.

Riffraff remembered the first dozen times he'd done it. It was some of the most excruciating pain he'd ever experienced. He was about to describe how much it hurt but realized they were staring up at him, their large round eyes full of fear. He sighed and swallowed his original answer. He couldn't have them backing out on him now.

"Only a little. Just try to stay loose. Roll when you hit the ground, if you can."

"Hit the ground?!" Stop stammered. The little thing was starting to panic.

Riffraff sighed. He pulled out the wooden square. 2:58:22. Giving it a squeeze, he activated the mission and grabbed hold of Stop and Goaway.

"Close your eyes," Riffraff said as he did the same. The fall had never failed to make him sick if he did it with his eyes open. Riffraff had developed a sense for it now, however, and he could feel the world open up beneath them, could feel the stars bend past, could feel time folding upon itself. Then, the true fall. They were arriving. Riffraff opened his eyes. Below was a sprawling city. It spread as far as he could see. But it was dark, not a single light. Riffraff concentrated hard on his breathing, slowing his fall. He almost felt bad as he watched Stop and Goaway plummet at terminal velocity toward the street below. Lucky for them, the magic kept the fall from being deadly. But on more than one occasion it had made an assassin beg for death.

The streets were filled with people. Some were in a panic, while others were huddled together. Riffraff heard the vague sound of two splats as he floated. A moment later he landed softly on the street between four humans, his clawed feet making a light clicking noise. The people didn't even seem to notice him there, arguing in the dark about something. Stop and Goaway were moaning nearby, their gooey bodies almost completely flattened. Riffraff would've moved to silence them but they were as good as invisible in this place. Whatever was happening provided the perfect cover.

Riffraff smiled. A world of darkness and distracted people. It was an assassin's dream come true and he felt some of the anxiety leaving him like a soft wind. Maybe this assignment wasn't going to be so tough after all.

He pushed through the crowd to where Stop and Goaway were still stuck to the street. Riffraff grabbed Stop first, peeling him up. The creature cried out in anguish as his body began to regain its shape. He then repeated the steps for Goaway.

"It gets easier with each assignment," he said, hoping the hint of future assignments would help the little creatures get over the pain they were experiencing. They calmed slightly as people continue to move about on the street.

"We need to locate the target and formulate a plan to kill him," Riffraff said.

The sky lit up, illuminating the world below. Riffraff instinctively started chanting quietly, preparing to dematerialize his body. But then he realized it wouldn't matter. Every eye in the world was on the sky and the three monsters in their midst continued to go unnoticed.

"Located the target!" Stop said excitedly, pointing up.

Riffraff turned his large yellow eyes to the sky and sure enough, there was the visage of his target. Completely bald, barely developed, it was a child dressed in the clothes of a king. For a moment, Riffraff felt like he was back on the previous assignment, drawing symbols above a sleeping boy, setting in motion what should've been the boy's death. But as he joined with all those around him and stared at the sky, he could see the truth. The boy lived on, his same rounded cheeks and thin lips evident on the face of this, his countless times removed offspring.

The boy's face filled the sky, making him seem like the largest being in existence, and even though Riffraff didn't believe in fear, he understood why some of those around him were dropping to their knees and shielding their faces. Some called it god, a concept Riffraff knew nothing about. But he could see the shimmer and the movement. A master of illusion and magic, Riffraff knew the difference between a thing that is real and a thing that is not. This was a projection of the target, not the target himself.

The boy's miles-wide-mouth moved and a sound so powerful came down that it knocked Riffraff to his knees next to all the others.

The words were foreign at first, but Riffraff quickly recited a spell in his mind, moving his fingers slightly as he did. As he completed it, he could understand the boy.

"...everything I want to play with. You tried to hide it from me! I saw it first and then it went away, and they told me you tried to hide it from me!"

He was screaming. A child's tantrum.

"When I look up, I pick from all of the stars which one I want next, and we always come and I always take it. They're mine! MINE! And I saw yours and I said I wanted it and they said you tried to hide it!"

An elderly man in a flowing white gown rose. He spread his arms to the sky, hoping the angry god above could hear him. "We're sorry, Emperor. We meant no disrespect, we were just trying to protect our world. We thought by shielding it from scans we could keep bad people away, but we never meant to upset you."

His words were pointless and powerless and went nowhere. Riffraff looked at him with disdain. It was a pathetic display.

"When I wanna play, I tell them where we're going and they take me there. I want what is mine and I can play with any star in the sky. Do you know how many are with me? All I do is say where to go and we come! When I get done playing we get rid of the old stars and we go to the new ones, because there's always a new star."

He was getting angry again.

"But you didn't want to play!" His voice caused the ground to shake. The elderly man who'd stood and spoke was knocked backward, his head thumping against the concrete.

Out of the corner of his eye, Riffraff realized that Goaway had stood up and had stretched one hand to the sky. His mouth was moving and Riffraff realized too late what the dumb booger was doing. A purple lance of energy shot forth from his hand, racing into the sky. It grew in size as it soared, ablaze in arcane energy. Riffraff would've been impressed had it not been such a complete and total waste. Now the little creature had just two spells left.

Riffraff joined with the rest of the gathered masses and watched as the fiery purple bolt of energy passed harmlessly through the eye of the giant projection. At least it had been an accurate shot.

The boy was motionless for a moment as the projection reformed. Then its mouth opened, and out came the worst sound anyone had ever heard.

"Waaaaaaaaaaaaaaaaaaaaaaaaa!" It was a scream. A shriek. A wail. All at the same time. A baby demanding his way, a temper tantrum from the bowels of hell. Then came the light.

"Run! Now!" Riffraff said.

From somewhere in orbit a massive beam of pure light shot down, passing perfectly through the mouth of the projection. The child emperor's wrath was given form, and from his lips spilled out death and devastation.

Riffraff and the two boogers pushed through the crowd as fast as they could. As the blast hit, Riffraff realized there was nowhere to hide. They were at the epicenter. He threw his arms around Stop and Goaway and whispered an incantation. As the energy began to tear apart everything around them they disappeared and reappeared miles away.

Turning around, Riffraff saw the blast in the distance. There was nothing left. No buildings, no people, just a hole that may have extended all the way to the other side of the world.

They were still in the massive city that seemed to cover the entirety of the planet. A few people screamed as they saw Riffraff and the two boogers but most were too panicked and distraught to care. There was crying, fighting, fleeing. These people were fools. Nothing they had could stand against power like what they were facing.

"Now, let's play!" the child said from the sky.

A swarm of small ships broke through the projection and fanned out, heading for the surface below. They moved like bolts of lightning, one place one second, miles away the next. Almost like magic, Riffraff realized.

Soon the ships were touching down, their doors sliding open to release a flood of soldiers. Men in plated blue armor, their faces hidden behind visored helmets. There was no question what they were there to do. Mounted on each of the soldier's shoulders were energy cannons that tracked wherever their eyes focused. As soon as they saw a target they fired, orbs of white light erupting from the end of the weapons. Riffraff watched as one orb caught a terrified man in the back of the head. It splashed on him like water, looking harmless at first. Then it began melting his head. It ate through skin and bone, sizzling as it exposed and devoured the brain inside.

The scene of death and gore didn't bother Riffraff but what adorned the soldier's chests did. Instead of wearing some insignia, each soldier was plastered with a projection of the child emperor that matched the one in the sky. This one was more clear and Riffraff studied it for clues. The child emperor moved slightly, momentarily revealing a bank of windows behind him. And through those, stars.

Riffraff looked up. The target was somewhere in orbit.

"Why are you running away?" the emperor's projection taunted from the soldier's chests.

Stop pulled on Riffraff's leg.

"We should get out of here!" he said, fearfully watching the approaching soldiers as their cannons melted terrified targets more frequently now. Riffraff looked down at the little creature. He was pulsing even more now, the number of spells inside of him dying to get out. He was an arcane time-bomb, and Riffraff hadn't the faintest idea what would happen when he went off.

Goaway stepped in front of them. "I got 'em!"

As soon as he started reciting the incantation, Riffraff knew it was wrong.

"Stop you idi—"

Goaway finished the spell but instead of casting it outward, it reflected back on him. A shimmer of blue energy passed over his body and his eyes went wide. He looked at Stop, a desperate fear in his eyes.

"Help me."

There was a flash, then Goaway exploded. A gooey, slimy shockwave sent Riffraff and Stop flying, sending them over a nearby wall and into a small courtyard. Riffraff landed on all fours, digging his claws into the pavement to slow himself as he slid across the ground. Stop bounced twice, then rolled into the far wall, sticking to it.

Riffraff stood and began wiping the gooey remains of Goaway out of his fur. Sometimes mishandling magic could result in beautiful disasters and the discovery of new spells. Other times, it exploded an assassin from the inside out. Sounds of the emperor's soldiers killing everyone in sight spilled over the walls, but for now, Riffraff was free to think of a plan. He started by pulling Stop free of the wall. The booger fell to the ground, square, gelatin tears plopping from his eyes as he mourned the loss of his...whatever Goaway had been.

The show of emotion annoyed Riffraff but he needed a little time to think. He used his claw-like feet to help him climb the wall and peered over the top. The child emperor was laughing as his soldiers killed. They were ruthless and fast as fire, clearing an area and then returning to their ships.

Riffraff smiled and hopped down. He ran over to Stop and kicked him gently. "Up, up, we've got a ride to catch."

Stop ignored him. His emotions were out of control, which meant his hold on the magic stored in his body was as well. He looked up at Riffraff but instead of his normal eyes, there was a storm of color raging there. The small creature was coming unhinged. It was a frightening situation but one that could prove useful.

Riffraff thought for a moment, then reached down and picked Stop up in his arms. He held the small creature with one hand, angling him up in the air. He whispered an incantation, but waited to speak the last word. One of the ships appeared in the sky, returning from the surface back to orbit. Riffraff studied its movements, holding his breath. It disappeared, but soon another one took its place. Knowing time was of the essence, Riffraff closed one eye and took aim. As the ship zipped from one spot in the sky to another he spoke the final word of the incantation.

Stop shot from his hand and into the dark sky. Just as Riffraff hoped, the ship blinked again, right into the path of where he'd launched the booger. He could barely make out the small round shape of Stop as it slammed into the belly of the ship.

Riffraff realized he should've warned Stop to hold his breath once the ship left the atmosphere.

Turning his attention to his own situation, Riffraff climbed the wall again. A group of soldiers was jogging by. Riffraff focused on the soldier in the back of the group. He drew a sigil in the air with his finger, knowing it needed to be precise in order to work. He then took a deep breath and prepared himself for what was sure to be an unpleasant experience. He finished the sigil and spoke the final word, teleporting himself forward.

The sudden darkness, wet warmth, and squishiness told him it had worked. The other soldiers turned to look as the fourth soldier lurched forward awkwardly, nearly falling over. The soldier let out a horrified gurgle.

"What's wrong?" a voice somewhere in the helmet asked.

Riffraff wasn't as tall as the man, so he had to claw upward to get to the head. His hands tore through organs and tissue, blood and bile soaking him as he moved up through the man's stomach and chest. The soldier was dead now and it was taking all of Riffraff's strength to keep the body standing upright. He thrust his head up through to the neck, then chewed a hole there so he could breathe and speak.

"All's good," Riffraff said, trying to sound natural. "Let's go."

The soldiers continued to stare. Riffraff desperately clawed his arms down the man's upper limbs, shredding the muscles to make room in the sleeves of the armor. He then forced the body to shrug, hoping the motion would set the other soldiers at ease. Instead they took a step away, looking even more worried and suspicious.

"Squad 77, return to mothership, your sector is clear," a voice said inside the helmet.

The other soldiers turned their attention away from him.

"Get it together and come on," one of them said.

Riffraff tried to nod, but it nearly caused the body to fall over. The soldier nearest him shook his head.

"You need help, Greer."

Riffraff tried to follow as the soldiers walked back toward their ship, but he was having trouble manipulating the left leg of the body. He tore away as much of the remaining flesh as he could with his feet, then wriggled his body, sinking deeper into the corpse. This made it a little easier to work the legs but harder to keep the upper body from becoming unbalanced and collapsing. It tilted forward and Riffraff broke into a run to try to keep from toppling. He passed the other soldiers and turned the body toward the waiting ship. The door was still open and the body finally fell just as Riffraff reached it. The corpse slid face first into the ship.

As the other soldiers caught up, one of them nudged the body with his boot, then touched his helmet.

"Have medical on standby, something's gone wrong with Greer."

Riffraff chuckled darkly. Something had most certainly gone wrong with Greer. As the ship lifted off, Riffraff crawled around inside the Greer-suit, trying to get to a place where he could breathe. The corpse convulsed on the floor of the ship, causing several of those nearby to eye it with worry. Someone knelt beside him and spoke reassuringly, telling Greer it was going to be okay. Riffraff stifled a laugh.

It took just a matter of seconds before they broke through the atmosphere. Riffraff couldn't see but he'd traveled through time and space enough to know when he was in the company of the stars.

"Docking bay 2278, cleared for approach," a voice announced inside the ship.

Riffraff prepared a spell, knowing he'd need to act fast once they stopped. The ship shuddered, then settled to a stop. He could hear the other soldiers moving around, could hear the door opening, and he spoke the final word, dematerializing and falling through the body. He guided his ghostly form through the wall of the small ship, then stopped suddenly. The inside of the mothership was the most enormous thing he'd ever seen. The docking bay stretched on for well over a mile, ships buzzing about like insects. There were thousands of them and tens of thousands more already docked. Riffraff wondered where he would find the ship Stop had stuck to. Could the little booger have actually survived?

A soldier jogged by, then paused and turned back. Riffraff watched him closely, wondering why it felt eerily as if the man could see him. The soldier tapped his visor several times, then spoke.

"Command, give me a mist scan near docking bay 2278. My spectromener is going haywire, I think we got some kinda spirit here."

A liquid began spraying from nozzles somewhere in the ceiling. It hit Riffraff despite the fact that he was in his ghostly form at the moment. The soldier took a step back, his shoulder mounted weapons activating.

"Command we got a..."

Riffraff surged forward, one deadly claw out-stretched. He drove it in just beneath the helmet, right in the under-armored fleshy neck. The soldier choked on his final word. Riffraff twisted his claw, severing the man's head from his neck. The only thing holding it on was armor. Riffraff pulled his claw back, allow-ing the body to fall to the ground. As he stared at his blood covered hand he smiled, reminding himself that sometimes good old fashioned murder could get the job done better than magic.

His moment was ruined as alarm klaxons blared.

"Intruder near docking bay 2278, spiritual abil-ities, eliminate on sight," a booming voice announced to everyone on board.

Within seconds, Riffraff was dodging energy blasts. He was forced to burn a forcefield spell that he'd hoped to keep in reserve. It bought him thir-ty-seconds as nothing could get through the forcefield. As more and more soldiers appeared and opened fire, he looked around, trying to plan his next move. There were too many of them. No matter what he planned next he was going to lose to their sheer numbers.

Instead of focusing on escape, Riffraff began re-citing the incantation for an offensive spell. He knew the time on the forcefield was running out, but he still took the extra few seconds to pull chalk from his pouch. He drew in the air, glowing runes that pulsed with a power as ancient as time itself. The spell would've worked without the chalk and the runes, but they gave it extra power, and Riffraff was going to need every bit of power he could get.

Just as the forcefield fell, Riffraff spoke the final word of the incantation. The glowing runes in the air faded as a black spiral erupted from them and went spinning wildly, growing as they moved. The soldiers continued firing at Riffraff but the orbs of light from their weapons veered suddenly. Soon, everything was being pulled into the spirals. First it was just loose objects and those who were unlucky enough to be too close, but as they intensified so too did their gravitational pull. Soldiers were sucked into them.

The smaller docked ships began to quake and groan. Metal bent and bolts snapped and the spirals began swallowing ships whole. The walls and floor of the enormous docking bay audibly protested as the spirals threatened destruction.

It was the most powerful spell Riffraff had at his disposal. He was sad to see it go but it was buying him the time he needed to escape. The spirals might even expand enough to swallow the whole ship, finishing the assignment and getting Riffraff back home.

"Purge protocol, sections 2234 through 2397, evacuate immediately!" a voice boomed throughout the area.

Blue sirens went off and Riffraff looked around, trying to make sense of what was happening. Then he saw the ship begin to come apart, section by section. Including the section he was standing in. He quickly recited an incantation and set his sight on a point in the middle of the docking bay, disappearing and reappearing there in an instant. Riffraff looked back just as the section of the dock he'd just left jettisoned out into space, taking the menace of the spirals with it. Force-fields appeared, sealing off the rest of the dock from the open wound left from the jettisoned section.

Riffraff was annoyed but impressed. Sacrificing a portion of the ship and the people on it was a shrewd tactic, one that had saved the rest of the ship. He tore his eyes away, looking for the nearest route that would get him out of the expansive docking bay and into the ship proper. In his current position he had no where to hide, but if he could get deeper into the ship he knew he would be able to skulk his way to wherever the child emperor was hiding.

Seeing a door, Riffraff ran for it. When he neared he saw a forcefield active over it. He swiped at it with his claw, curious how strong the technology was. An electric current surged unapologetically through him sending him reeling backward. The back of his head smacked hard into the metal floor and he slid several feet before coming to a stop. Riffraff could smell something burning and looked down to see the end of his claw completely burned away. He wanted to weep, not because of the pain, but because it was his favored killing claw. He'd taken many lives with that claw and his effectiveness as an assassin would be forever diminished without it.

He cursed the child emperor as he stood, more resolved than ever to take the life of the bald headed boy. Out of the corner of his eye he saw soldiers pouring into the area, surely coming for him. But his focus remained on the door. A slight smile pulled at the corner of his mouth, black lips parting slightly as he thought of a particularly nasty spell. He'd held onto this one for years, waiting for a day when he'd really need it.

Just as he started silently reciting the incantation he noticed something descending from above. Instinctively leaping backward, Riffraff barely managed to avoid the glowing energy net that had fired from the ceiling. It crackled with electricity as it danced along the floor. Riffraff looked up as small nozzles appeared, each humming to life with energy. He rolled to the left as a cascade of electrified nets fired. He fixed his gaze on the top of a nearby ship that was docked and quickly rattled off an incantation. He appeared atop the ship in an instant, but the moment he did nets fired from multiple directions. Riffraff leaped off the ship, hoping to get lucky while knowing he wasn't. As two of the nets hit him in midair he cursed himself. He'd gotten predictable and used the same spell too many times, something that this opponent had been ready for.

The nets bound him tightly and he slammed hard into the metal floor. He was momentarily stunned and the current running through his body made it impossible to think. His body convulsed. He could hear footfalls, getting closer. It was the end drawing close.

Riffraff raged with all he had, rolling and ending up on his side. Nothing he did seemed to make a difference, and the more he struggled the more the nets hurt. He stopped, trying to figure if there was another move he could make.

And then he saw the goo.

Oozing out from under a nearby docked ship, looking just like a smooshed booger, still pulsing with arcane power. It was Stop. Or his corpse. But either way, all that magic was still inside of him.

Riffraff couldn't concentrate enough to cast a spell, but another idea occurred to him. He could concentrate enough to transfer spells. With no idea how much of his magic he was giving up he spoke a simple word and focused on the part of Stop he could see. The sound wave of his spoken word was visible, sparked to life with arcane power. It hit the booger.

All he could do now was wait. He could sense that he'd sent most, if not all of the spells he had memorized, which meant that Stop's small body now held hundreds upon hundreds of spells. More than any assassin had ever had inside them. Riffraff knew they were in uncharted territory. There was no way of knowing what would happen next. Magic on top of more magic equaled...super magic? An arcane bomb? Riffraff could hear the soldiers. They were almost on top of him, their attention focused completely on the furry monster netted on top of the ship.

And not on what was happening underneath a different ship.

The part of Stop that was visible was strobing now, every color in existence taking turns flashing through his gooey body. The ship he was under began to shake, then lift. What emerged from underneath wasn't some small booger. It was a technicolor atrocity, a creature unlike any that was ever meant to exist. And it was pissed off.

The creature formerly known as Stop lifted the ship it had been stuck under, raising it up over its head before letting loose a fearsome roar. Now the soldiers saw it. Stop threw the ship. Riffraff's eyes went wide, realizing that he was right in the path. He fought against the nets, forcing his body into a roll and getting out of the way just as the ship smashed down and tumbled into a huge gathering of soldiers. They screamed ever so briefly before being crushed to death by the ship.

All eyes were on Stop now. Soldiers opened fire, nets shot from the ceiling and all of it just served to make the creature angrier. Spells just spilled out of it. None of them appeared to be thought out or even aimed, which in a way made the creature even more dangerous and destructive. It went invisible for a moment. Appeared further away. Launched a fireball from the back of its head. Leaped with unnatural speed and smashed a hole in the ceiling.

Riffraff laughed. It was a perfectly beautiful bit of mayhem and if he didn't have pressing business he would've loved to stay and watch. With the soldiers all distracted, Riffraff used his one good claw to begin sawing through the net. The progress was slow, but Stop wrecked the entirety of the docking bay and wiped out anyone foolish enough to approach. Riffraff had plenty of time to cut through without being noticed.

Once free he stood and looked around. Stop had thrown a console through the wall, creating an opening for Riffraff that led deeper into the ship. The inner halls were quiet and mostly empty. Two men came through a door, their eyes going wide when they saw Riffraff. Before they could say a word he slit their throats, using one dramatic swipe with his remaining claw to go across both necks. As their bodies fell to the ground he was already on the move. With no idea where exactly the child emperor was, Riffraff just resolved himself to keep moving. Eventually, he knew he'd come across his target.

His confidence waned with each minute he spent lost in the hellish maze of the mothership. The higher he climbed the closer he believed the target to be, but getting up a level took time. Too much of it, and he had precious little to spare. Patrols, forcefields, traps, sealed bulkheads, everything was against him, and with nothing to rely on other than his agility and claw, it was an excruciating undertaking. Every now and again the ship would shake and a distant alarm could be heard. Stop was still on the loose.

As he got closer to the top of the ship, Riffraff finally chanced a look at the wooden square. He estimated that he had at least thirty minutes left, but his eyes went wide when he saw the real number. 0:05:14.

Barely five.

Riffraff was exhausted. He was covered in blood, having killed twenty-six people as he made his way through the ship. He breathed heavily as he crawled on his hands and knees in the small maintenance corridor. He paused at a vent and looked down, realizing that he'd finally reached his destination. There below him was a lush throne room. Fit for a king. The perfect setting for a murder.

Alarms rang out all around him. The vent opened and the entire maintenance corridor tipped, sending Riffraff tumbling out. He landed awkwardly on his side, again both impressed and angry over how well-equipped and prepared the child emperor and his people were. No mission had ever been even a fraction as difficult as this one.

Four soldiers rushed in, surrounding Riffraff and aiming their shoulder weapons down at him.

"It's fine," a childish voice said from across the throne room. "Let the monster in."

The soldiers backed away in unison. For a moment, Riffraff thought it was a trick. He eyed them suspiciously, waiting to see which would fire first. But they did as they were told, leaving the monster alone.

Rising cautiously to his feet, Riffraff looked across the throne room. Sitting on the floor in front of a wall of windows was the child emperor. In his hand was a toy and he was intensely focused on it, using it to knock over a stack of other toys.

Riffraff thought about the timer in his pouch, estimating he had less than two minutes to complete the mission. He walked across the throne room with murderous intent, never taking his eyes off the emperor. Soldiers lined the walls and sentry guns lined the ceiling. Riffraff was all out of magic and was down to one claw. As he drew closer to the target, he realized there was really only one thing left that he had.

The element of surprise.

He sprang into action, rushing forward and raising his claw above his head. When he was just a few feet away from the emperor he noticed a shimmer in the air. It caught him, stopping him in his tracks. It was an invisible wall. Riffraff tried to push through it, tried to cut it, but nothing worked. It was impenetrable. One final impenetrable barrier between him and his target.

The emperor continued playing with his toy for a few moments, then finally looked up. His bald head gave him an unnerving appearance but there was no malice on his face. He almost looked frightened as he stared at Riffraff.

"Are you a real monster?" the child asked.

Riffraff smiled, hoping it would unnerve the small boy.

"That's exactly what I am."

The emperor stood slowly, taking a step toward the barrier, then stopping and taking a step back.

"I used to think that monsters didn't exist. Someone told me a bedtime story once about monsters but when I asked if they were real they said there were just made up. We checked my room every night because the book said monsters lived in closets but there were never any monsters there."

He paused, a question occurring to him.

"You don't live in closets, do you?"

"I live on a planet made of trash."

The child emperor shrugged, the statement going over his head.

"Well, we checked my room every night, but we never found any monsters."

It appeared to be a pleasant memory, but soon the boy's expression darkened.

"But some of the stars we went to play at, they had monsters there."

He paused and looked around, a child searching for reassurance, maybe the calming presence of a parent. But there was no one around. Finally, the boy looked directly at Riffraff.

"And now there's you."

Riffraff stood a little taller. After a lifetime dedicated to violence and murder, it warmed his black heart to know he struck fear in even someone as powerful as this tiny emperor. His moment of pride was short lived.

"You're not so scary," the emperor said, a look of defiance settling on his face.

Riffraff tried again to pass through the invisible wall. Again, he found it impossible.

Then the child emperor did something he didn't expect. The boy lurched forward and extended his arm, slapping Riffraff hard across the face. He had no problem passing through the invisible wall. As the shock of the blow wore off, Riffraff tried to retaliate, but the child quickly pulled his arm back through the barrier, safe from retaliation.

Riffraff roared, swiping and kicking at the wall.

"Haw haw, you're too slow," the child said, taunting Riffraff.

It felt impossible to Riffraff that this was how it was all going to end. He knew there could only be a few seconds remaining on the timer, meaning he was about to be pulled back through time and space to his home. A failure. And the committee had made it sound like failure wasn't an option on this one. Yet here was the one who had bested him. A small boy who was afraid of monsters and still played with toys.

"I thought you'd be fun to play with but you're bo-ring. Capital B, boring. I'm bored with you. Guards, why don't you…"

Before the emperor finished his command the floor beneath him erupted. Riffraff's eyes went wide and a crooked smile spread across his face as he watched an overgrown, glowing booger come crashing through the floor. Stop's head was half melted, and one of his stubby limbs was missing. Some strange vegetation was growing out of his back and in his mouth was the severed head of a soldier. He'd apparently been busy.

Riffraff could feel the shift beginning. The timer was at 00:00:00, and there was no stopping the pull of the future. He was about to shift back through time and space, back home, back to face the committee and tell them he'd failed.

But the arrival of Stop had changed things. As he exploded through the floor he knocked the child emperor off balance, sending him stumbling. Right toward Riffraff. The boy passed through the invisible wall just a second before Riffraff dematerialized from this place.

A second was all that was needed.

Riffraff swiped upward with his remaining claw. Lightning fast, deadly precise. The cut started just under the chin and went up through the face, taking off the nose, continuing up all the way to the forehead. He sliced the child emperor's face clean off. The assassin had never seen a sight quite as lovely. The flesh fell away, revealing two shocked eyes and a whole lot of blood and grossness. Riffraff wished there was some way to take a picture so he'd never forget this moment.

"Haw haw," Riffraff said as he was pulled from this place.

He didn't bother to close his eyes as he was unhinged from time and space and flung across the cosmos. Since it was only a hundred years difference between this assignment and his own time, the trip was quick, and in an instant he was back home, standing amidst an ocean of trash once more.

But something was wrong. The automated trash barges weren't in the sky. Nothing was in the sky. There wasn't a single star visible. Just a true darkness, the kind of void that made even a creature like Riffraff uneasy. Where had all the stars gone?

A sharp pain passed through him from behind. His mouth dropped open as the pain held him in place. The blade pushed again, piercing all the way through him until it came out the front of his chest. Riffraff looked down, his brain barely registering what just happened. It wasn't until he felt the tip of the blade with his own hand, allowed it to draw blood, that he realized. Someone was behind him, and they'd impaled him.

"I've waited a long time for this moment."

The voice was old but tinged with excitement.

"Lotta planning, lotta killing. Took a lot to get to this exact spot at this exact time but I did it. And I gotta say..."

He paused and walked slowly around Riffraff. Still unable to move from the shock of the blade that was stuck through him, Riffraff could only stand and stare in disbelief at the figure before him. A fully grown man wearing royal garments. The body of a man but the face of a child emperor. A projection, just like the one in the sky on that planet a hundred years ago.

"I..." Riffraff croaked, barely able to speak. "I killed you."

The child emperor shook his head. "All you did was take my face."

The projection disappeared for a moment, revealing a gruesome scene. Bone and exposed muscle and cartilage, an open nasal cavity. The child emperor, all grown up without a face.

The projection returned.

"You took my face and you took my fun, and I knew from that day forward that I was gonna take your life."

Riffraff's mind was filled with questions but he didn't even have the strength to ask them. He was dying. He fell to his knees, trash crumpling beneath him.

"Good idea," the emperor said. "Kneel."

Looking past the menacing visage of the child emperor, Riffraff stared at the empty sky. Normally he liked the dark, but not this dark.

"What'd you do?" Riffraff asked, barely able to keep his eyes open as death slowly claimed him.

The child emperor smiled.

"I wiped out everything. Not only did you leave me alive but you left something else behind."

Riffraff knew what he was talking about before he said it. Stop, that detestable little booger.

"It took us days to get your friend under control. But once he'd expended all his magic, it was just a matter of time before he broke under our interrogation techniques. He told us everything. About the Assembly of Assassins, all dead, by the way, about the point in the future you'd come from, about how at night when you think no one is looking you like to lay among the trash and stare up at the stars."

The child emperor was quiet for a moment, staring intently at the dying creature in front of him.

"I was angry, so I did the only thing I could think of. You took my face from me, I was gonna take everything you loved."

He sat down beside Riffraff. The two remained silent for a long moment, each staring up in the empty sky.

"I used to love playing with the stars. Each one was different and all the people were different. It was a game I played, destroying them. It was fun. But after you, well, I knew I had to get serious. Fun time was over. Systematically wiping out a universe is no simple task and it's not all that fun, but if you loved staring up at the stars I knew I had to take them from you. So I took them all."

He shook his head, then stood up.

"You took my face and you took my fun. I didn't enjoy my life much after you came into it but there was one thing I held onto all these years. One simple pleasure I knew I was going to have coming to me. A single moment in time that was going to make all the other moments worthwhile. One last piece of fun."

He reached into his robe and pulled out another blade. This one was jet black and adorned with jewels.

"A good, old fashioned murder."

The child emperor raised the blade, then brought it down swiftly. It was a strike he'd practiced ten thousand times, and the blade cut perfectly through Riffraff's head, taking his face clean off.

Riffraff fell over onto his side. Blood gushed from the place where his face had once been. He took one final breath, a deep sadness filling him as he realized that without his nose he could no longer smell the aroma of his beloved trash.

ABOUT THE AUTHORS

HALL AND BEAULIEU are an author team from Fort Worth, Texas. Their debut novel Brother Dust: The Resurgence can be purchased here.

Aaron Hall was born in 1981 in Fort Worth, Texas. He has spent a majority of his life writing, finding a love of creating fiction at an early age. After spending a decade as community journalist, Aaron now works in communications for his hometown municipal government. He loves spending time with family and friends, watching TV and movies, and above all else, his savior and lord, Jesus Christ.

Steve Beaulieu was born in 1984 in East Hartford, CT. Having spent most of his life in Palm Beach County, Florida, he and his wife moved to Fort Worth, Texas in 2012. He works as a Pastor and Graphic Artist and loves comic books, fantasy and science fiction novels.

He married the love of his life in 2005 and he fathered his first child in 2014, Oliver Paul Beaulieu. His namesake, two of Steve's favorite fictional characters, Oliver Twist and The Green Arrow, Oliver Queen. They are expecting their second child on July 30th, but Steve secretly hopes she'll be a day late so she can share a birthday with Harry Potter.

Chat with Steve and Aaron about anything from books to religion over at Facebook: www.facebook.com/hallandbeaulieu/

RE:EVOLUTION AND THE RADIANT MACHINE

A.K. MEEK

MONSTERS DON'T COME from swamps or graveyards. In fact, they don't realize they're monsters at all. They begin their journey thinking they're heroes, doing something great.

—BERNARD'S JUSTIFICATION ON why he caused the Radiant Machine to flip out and kill all those people.

An auditorium

"Since it's human consciousness we're talking about," Nelson brushes a stray lock from his eyes, a millennial Superman, "we can exclude the International Consortium of Ethical Machine's regulatory protocols. Forget about them, because, after all, humans aren't androids."

In Re:evolution's auditorium, three hundred colleagues and reporters hold their breath, watching Nelson center stage, a technological pirate, a digital Blackbeard, riding the waves of the eighth sea.

Nelson pauses for effect and scans the crowd over weepy, Abercrombie underwear model-turned-tech mogul eyes, sees the old heads, the lifelong researchers that should be retired by now, playing golf at Shady Oaks Rest Home for the Old and Decrepit and eating dinner at three p.m. Or maybe knitting mittens for snot-bubbling grandkids.

They're the ones who said it couldn't be done.

No, they're the ones who said it *shouldn't* be done.

They can't see what he sees. Their scope is too limited. They cling to their outdated ethics and dead-god religion. That's all well and good for the everyday cavemen, but it's not good for business. Or for progress. These old heads, these monsters, need to become extinct, like the dinosaurs. There's no place for them in this new and shiny world.

Re:evolution began life as a fleeting epiphany ten short years ago as Nelson was shaving his forearms for a photo shoot. The creative director thought body hair didn't fit the advert campaign's aesthetics.

Nelson thought it would be great if he didn't have to worry about shaving again. That would mean not growing old. He decided to create a body that wouldn't grow old and die. So he gave up his modeling career, cashed in his inheritance, bought Dynamo Robotics tech, hired smart, nerdy men that understood android tech, and then worked tirelessly for years spearheading the creation of the perfect body. With that done, he needed the perfect man.

That was the gist of his epiphany.

How ironic that the first soul selected for complete integration, for evolution, would be one of these same old heads? Admittedly, Dr. Charles Gleason isn't your typical engineer. He holds many progressive views of genetic evolution. In fact, Nelson's own basic understanding of the dynamic nature of biomechanical overlaying was formed as he poured over Gleason's groundbreaking research.

Gleason's only misfortune is that he was born sixty years too early. That, and the Parkinson's that left his body to rot.

The old heads become extinct, starting tonight.

"And now," Nelson begins, struggling to swallow the euphoria welling in his throat, "after over a year of screening candidates, the committee has overwhelmingly supported one name. The first person to step on the next ladder rung of human evolution is none other than the founding father of biomechanical layering. I give you Doctor Charles Gleason."

The room erupts with applause. Everyone knew it was going to be him, but they still had their part to play. They spring to their feet and wear their hands out with thunderclaps of applause, support for the committees' decision. Nelson steps to the side of the auditorium stage, confident in Re:evolution's choice for the first person to be completely fused with a machine.

Gleason is wheeled onto the stage by his bombshell nursing assistant, Daphne. She waves and smiles and blushes like all the applause is meant for her, though it's not. Gleason can't wave back because he can't move on his own.

Clapping dwindles to excited whispers of electricity. Nelson raises his arms to quell the noise. He moves to the edge of the stage as Daphne parks the wheelchair over the duct tape X, at the center, marking where she's to stop. "I'll now answer a question or two," Nelson says.

Hands in the front row shoot in the air. Questions shouted out from the press pool range from, "is it true you and Daphne hooked up?" to, "are robot pets next on your list?" But one question gains traction and is soon picked up and repeated by others. And it's this: "What do you have to say about the failed prototype, about Timmy Bordeaux?"

Nelson bites his lower lip and his weepy eyes turn steely. The first human soul transfer always pops up. The media always wants to focus on the one negative while disregarding the countless positives they've achieved over the years. They're not much better than the old heads.

But he doesn't let the question derail his momentous occasion. Instead, he flashes an easy smile, a smile that has swayed millions. A used car salesmen smile.

"Timothy Bordeaux was sad and tragic," he elaborates for what seems the millionth time. "An unfortunate circumstance. But until his mother killed herself and her robotic son, Timothy performed exactly as expected. Again, I've said this over and over: the prototype didn't fail because of an unstable overlay or mechanical chassis defect, but because of an unstable parent killing her child. That's the worst kind of monster. That won't happen again."

Reporters hurl more questions, but the Timothy question puts a cloud over his head and he doesn't want to answer any more. "We're running a little behind," he lies as he glances at his watch. "Let's move on, shall we." He breathes in, reassures himself this is a great moment. "Now, let me introduce you to the other half of the radiant machine."

Instantly the crowd shuts up—he knew they would—and holds their collective breath, waiting for the grand unveiling. Nelson has always thought of this as one of those defining moments that he'd read about in history. Like Pearl Harbor or Kennedy's assassination or the Singularity. This will be one of those moments.

The curtains behind him sway, tall, dancing ghosts, and separate to reveal a solitary figure. The stage goes dark, then spotlights burn to life and intersect on the lone man. But it's not a normal man.

Twinkling shafts of golden sunlight reflect off its skin back into the auditorium. They gasp in unison. An older man's heart can't take the strain and he collapses in his seat.

Three hundred colleagues and reporters are in amazement and chalk up one more event in their ever-growing journal of significant events, right next to Pearl Harbor and the Singularity. But they're not just watching another robot milestone, they're witnessing human evolution.

Two years before the Radiant Machine makes his debut

When the opportunity to be selected for Re:evolution's Project Alpha became real, Gleason couldn't agree quick enough. Through a succession of eye blinks, he said, 'yes,' to the proposition.

Re:evolution's selection committee had visited him while he was collecting sun on his perpetually cold bones on his front porch in what started out as one more miserable day of lingering existence, following a previous miserable day of the same.

Once they'd left, Daphne repositioned his chair so that he could watch the geese honk on the bank of his private pond. He hated them but had become a prisoner in his body, driven by the whims of his nurse to silently oblige wherever she pushed him.

She said through smacks of her gum, "I have no idea what those guys were saying, but it sounds exciting." She leaned over him and dabbed the corner of his mouth with a spit-yellowed handkerchief. "Oh my, Mr. Gleason, you're leaking again." She smiled and wiped with exaggerated movements, performing for an unseen audience.

He hates when she says that, especially in that tone. He's not a child. Or a drooling idiot. What Re:evolution offered him was a chance to escape the helplessness, the slow, demeaning death that awaited him. He'd given up on religion long ago, once the Parkinson's ravaged his body to uselessness. But now, a door has been opened.

"There you go, good as new." Her smile didn't crack. She plopped onto her Adirondack and went back to work fixing her hair, checking her mascara.

Gleason's work wasn't so much technical as it was philosophical. And his biomechanical layering theories weren't so much a rigid scientific process as they were his new religion. Through years as a research scientist, he'd slowly developed his complex philosophy on human evolution. He outlined his twenty plus years work in his best-known book, *The Radiant Machine*. He coined the term as the summation of man, including every man-made advancement and achievement throughout time.

Biomechanical layering in a nutshell: evolutionary processes are infinite. Unfortunately, bodies aren't.

People think, their minds active, until the moment they die. That's as plain as day. But human bodies are finite. They're an ember that flickers out too soon. In the unending mind, there's the driving, instinctual need to evolve. A desire limited only by the frail body.

He postulated there's a point in development where 'natural' processes are no longer able to evolve or become too slow for quicker environmental, societal changes. This includes the death of the body, which he considered an annoying environmental change. Given these conditions, it becomes the responsibility of the species to continue with the process. Biomechanical layering was Gleason's answer to the eternal problem.

Take the mind, soul, essence, call it whatever, but it's the undying portion of our being, and transfer that undying portion out of the dying body into a new body. In this case an android body, designed by Nishimora-Dynamo Robotics.

Biomechanical layering now becomes the new evolutionary process, and the Radiant Machine continues to exist. Forever.

Building gods.

And Nelson and his Re:evolution wonder boys are making it happen. To him.

Begin the warranty period

"How do you feel, Doctor?"

Gleason opens his eyes to a new world.

The laboratory, which is more like a hospital room fused with a mechanic's garage, overlooks an artificial lake. Outside the window, the sun is peaking through nighttime storms slowly breaking on the horizon. A pair of sparrows are holding a mid-air joust, fighting for some mate tucked away in waiting branches. Their passionate tweets are discernible even through hospital ambience.

"How do you feel, Doctor?" Engineer Paulson repeats. He's been on shift since midnight monitoring Gleason's vitals as they blip across monitors, a video game of life. His moment of thrill that overcame him once he saw Gleason stir in his bed is slowly descending into worry as he waits to see if the Radiant Machine is aware, if he can even speak.

The early android prototypes that were merged with human consciousness, such as the tragic case of

Timothy Bordeaux, were quite different from the Radiant Machine. For them, it was like a cassette in a VCR; the entities were separate but worked together.

The Radiant Machine isn't a dumb android running algorithmic recordings of thought patterns and deciphered emotion fed off a magnetic tape.

Magic has merged with technology. The spirit of man is integrated into metal at the subatomic level; a marriage of soul and steel. A truly blessed and unbreakable union. They are one. Gleason has been biomechanically layered. Gleason has evolved.

He's attained a higher order, he's made that leap from water to land, ascended the plane, climbed down the trees for huts of sapling branches and fronds. Gleason has become the poster boy, the golden-skinned calf of a new world, a golden Age of Enlightenment.

He lifts his arms, first his left, then his right. It takes no more thought than he remembers. His hands flap in the air, mimicking the sparrows. His legs work and he swings them off the hospital bed. They're restless. He wants to sit up, to crawl from his incapacitated cocoon that has tormented him for the past decade. He wants to run outside, around the lake, around the world. He knows he can do it in this new golden body. There will be a time for all this and more. So much more.

He clears his throat and smiles at the young engineer. "Why, I feel capital."

A squalid, rent-controlled studio apartment on the west side

"Bernard!" a piercing voice cuts through the wafer-ceiling, penetrating drywall like the very lungs of Hell have shuddered and coughed up a hairball, dislodged after a millennium of soaking in phlegm. "Shut that music off or your power's cut!"

"The cops said you can't cut it again," Bernard screams in return. His ceiling thumps and the 70's Budweiser fluorescent sign hanging from a chain swings as the slum-lord super stamps his frail foot, just to make sure Bernard gets the point.

"Alright, You crazy old goat, I'll turn it down," Bernard says. "I hope you break your leg," he adds. He has no real intention of turning his speakers down, and in fact, turns his stereo up to eleven. Classic Iron Maiden wails.

In his darkened apartment, hunched over his laptop connected to the cloud and all of its magnificent knowledge through hundred-thousand miles of electric cables, Bernard frantically types in a private chat. He's in a race to see and share every vast moment of history before the sun comes up.

When the daytime sentries that keep all men in check punches the clock and heads home for the evening, that's when the night comes, with its darkness and foul thoughts. It spreads illness over the land. And the few that have reviled but endured the daytime rejoices at the coming, laps up the night with parched and dry tongues, spits it back out as vile intentions and actions.

No kidding, I'm laughing out loud.

Bernard types with trained sausage fingers that barely touch the keyboard, gliding as gracefully as a seamstress hemming a skirt.

StarMan22 streamed me one cut in half in a construction accident. A Dynamo 1000. Legs and lower torso walked for 15 min! Great stuff. Let me find the vid & I'll patch in a sec.

Bernard pulls up his directory of thousands of illegal files, files of androids coming to their end in gruesome ways, files that'd get him prosecuted for hate crimes. He locates the video and patches it to NishRUs.

NishRUs—*Thanks. Sorry about losing your job, @StudHitman. Bummer. Those lousy androids are a plague.*

StudHitman—*U don't know the half. Doc said I was exhibiting classic machi-phobia. That was grounds for termination. All because I refused to share my cubicle with that machine. If you knew me you'd say I'm completely stable.*

Bernard slaps the Enter key in unemployed anger as he remembers the steamy summer Monday morning, three months ago, when he arrived at work to a waist-high computer sharing his cubicle. His boss, Mr. Randall, informed him he had been selected to field test the Nishimora Computational Device. But Bernard knew better. Corporate wanted him out.

Ever since he threatened to sue after eating a spoiled Yummy Nougats candy bar from the Nishimora Vend-O-Matic and coming down with a severe case of dysentery, they were out to get him.

NishRUs—*I completely think you're capable. You have some great vids.*

StudHitman—*Don't you know it!*

NishRUs—*Oh, almost forgot. Found a reso stick on Pirate Bay. You got the frequencies, right?*

StudHitman—*I've had them for weeks. Send me the link.*

NishRUs—*Sending now. This'll be epic!*

Bernard leans back in his computer chair, rests his arms on his protruding belly in smug contemplation. The reso stick was the last item he needed to put his plan into work. Now he can start tracking this so-called Radiant Machine's whereabouts, which should be easy enough given his knowledge of the interwebz.

His stomach growls, breaking his thoughts. He rifles under his bed for any missed Yummy Nougats bars.

This is going to be epic.

Unremarkable city, remarkable man

In an instant, Gleason becomes the most interesting man in the world. He zooms up the celebrity alphabet past the C and B-list actors straight to the top of the A's, an A++, without a single movie to his credit.

The Nobel Committee begins the nomination process for his Peace Prize because they know he'll bring great things.

His album hits double platinum, even though he hasn't cut a song.

Paparazzi redirect yearly budgets to keep up with him. One entrepreneurial Refuse Collection Agent squirreled away Gleason's household trash, and within a week was able to retire with the money he bankrolled selling it on Pirate Bay.

Kids trash their second-grade reports where they list mom and dad as their heroes. They rewrite them to say they want to become mechanical when they grow up, just like the Radiant Machine.

The Vatican rewickers their canonization process to fast-track his sainthood.

He's the 22nd Century Star-Darling. A post-millennial Singularity god of gold.

A year later along a nondescript sidewalk, and the universe sings a song, continually. Twinkling stars millions of miles away are all part of a celestial chorus. And it's near, too. The song is sung across the earth. It's in every heartbeat, fueled by the electricity of life. Every machine resonates in harmony as one of many players in the celestial chorus. It cannot be escaped. The Radiant Machine is no different.

And as the universe sings, Bernard passes the time hiding in a dark alleyway, humming out of tune to a song he doesn't know the words to. A drop turns into a sprinkle turns into a light and steady rain. He pulls his hoodie over his face to keep the cold out. He waits.

Another thirty minutes and he hears a tune that sounds like an impromptu London Philharmonic Orchestra rattling out Beethoven's Second Symphony. The rain lets up.

After the third Yummy Nougats bar, Bernard has finally built up enough nerve to go through with his devious, conceived in the dead of night, plan he laid out months ago. It's risky, but nothing risked, nothing gained. He discards the wrapper before placing his hand over his robes, where the modified reso stick is safely tucked away in an inner pocket.

If he was caught with this reso stick—resonance stick—a riot police vertigo-inducing baton, it would instantly net him a 5-year sentence. Minimum.

Bernard worked in marketing support for Dynamo Robotics when he was sacked for machi-phobia. He wasn't privy to corporate secrets, but he was privy to other employees and had formed a gaming league during his time at Dynamo. Willie, or Glumly, a neutral–neutral dwarf from the Northlands, had a second cousin who was a Dynamo engineer. That was enough.

Through Bernard's dangled carrot of an iron-clad guarantee he would find the *Wand of Total Destruction* during their next tabletop RPG campaign, Willie spent the weekend at his cousin's. After an evening of home-made screwdrivers, his cousin hinted at the operating frequencies of Nishimora-Dynamo robots. Through the night, Willie pried the corporate codes from his unsuspecting, stinking drunk cousin.

All through school, Bernard's counselors had labeled him an overachieving mind wrapped in an underachieving body. Now he put that overachieving mind to work.

Bernard had spent the last of his severance package from Dynamo to purchase an illegal reso stick for reprogramming. He also picked up a copy of *Physics for Dummies* to learn the basics of harmonic resonance and fundamental electronic theory. The fact that Dynamo's money would fund their own destruction was icing on the cake. Bernard was all about the irony. And the cake. Bernard likes cake.

He'd dressed in his best gaming outfit of a black friar, along the lines of chaotic–neutral. His mother, a seamstress, turned some discarded blackout curtains into his rocking getup. The black robes and heavy hood would prove perfect for his nighttime mission.

That's what this is, a nighttime mission.

A mission more important than destroying a vampire, goblin king, or rogue dragon. This is to destroy a monster. The worst kind of monster, the kind of monster that's lifted up as a hero, but in fact, is terrible.

He'd stood by and watched while Dynamo Robotics propped up Timothy Bordeaux as the first successful transfer of human consciousness into robot. They created a Frankenstein while the world clapped and cheered them on. And now, the Radiant Machine is the next step. The true merging of two things that should never be joined.

Bernard had his ongoing issues; his lower back pains, spontaneous left arm numbness, occasional heart palpitations, chronic bad breath, and acne. If anyone deserved a new body, it was him. He had given the best two years of his life to Dynamo and let them know that on the application for selection to evolve. That's what Bernard wanted, a better body that wouldn't die. That's what everyone wants. And he resented those that got it while he stood on the sideline.

Instead, they picked some dried up doctor with Parkinson's.

To add insult to injury, Dynamo sacked Bernard because he wanted compensation for the crippling diarrhea. They used the machi-phobia as the reason. But it wasn't. It was all too much to bear.

It had been a year since the Radiant Machine had been created, brought to life by the Re:evolution sorcerers with electricity and magic. This monstrosity has gone on long enough.

He chose this night because the big and bright moon had just faded with the month. A new one was still in the process of being born.

After the ruckus of stardom, Gleason had settled into a fairly routine life, for a superstar. He soon desired those moments away from the gawking mass of humanity. He took strolls, just after dinner, around the city block. He had done it so much the local community had gotten used to him, and somewhat respected his desire for privacy. That would prove great for Bernard, not so great for Gleason.

Tonight, Bernard slays a god.

Not just anyone can whistle like the London Philharmonic Orchestra. He knows Gleason is near.

Quietly, like a stealth Jedi-ninja, Bernard slips his modified reso stick from within the folds of his robe. He needs to activate it just before impact.

As Gleason passes along the darkened sidewalk, Bernard steps from the alleyway to intercept him. For a second he is taken back, startled by Bernard's sudden presence in his path. Quickly he recovers and stares at the large, curtain-wrapped man.

Nerves get the better of Bernard now that he's on the spot. He tries a fake smile and stammers, "H-hey, I know—you're Gleason. Doctor. I mean, you're a doctor. Can I get *my—your* autograph?"

Dynamo's engineers have taken great care to craft facial nuance. Bernard has seen annoyance enough in his life to instantly recognize it, and Gleason's carefully crafted facial nuances are exceptionally cruel.

"Hey there, big guy," Gleason says, his voice reinforcing his facial expression, "you headed to a Halloween party? You're about six months too late."

More stammering instead of responding.

"What are you a druid or something? A warlock?" Now Gleason's voice cracks with amusement as he eyes Bernard up and down, full of disdain.

Like he'd practiced on his pillow so many times over the past year, in one smooth motion Bernard whips the stick from under his robe while simultaneously activating the modified frequency generator. It hums faintly as tickling electricity spiders up his arm. He brings it around. Before Gleason can react, the stick glances off his head. In full Jedi-ninja mode, Bernard dissolves into the darkened alley, into shadow and night.

Gleason staggers as the reso stick frequency contradicts his resonance, overwhelming him in dissonance. His neural processors glitch and reset incorrectly. His gyroscopic sensors are in disarray and tell him up is down, slide left is actually slide right.

He's in bad shape.

Dropping to the ground, he heaves in a mechanical way which sounds like a septic truck draining a full tank. He throws up *ones* and *zeroes*. They trickle into the nearby street drain to become one with the city's sludge highway.

His body spent, his senses reeling from the shockblast to his faux-human cognition, Dr. Charles Gleason, the Radiant Machine, the 22nd Century Star-Darling, passes out like a common drunkard in the gutter.

The illusion of science and magic

"Dr. Gleason? Can you hear me?"

"I...think...I can...hear you," comes the voice, spoken from under water.

Nelson is the only human in a recovery room located in Re:evolution's basement. The temperature is a dry 92.7 degrees, exactly. That's the optimal climate for the advanced circuitry. In the center of the room is a vat filled to the brim with ionized water. It's large enough to hold a man. Inside, Gleason rolls and tumbles in the churning fluid, a priceless garment in a washing machine. The induction bath is the final step in the process of fixing Re:evolution's flagship man.

Nelson bites his nails as he watches the last ten years of work hang by a delicate fairy thread. "You can't be broken," he whispers. He prays to Gleason, "you're perfect, just perfect, unbreakable," and waits to see if the magic elixir of life will work.

As Gleason tumbles, he hears Nelson's plea. His partially fried circuits reassemble his thoughts like the horsemen putting together a cracked egg.

They promised him immortality and perfection. They may have built the perfect body, but they couldn't fit in the perfect man. His anger, his pride, his lusts never left. Those base, sinful emotions, those imperfections that resided in him before never left. The anger never left.

Anger of life, anger of disease, anger at being packed in a disease-ridden human body like a sardine in a dented can, forever. One diseased body traded for another. Forever. An existence eternal as an undying company prop, to be hauled out every party and national holiday.

Gleason sees it now. It took the trauma to clear his head. To burn away the cobwebs.

What is life if there's no death?

In his biomechanical layering theories, he'd sought to find that well of life, that magic fruit that would grant immortality. To go on and not know death. An endless hum of existence.

He can't die.

He can't die, he can't feel the exhilaration of a roller coaster because there's no gamble, he can't wholeheartedly love a woman without the fragile fear that he's sure to bury her one day. He can't appreciate the complex but simple beauty of a daisy. No longer can he enjoy the thrill of taking one breath after another; it's a given. It's enough to drive him insane.

And insane he goes.

Nelson, in all his boy band fervor for his creation, steps close to the vat. His heart leaps. The elixir seems to be working.

Gleason explodes from the rejuvenating water, grabs Nelson by his $200 tailored shirt and drags him into the vat.

The tech mogul screams but takes in water that tastes like liquid battery. It burns his skin and throat. He punches at the golden man but his twice a week toning classes never planned for attacking robots. His resistance is futile.

Gleason pins Nelson to the bottom of the tank. He thrashes as he knows he's going to die.

Just like Gleason can't.

Another thirty-seconds and the bubbles stop. Superman is dead.

Gleason has just given his creator the greatest gift he could give: death. It feels good to give, consoling in an odd way. He needs to give more. As the Radiant Machine leaves the induction bath, creeping up the basement stairs half-lit by emergency lights, he looks for more people that would love his wonderful new gift.

Captain Cluck's Wingery

The celebration lasts well into the night. Chicken wings and Pete's Red Ribbon beer are involved. Once he's had his fill, Bernard staggers from Captain Cluck's Wingery to his apartment a little down the street. He makes his way to the elevator, lets out at the fourth floor, and spends the next five minutes fishing for his keys in the wrong pocket. Once he sheepishly realizes his mistake, he quickly unlocks his door and slips inside.

He disrobes from the sweat-and-rain-drenched friar's outfit, he finds his favorite pajamas on his hamper and puts them on. Ecstasy is still rushing through his veins as he thinks of what he accomplished tonight.

He killed a god.

The man who stole his body, who had ripped fame and fortune from Bernard's chubby hands. Revenge is sweet. Candy bar sweet.

A satisfactory smile creeps across his face. A night-time snack is in order. He opens the box of Yummy Nougats on his counter, grabs one and drags it under his nose like he's taking in a fine Cuban. A good candy bar, maybe some gaming...but first, he needs to let NishRUs know the mission is accomplished.

He sits at his workstation and his desktop/laptop hybrid senses him and boots up. By the time he plants his butt in the molded seat his screens are active with chats and boards and news feeds.

Something catches his eyes. A news scroll of breaking events. He clicks and brings into view the WXWY late-breaking video feed and closes one blurry, intoxicated eye to see what's going on.

Police cruisers have surrounded the downtown Re:evolution office building, red and blue strobes playing off shadows. Police drones, basketball-sized chrome spheres with multi-viewing lenses, spotlights, and flashing LEDs, zigzag around the building from top to bottom, spying through every curtain crack. The feed is piped into WXWY and played across the city in hi-res footage.

The news scroll states a hostage situation is on-going. Someone inside the building initiated the lock-down protocol. Blast doors have cut off exits. There's no way out. An hour ago, a security guard managed to get a call out saying that a machine had gone rogue and initiated the protocol, trapping approximately thirty researchers and security inside. The call ended abruptly with a scream.

In a moment of clarity, Bernard knows his plan didn't work the way he intended. Not completely, any-way. The plan was so simple he didn't think it could fail. A simple way to get revenge on a corporation and their monstrosity. He knows it's Gleason in the build-ing. The blow to him must've glanced off, not made complete connection.

Bernard didn't slay a god. He came close, but no cigar. Not yet. Then, as he stares at the scrolling feed and strokes his pockmarked face, a brilliant idea strikes him. He can fix this.

Rushing back to his soggy robes, he grabs the reso stick. It's so simple, he can finish the job and even earn points. The city—no, the world will see him defeat the monster. He'll be a hero. He doesn't need a robotic body to be famous, to live forever, he just needs to defeat an evil robot. That'll be enough. And everyone will soon know the name of the black friar, Stud-HitMan, Bernard Shively. Just as soon as his head stops spinning from the cheap beer so he can grab a snack.

Re:evolution Headquarters

Alpha Team Bravo began the ordinary night shift as a ten-person security detail. Only Clive is left. And he's not faring too well.

Inside Re:evolution's main facility, emergency lights strobe in sickening flashes of cut scene movement, chopping reality into bite-size chunks of brightness for easier consumption. Blast doors have blocked all the exits. Everything is working according to safety protocol Z13. Of course, Z13 was meant for outside intrusion, not for invasions that come from inside.

Clive hates protocol Z13. It keeps him from escaping.

He'd made it down to the first floor and came within twenty short yards of exiting the building. That's when someone initiated Z13. The blasted blast door fell and cut off his exit. He tried an alternate route, that's when he also met Gleason.

He'd barely escaped to the second floor with his life, a tremendous side wound evidence of his run-in with the maniacal robot. From there he decided to continue up. He had an idea, and if he could make it to the fifth floor, then there was a chance he could live. The soldiers might be that only chance.

On the fourth, he'd met Daphne, just as his strength gave and he was ready to give up.

"Blast," Clive mouths as he notices the wet, red stain on the side of his uniform spread. He's weak and needs to lean on her for support.

I didn't sign up for this, Daphne thinks. But this Clive fellow was insistent on her helping him to the next floor. She reluctantly agreed, and now struggles to help him up the stairwell, careful to keep him from bleeding on her new purse.

How did I end up here? she asks herself. They were headed for a wild night on the town, full of swanky sushi bars and throbbing dance clubs when Nelson got the call from the police that they had found Dr. Gleason unconscious. He told them to bring him straight to Re:evolution's facility where there would be staff waiting to tend to him.

She hung out in the executive lobby picking green M&Ms from a fishbowl candy dish. Then sirens sounded and lights flashed. Everything fell apart. Everyone scattered, leaving her behind like they all had certain places to be except her. She followed a couple of men in lab coats up the stairwell to the fourth floor, to a small foyer. There she'd lost them as they knew where they were going and she didn't. So she hunkered underneath a receptionist's desk, gripping a pair of scissors. Screams rose from below. Clive found her there.

The two make it to the fifth floor and exit the stairwell.

It's mostly auditorium surrounded by various utility rooms. Clive leads her across the expansive room to a small alcove, set off in shadows. A narrow door leads to a room full of complicated control panels with hundreds of knobs and switches.

Through spasms of pain and teetering on the verge of passing out, Clive attempts to tell her the input sequence to activate the robots. Daphne grabs wildly at knobs and enters codes on keypads with nervous fingers as she tries to follow his confusing instructions.

On the way up the stairs, Clive had mentioned they just needed to stall Gleason long enough for the safety protocol to reset. Then the doors would open and they would be able to get out. Hopefully.

Re:evolution's parking lot

Patrolman Kenney, a six-month recruit, after listening to Bernard whine, beg and threaten for the past thirty minutes, finally gives in and takes him to Incident Commander Chief Raston, yards from the entrance to Re:evolution, amid the swirls of police lights against the breaking dawn background.

He patiently listens to Bernard's plan for five minutes before saying, "So you're telling me, Mr. Bernard, you want to go in there?" He thumbs over his shoulder to the entrance doors. "You have the means to stop Dr. Gleason?" Chief eyes Bernard, in his black friar robe, up and down, and is completely not impressed. "What are you, some kind of ninja?"

In a smugness brought about by several glasses of beer and an unhealthy amount of comfort food, Bernard smiles as he finishes his second Yummy Nougats. He wads the wrapper and tosses it to the ground. "That's what I said. I hold the keys to shutting off this monster. I hate to state the obvious, but if word gets out that you knew this, but failed to act, I'm sure the mayor would be pretty upset."

Chief lowers his head, stares at the discarded wrapper. He mouths without words, like he's voicing his options to himself. Finally, after internal deliberation, he shrugs. "Hmm, let me check something. I'll be back in a couple minutes, ninja," he says and hurriedly winds around parked cruisers to his unmarked vehicle and sits in the driver's seat. He closes the door.

A mechanical swoosh emits from the entrance. Bernard spins around in time to see the blast door that was blocking the entrance suddenly lift into the ceiling. This is his golden moment. He races to the entrance and through before anyone can respond. Inside, he pulls his club from his pocket in his fluid, pillow-beating movement. Now to find the killing machine and finish the job.

The Radiant Machine

After helping the twenty-third person realize their full potential, Gleason pauses to consider the magnificent work he has done. They fought and kicked, but it was all no use. They didn't know what he knows, the wonderful elation of freedom that he offered each of them. The experience to die. Something only a true human can fathom.

If they could only understand, they would welcome the gift. They'd all come and lay before him, their electric god of chrome and brass. They'd worship him as they offered themselves to him on an altar. Sacrifices to a god. Yes, that's what they are.

He's made it to the fifth floor and stands just beyond the doors leading to the auditorium. It has been such a long time since he was last here. A different body, a different mind. A different time.

The doors swing open unexpectedly and proto-type peacekeeping bots pour through. Their weak AI isn't capable of performing complex reasoning, not like Gleason. They can target and fight, but beyond that are dumb to the world. Under Clive's direction, Daphne has input a command code so that they select Gleason as a hostile target.

The first to respond to the kill command is a K.97 peacekeeper bot, nicknamed a "slugger." Instead of arms, it wields two 18 gauge shotguns. But its internal targeting system hasn't cleared beta tests yet and due to a coding error on line 25,754, sets its sights on a peacekeeper bot nearby. It unloads six uranium-tipped 18 gauge slugs into the combat bot's chassis. The poor unsuspecting thing sputters and spits sparks through the holes in its chest as it falls forward.

Two bots holding 9mm pistols unload their banana clips into Gleason. Then they order him to stop.

He staggers, internal sensors screaming that his chassis has endured trauma. He inspects his naked chest, fingers the holes in him that are leaking red and black and smell of motor oil.

In the bath that rejuvenated him, his self and body began to separate. The evolutionary union that was supposed to be eternal had a flawed seam. He should've felt the bullets like a real person. But he doesn't. The neuro-pain protocols should've made him react in an artificial way commensurate to real life. But they don't. He doesn't feel.

With a primal scream of an unstoppable monster-god, Gleason lunges for the shock troops with his clawed hands. They need to be freed of their robotic inhibitions.

He rips and tears and rends, gets shot, rends some more. Till all the peacekeepers are torn apart, their dead bodies cast aside, magazines spent. He's made it across the auditorium and makes his way to the control room, a red oil slick trailing behind him.

Daphne screams as the door's kicked in. Clive had left his service revolver on the counter before tumbling to the floor, unconscious. She lifts the heavy gun with perfectly manicured hands and tries to keep it steady.

She unloads the weapon at Gleason. Bullets embed in his pliable exoskin, yielding to force, but not giving in to the violence.

He smiles, but three bullets have shredded his facial expression protocols, so his mouth is frozen in a sneer, much like his old organic body with Parkinson's. "You can't kill me," his voice slurred because of an uncooperative tongue. "Don't you know I've evolved? I'm immortal. I'm a monster that can't be killed."

The gun obviously didn't work so Daphne drops it. She doesn't know what else to do but maybe reason with him. "We're all monsters," she says, lips quivering. "You can do horrible things, but one day you wake up and find out you're no longer a monster. You can be a human again." She nods so he can see she truly believes what she says.

"I can release you from your body. You'll thank me."

"Please," Daphne sobs, mascara running as black tears to outline Botox lips, a sad clown in the making. "Please don't kill me. I took care of you. We watched geese together."

Gleason's sneer is unrelenting. "I hated those geese. I was a drooling idiot to you. I was a stage prop for your audition before the world."

"No..." she shakes her head.

"You would as soon push me over a cliff or feed me to the geese as care for me. But I have something better for you."

"No, that's not true," she whispers, her voice a defenseless child's.

"I can release you from the dull trappings of your manufactured life. I can show you so much more, show you what I know is the greatest gift of life: death."

He moves to her as her legs fail and she falls to the floor, next to where Clive has collapsed. Grasping her tiny wrists, Gleason effortlessly lifts her and she dangles like a shot rabbit ready to be skinned. He drapes her over the control panel. "I can release you from all this... fakery. You'd thank me if you knew what I'm doing for you."

She doesn't resist anymore. She accepts the fact that she's going to die at the hands of the monstrous robot her boyfriend created. And all the moments she wasted on her exterior are nothing because she knows, in the end, it's not about that. Her soul is fearful, empty, and wasted.

Dr. Charles Gleason, the Radiant Machine, raises one bloody golden arm over his head, ready to plunge it deep into Daphne's chest.

A sound of metal on metal breaks the odd, tense silence.

If Gleason's face was registering emotion properly he would show surprise, eyes wide and mouth agape. Instead, he lets go of Daphne and staggers to the side, like his head has suddenly gained an extra hundred pounds. He grabs at his ears in the hope that cupping them will steady his reeling gyroscopes. Leaning left, he gains momentum until he crashes into a cinder block wall. The wall doesn't give but he does. He bounces off and falls backward to the floor, his circuits dead.

Where Gleason the killer robot stood moments ago now stands a large, robed figure. He's breathing heavy, sweating profusely, and holding a police baton.

Bernard smiles at the bombshell he just saved and gives her a quick nod and salute with his reso stick, like he's a cowboy that just rescued his favorite bar girl from the drunken gambler. He looks to where Gleason has collapsed, still. "Your evolution has failed," he says in welling pride and manliness.

"Mr. Bernard!"

He spins on his chubby heel at the familiar voice. Chief's standing at the doorway of the control room flanked by three of his officers. Patrolman Kenney cautiously moves to Gleason, his service revolver aimed for a shot at center mass, if needed. The other two tend to Daphne and Clive. "So you stopped him with that resonance baton?" Chief asks, his eyes pointing to the illegal device Bernard is holding.

"Yeah, dead in his tracks."

"That's great." Chief thinks for a moment. He crosses his arms. "And you like Yummy Nougats?"

Bernard, expecting a pat on the back and a 'job well done' statement from the Chief, doesn't expect the question and hesitates momentarily, wondering where this is all going. "Uhm, yeah. Why?"

"When I was investigating Dr. Gleason's attack yesterday, Nelson said external trauma caused him to glitch. Maybe something like that hacked baton?"

"If you're asking," Bernard suddenly finds himself playing defense. "I don't know. Maybe. Who knows." He's sweating more. "There's lots of things that could've affected him."

Chief nods. "At the scene of the crime, where Gleason was attacked, I found something curious."

Bernard's sweating to the point he can smell himself. He isn't sure if the air conditioners are working or if it's because he's draped in blackout curtains. Either way, he's lightheaded and wants to sit down.

"Yeah," Chief continues. "The most curious things, candy wrappers. Odd, huh?"

Bernard's overachieving mind knows Chief has put together that he's the one that drove Gleason to begin the murderous rampage. But he feels completely justified because he ended up saving the day by bringing him down. "Monsters don't come from swamps or graveyards," he says in his sure-fire defense. "In fact, they don't realize they're monsters at all. They begin their journey thinking they're heroes, doing something great."

The words are deep and profound, and Bernard knows that they cut to the heart of the situation. It's just a matter of making Chief understand.

And as Chief stands there, staring at the scene that has unfolded, he considers Bernard's words, chewing on the inside of his mouth for a minute or two as he contemplates. Finally, he says, "Do you think you're responsible, that you're the monster because you caused all this?" He gives Patrolman Kenney an almost unperceivable eye glance for him to get ready the extra-large handcuffs.

Now Bernard considers the Chief's words. He rests his arms on his stomach in introspection. "Hmm, I never thought of it like that."

ABOUT THE AUTHOR

AK MEEK IS a mild-mannered management engineer by day, a mild-mannered writer by night, Anthony writes speculative, slipstream science fiction and fantasy. He has penned alternate realities where robots are treated as gods fallen to earth, built cities filled to the brim with artificial animals, and crafted stories of alien invaders that can see human thought. He has also dipped his hand in "Jericho" style post-apocalyptic fiction and birthed a fantastic world where truth and lie can occupy the same space. He lives in the Deep South, among the mosquitoes and magnolias, with his wonderful wife and menagerie of dogs and cats, and a wild rabbit that occasionally strays into the back yard for a visit.

MONSTERS IN OUR MIDST

OUR MIDST

MARTIN T. INGHAM

RAPID EXPLOSIONS SHOOK the ground as the midnight sky lit up brighter than the dawn. The faint sound of sirens echoed in the distance, the shocked cries of a city under siege. The bombardment was only just beginning, though the war was nothing new. It had been years in the making, this assault on the colony world, Bellaris IV.

Brex Katrine cringed, as the blasts grew closer. He was on the outskirts of the small town of Alden, away from the main assault, but it was spreading outward, growing closer with every tick of the clock. Before long, even his relatively remote position would be a target. The enemy was determined to leave nothing standing. Any construct that could be used for shelter or a sign of civilization was to be decimated. That was the intent of this strike, to terrorize and demoralize. If it was merely about killing, a single tactical fusion bomb would have turned the surrounding area to glass.

But this enemy didn't believe in wholesale slaughter. No, they were only interested in conquest, and there were times Brex had to wonder if they weren't justified.

"We must get to the woods," Brex said, as he adjusted the straps on his backpack. He'd been prepared for this contingency, and the bug-out bag weighed him down with everything he'd need to survive in the wild.

A silent nod was the only response his companion gave, but it was all Brex needed. The two had a way of communicating beyond words. The past two years had taught them that, since verbal communication had proven problematic. So, of course, necessity being the mother of invention and all that, they'd learned to talk in other ways.

For how was one supposed to converse with a monstrous alien?

Simple grunts seemed to be the best that the hairy beast could utter. Its vocal cords were sadly inadequate to produce a regular syntax. Brex had tried to understand the low mumbling sounds that his companion would make, though it had proven futile. They had worked out a form of sign language so the monster could express itself, and it clearly understood Brex's speech.

How strange that this curious monster would be his best and only friend at the worst of times.

Brex had always been a loner, an outcast, a socially awkward individual. He didn't understand why. His parents had been very sociable and well-liked by their peers, yet he found himself lacking social skills. As a child, it had bothered him, but as he grew up, he found he didn't really care. Other people didn't interest him, as they hadn't been interested in him. So, he was happy on his own.

Only, now he finally had his first friend, and that made him do crazy things.

• • •

BEWARE THE MONSTER INVADERS

The sign was plastered at the bottom of billboards and in the headers of most military dispatches. It had become a catchphrase of the day as interstellar conflict intensified. The long reign of peace amidst the stars had been a fleeting concept. It seemed when peace was finally achieved on the homeworld, there would be new foes found in space.

Brex could scarcely remember the era of peace. It ended shortly after his birth, and twenty years later it still raged on. When he came of age, he was drafted into the civilian military corps, something all able-bodied adults experienced these days amongst the Confederated Worlds. The draft was necessary for survival, as the monsters continued their incursions and sought to exterminate every living being in their path. At least, that's what the popular line was. Enough ships went missing that it was easy to believe.

It was something Brex never truly believed. He couldn't understand why an intelligent race of space-faring beings would be interested in bloody conquest..

The true form and nature of the enemy was not discussed, and few had ever seen their faces—the monsters preferring to hide behind their technology. Popular media depicted them as hairy barbarians with massive teeth. Modern horror films showed the monsters eating people alive as they ventured deeper into Confederated space, and such depictions only aided the war effort, stirring citizens into servitude to defend against impending doom.

Living on an outer colony world, Brex didn't really care for the horror stories, and when drafted he was content to do his duty, serving as a mechanic and sentry at various military bases across the central continent. He put in his time, as everyone did, and for years it was tedium and regularity. Nothing ever happened in the backwater world his grandparents had helped to colonize. The war was on the other side of Confederation space, over a hundred light years away.

Manning stations and running combat drills seemed pointless.

Then, it came.

With three months left to serve, Brex found himself in the hot seat for the first time. There was a firefight in the upper atmosphere. A pair of Confederation cruisers had chased an invader spacecraft all the way here, across so many star systems, and there was no telling what would happen next. The minutes ticked on, as Brex and his comrades listened to comm-traffic as the incursion continued. It was the tail-end of a fight that had been ongoing for days, and finally, as everyone's nerves grew sharp, it was over. The Confederation cruisers forced the enemy vessel down. The battle was won.

Before Brex could catch his breath, his unit was called up. The remaining hunk of the enemy craft had crashed in the marshes several hundred klicks to the west of their base, and it was largely intact. Now was the time for the mechanics to shine, to dismantle the vessel and learn more about its alien technology.

For the first time, Brex felt that his service wasn't pointless. The war was here and he had a purpose.

The flight out to the crash site gave precious moments for introspection. Brex knew he should be scared, terrified even, but he wasn't. The thought of boarding the remains of an alien spacecraft and the monsters within frightened his colleagues, but he didn't fear the enemy. The prospect of meeting a true alien intrigued him, but there was a combat unit flying ahead, ready to comb through the wreckage before the mechanics took their turn. The enemy aliens would be routed, their living captured or killed, and their dead bodies removed from sight long before Brex got there.

The techs and mechanics would never look the enemy in the eyes, allowing them to do their duty with peace of mind.

A cloud of smoke obscured the view of the green and purple foliage in the Amba-Da-een Swamp. As the landing craft set down near the dark plume, Brex saw the cause of the cloud, as dozens of soldiers in full body suits piled cloth-draped bodies upon a raging pyre. The bonfire glowed brightly, as a dozen automated flamethrowers intensified the inferno, incinerating all trace of the enemy corpses. The soldier boys had done their job, cleaning out the alien craft.

Brex followed his unit out of the lander, trapped amidst the crowd of technicians, specialists, and mechanics. They were a mixed crew who had spent their draft years studying schematics and performing maintenance on military hardware. You could say they had trained their whole careers for this moment.

The alien vessel was hardly impressive from the outside. It was a charred, crumpled wreck, little more than a giant, silver crate. Several holes had been cut into it for easy access to the interior—much easier to remove the corpses that way.

Brex felt a shiver of excitement roll down his spine. The tools in his sack jingled slightly as he walked the makeshift gangplank leading up to one of the cut openings in the alien craft. He was caught in the thrill of the moment, and a few of his fellow technicians gave him confounded looks. They couldn't understand why he would be so jovial at a time like this. It wasn't bravery or attention to duty but actual joy on his face. Nobody else was smiling, leaving Brex the outsider once again.

The interior of the alien vessel was eerily familiar, not all that different from Confederation designs. The sterile metal walls with computer consoles filled the cramped room, which Brex imagined to be the command bridge of the crippled craft. Several doorways led away from the central room, giving access to the rest of the ship.

Brex was a technician "second class," which made him one of the more senior members of the team, giving him top pick of assignments. His chosen task was to dismantle inner hull panels for metallurgical analysis and to photograph the framing of the ship to document its construction. What new secrets could they glean from this captured prize? Brex felt honored to be a part of the research.

The stink of chemicals and the acrid smell of electrical smoke assaulted his senses as he descended into the craft. There was little light in the lower decks, but Brex had his trusted headlamp to show him the way. He started pulling things apart methodically, the whirring of his cutter and drill echoing through the empty space, joined sporadically by the sound of other tools in disparate parts of the ship. His fellow workers had their assigned sections, but he kept himself isolated, alone, in a section of the ship deemed to be of low priority. That way, nobody would bother him.

Panel after panel came off, and as he removed each section of inner plating, he marked it with a digital etcher and documented where each piece came from. Once cataloged, a piece would go on an anti-gravity dolly capable of lifting several tons of cargo. Its only limitation was the narrow hallways of the vessel.

After removing a dozen plates in the same manner, the thrill was fading. Brex felt the cold boredom of the mundane. He could have been dismantling scrap in a junkyard to the same effect. Despite the alien origin of the vessel, it all seemed so ordinary, and his assignment was the dullest of the dull. Yet, he had a job to do, so he did it.

As the stack of panels grew large, almost sizeable enough to call for a second anti-grav dolly, Brex turned his attention to an odd looking floor plate. It was different from the rest of the structure, and after quick inspection, it became clear that it was a hatch of some kind. A storage compartment or maintenance access, perhaps. Brex took a moment to examine the layout and recognized the opening mechanism. It was a simple enough configuration, but as he tried to turn the mag-locks holding the plate down, he found it unwilling to budge. It had been sealed before the ship had lost power, leaving the metal locking bolts in place.

Firing up his cutter, Brex burned through the sections of the hatch that held it in place. It wasn't very hard to do, and within moments the plate was free. A quick yank and the panel came off.

How quickly the thrill returned.

• • •

The rumble faded with the dawn.

Brex leaned against a sapro tree that grew on a forested knoll overlooking the wooded valley and the flattened city beyond. It had been eight hours of hard march through darkness to reach this vantage point, and it gave him little solace. They were far from safe. The bombs had finished, leaving so many questions for the future.

A series of low-frequency grunts sounded, and Brex turned to his companion, who proceeded to make hand signals—the complex form of sign language they had developed. It had been awkward for Brex to learn, since the monster's hands were two fingers short of normal and pretty stubby, though the alien had been patient. Brex was now an expert and translated these latest hand signs to mean, *"I'm tired. Can we stop?"*

"No, we have to keep moving," Brex said. "We need to find shelter, but we're still too close to the city. We should head deeper into the hills."

"I Need rest," the monster signed. *"Water."*

Brex had to remind himself that his companion wasn't quite as resilient as he was. The monster seemed to sweat all the time and had diminished stamina. His physiology wasn't that robust. Their homeworld had to be such a gentle place.

The relative frailty of the monster had been an endearing quality for Brex. He felt sympathy for the creature, and after nearly two years of discussion, he had learned much. This thing's race weren't horrible warmongers, as the Confederation media reported. Far from it.

"We'll find you some water," Brex assured his companion, even as he glanced back at the smoldering remains of the distant city. The plumes of smoke obscured much of the view, though there wasn't much left to see. Not a single building stood.

Brex turned back to his companion and ventured deeper into the forest. The undulating terrain and thickets of thorny underbrush left them zigzagging through the woods, putting greater distance between themselves and the devastation.

The further, the better.

•   •   •

"These battery modules are unlike anything we've ever seen before," Ari Mausk, Chief Technical Officer, said.

The meeting room was packed with every tech from Paladin Base. Mausk stood at a massive podium that seemed to dwarf him, as did the large-bodied military veterans seated at the on-stage table beside him.

A picture came up on the wall behind Mausk, displaying the modules in question. The discovery of the oval pods had been Brex's, the dozen interlocking pieces having been set in a ring within the secure floor hatch. The picture showed them as he had first found them, and then shifted to reveal their removal from the ship, and other scans of them at the base labs.

Mausk went on. "Preliminary scans reveal that they have enough power stored to feed our largest city for a year."

The revelation was frightening, though hardly unexpected. The monsters had raged war against them for so many years, with technology that continued to astonish. How did these creatures gain such advanced knowledge, and why didn't they utilize this power to its full extent? They seemed to have the means to decimate their enemies, yet their strikes remained minor. That left Brex wondering about their true intentions.

"The true purpose of these batteries is unclear," Mausk said, as a slideshow of alien technology slowly shifted on the wall behind him. "It doesn't appear they were part of the vessel's primary operating systems, nor do they appear to have been disposable ordnance. It's possible they were part of a disabled self-destruct, or possibly a suicide weapon. If all of them detonated in tandem, it would spell destruction for this entire colony world, and any space vessels within close proximity."

Mausk turned and nodded to a group of men seated at the table beside his podium. One of significant stature stood up and took over the briefing.

"Unlocking the secrets of this technology is of utmost priority," General Hugh bellowed as if barking orders to grunts. "This power could turn the tide of war drastically. The enemy has it. We need it. Your job will be to figure this out, no matter the cost."

• • •

Brex and his monster set up camp on a small sand flat beside a stream, eager for a mid-morning rest. The foliage gave them sufficient cover, and the thickets provided a suitable alarm system. Nobody could get close without snapping branches and alerting them.

"*I'm Hungry*," the monster said with his hands.

Brex dug through his bag and retrieved a nutri-bar, which he tossed at his companion. "This will have to do for now."

The monster tore open the silvery wrapper and took a bite of the foodstuff. It was packed full of vitamins, and you could taste it. Brex was no fan of the rations, but they were good for emergencies. Looking through his bag, he wished he had grabbed more of them. They'd be getting hungry in a few days.

Brex had assembled his pack ages ago, anticipating the inevitable. He knew he'd have to get out sooner or later, whether running from aliens or his own people. Though he had hoped for more time to prepare.

As it was, he had only packed the barest essentials, and he hadn't spent much time scouting the forest. He had never been much for the outdoors, and had never been this deep into the unknown wilderness. It left him wondering where to go from here.

A small canister of fishing line fell out of the pack, tempting Brex to try his hand at the stream. It was too soon. They were still too close to the fallen city. He wanted a few more days between him and the bombed settlement before he would be comfortable enough to dig in and start angling. That, and he'd never fished a day in his life, so it might take some time to learn.

Returning the fishing line to the bag, Brex retrieved a sheaf of papers. The topographical sketches had been copied from aerial scans and revealed the terrain ahead. It would have been easier to have the data logged on a tablet, but he'd left all technology behind. Tech could be tracked and there was no telling who was out there looking for survivors.

How strange that someone whose professional skill-set was tech-based would find himself in the woods without a speck of technology.

Laying the papers out on a dry patch of ground, Brex found their position and reviewed the possible travel routes ahead. He waved his companion over to assist him in his decision.

"I've mapped out four separate travel routes here," Brex said, tracing each colored line with his thumb. "The scans I drew these from showed the terrain to be passable, and the destinations to be suitable for our needs. We just need to decide where we want to go."

"What are our options?" the monster signed.

"Four routes, with two destinations. This first line leads to a series of caves in the lower mountains. We'd have shelter there, but it's a bit of a climb, and I'm not sure about the wildlife.

"The blue lines take us to the Trall Valley. Surveys reveal numerous streams for fishing, a lot of small game we can hunt and live off of, but it's exposed—a lot of grass and open spaces."

"*I like the valley,*" the monster answered.

"I'm inclined to agree," Brex said, grabbing one of the sheets and looking at his notes scribbled amidst the terrain. "We can find shelter in the hills, and venture down into the valley when we need food. It may not be as secure as the mountain caves, but it will be easier to survive."

"*I want to survive,*" the monster signed.

"I know," Brex replied.

• • •

Each of the twelve power modules was assigned to a trio of technicians for examination. Due to the dangerous nature of the research, separate facilities were set up all across Bellaris. Four were sent to orbital stations, and the remaining eight were assigned to planet-side locations, each in a different settlement far distanced from the others. If one of the devices detonated, the rest would remain intact...theoretically.

Weeks went by with little progress. Computer analysis baffled Brex and his two colleagues. The true purpose of the device eluded them.

"Why would anyone put this much energy into storage?" Helli remarked. It was the same question she asked every day. The diminutive lady took a sip from her stimulant-infused water and sighed in resignation.

"I'm sick of *'why,'*" Previa responded, the muscular woman who rounded out the team was the junior-most member, though quite possibly the brightest. Her mapping of the energy patterns in the device remained baffling, but it was her insight that had allowed them to stimulate the battery's inherent energy enough to measure its output. "I only care about *how*. That is our task. Determine how this power cell was constructed, and how we can duplicate it for our own purposes."

Brex sat quietly and listened to the same argument his female colleagues had held each day for the past four weeks. It was daunting, to say the least. He was less concerned with the how or the why than the *what*. What truly was the battery? It was a question he kept to himself. His colleagues weren't all that interested in his opinion. He was the weird guy they were stuck with, the oddball techie who didn't have their fervent ambitions or proclivities for fornication. What he showed them was the picture of a man who wasn't climbing the social ladder or looking to get laid—making him something neither of them could understand.

At night, he'd work alone and during the day, he'd sit back and let the girls run their tests, make their hypotheses and bicker. Their uncouth behavior left him firm in his decision to remain celibate.

Ignoring the drama of his current work environment, Brex pursued his task to unlock the secrets of the module. Working on his own, he had a breakthrough. Realizing that the module had to work en-tandem with other machinery, he had been studying various components of the crashed vessel, and after a great deal of examination, he discovered what he believed to be the larger mechanism the modules belonged to.

The mechanism in question had been destroyed during the firefight, but schematics remained locked within the ship's database. As more technical data was revealed, Brex was able to make the correlation between the missing part of the ship and the intact modules. He might have been the first, but he knew others would eventually comprehend the obvious, but he didn't care if or when they did. It only mattered that he had discovered something, and he worked quickly to prove his theory.

Everything he needed was lying around the lab. Working through a week of nights, he assembled a rudimentary chamber that duplicated the device depicted in the alien schematics. It was a monumental feat of engineering, and one Brex hoped would provide the final answer he had been seeking—the great, big *what*!

His co-workers didn't pay him much mind and figured he was just playing around. So long as he stayed out of their way, they didn't care what he did.

By the time the chamber was completed and ready to test, Brex had a working hypothesis about the true nature of the module. It was a matter storage unit, a cell capable of containing every particle of energy converted from a solid object. The chamber he had built would, in theory, be able to reassemble the energy into matter—a concept still considered to be science fiction by mainstream physicists. Yet, here, Brex was about to turn fiction into fact.

Connecting the module to the chamber, a blinding light filled the lab, followed by a shockwave that knocked Brex to the ground. As instruments and equipment rattled to the floor. The light faded, revealing a sight Brex couldn't have imagined.

Brex had assumed the matter inside the module would have been equipment of some kind, perhaps military ordnance. Yet the truth was astounding.

The face of the alien stared down at him, with frightening kindness.

"Hello?" Brex introduced himself, feeling strange in the presence of this creature from another world.

The alien monster didn't understand but made no hostile moves. He seemed strangely at ease in the unfamiliar setting—just as Brex felt in the face of this strange being.

A commotion sounded outside of the lab, and Brex realized he didn't have much time. The shockwave created by his makeshift rematerialization chamber had alerted security, who were on their way to investigate the disturbance.

It was then, in that moment, that Brex made his fateful decision.

"Quick. Hide," he said to the alien, hurrying the creature over to a storage locker. The alien complied, and Brex shut him inside, hoping to conceal him from prying eyes. This was his discovery and his monster. If anyone was going to unlock its secrets, it was going to be him!

It might have been crazy, but Brex was determined. As the security guards came in, he shooed them away, blaming the disturbance on his ongoing research. In the morning, his colleagues would discover the energy module drained, and he would have to explain how he "accidentally" discharged the energy, and they would spend the rest of their lives trying to figure out how he did it without leaving a giant crater in the face of the planet. That would be their problem. Meanwhile, he'd muster out of the Tech Corps, and begin his new job—getting to know his monster.

• • •

The snow came early to Trall valley. The global bombing was most likely the culprit. If a small settlement like Alden was a target, no doubt the enemy had struck the major cities, leaving enough dust in the atmosphere to lower temperatures. It was the dawn of a nuclear winter, and Brex had no way of knowing how bad it would get. So many times he regretted leaving technology behind. Just a few simple gadgets could have revealed so much.

Thirty days had passed since the bombs fell, and things were getting easier. After three days of hiking, they'd reached the valley, and found a sizeable cleft at the base of a hill. Bushy tree branches had been used to cover the open end in a hurry before the first snow, giving them shelter. It was dank and uncomfortable, but it kept them alive.

During the following weeks, the monster had proven himself to be an adept outdoorsman and provided much of their meat. Hunting and fishing was a time-consuming task, but the alien made it seem easy in the vast valley where predators were few, and the game was complacent.

Brex was still learning much from his companion.

It was midday, and the sun was poking through the clouds, daring to melt some of the previous night's snowfall. Brex was stoking the fire when a rustling sounded from the front of the shelter. His companion must have had a good hunt to be returning so quickly, but as he turned around a startling sight caught his eye.

"Looks like we got our survivor," the uniformed intruder said, keeping his slender machine gun pointed at the ground. "Clear!"

Three more armed military personnel in full riot gear entered the small shelter and gawked at Brex, who remained kneeling by the fire pit.

"Who are you?" Brex asked, not knowing what else to say.

"Commander Wu, search and rescue," the leader replied with a half-hearted salute, "and you're Brex Katrine, Technician Second-Class. We've been looking for you."

Brex simply stared. The fact that they knew who he was sent a shiver down his spine.

"Now, where's that monster you've been harboring?" Wu said sternly.

"Monster?" he asked sardonically. "I don't know what you're talking about."

"No use trying to hide it, Techie," Wu said. "We know everything."

"Nobody knows *everything*," Brex said, with a smirk.

Wu stepped forward, ignoring the man's insolence and raised his gun in a menacing fashion. "You think base security just let you walk off with that monster two years ago? That you were so good at hiding it from us? You're a smart one, so think. Do you really believe you'd have gotten away with harboring that monster if the higher-ups hadn't let you?"

Brex's worst fears were coming true. For so long, he'd convinced himself that he had, indeed been hiding his companion from the authorities, yet they'd known all along. He hadn't been clever enough, he'd merely been played the fool by those in charge...but to what end?

"Why?" Brex asked, staring down the barrel of a gun. "Why?" he repeated.

"Research," Wu answered. "I guess somebody figured it could be useful to observe you and that monster, see how it behaves, watch you two interact. Must have been good for something, seeing how they let you keep going for two damn years. Hell, if the monsters hadn't bombed the whole planet, you'd probably still be playing house with that thing."

It all made sense and left Brex feeling like an idiot. How could he have been so complacent? He'd been having so much fun interacting with his discovered friend, he hadn't bothered to see the obvious.

"What now?" Brex asked, dreading the answer.

"Our orders are to bring you in," Wu said. "After that, it's not up to me."

"So be it," Brex said, putting forth his hands in surrender.

"Not so fast," Wu said. "First, you're going to call back that monster of yours. We're taking it in, too. Our orders are to attempt a live rescue, but we'll bring it in dead if there's no alternative."

"What do you expect me to do?"

"Call for him, get him back here, and then tell him to surrender."

"I can't do that," Brex said.

"You'd rather we kill him?"

"No, I mean I literally can't. Do you see any communications equipment lying around here? No. We don't have technology. I figured we'd be harder to track without it."

"Yeah, you were. Must have run across a dozen other survivor encampments during the past few weeks while looking for you."

"Hey, I thought you'd tracked my every move, knew *everything*."

"I never said that. I said some people knew what you were up to. Don't ask me how much they knew, or why they ever let you keep that thing, but that's not my business. Everything's gone to hell since the bombs fell. The planet's a wreck, nothing but leveled cities full of freezing refugees. Millions are dead, and millions more are starving to death! If I had it my way, your little friend would pay for it in blood!" The commander's true feelings were peeking out from behind his professional façade. "Too bad somebody thinks it might be more useful alive."

The commander's anger was understandable, considering all that had happened, but Brex didn't blame his companion for the destruction, and he hardly blamed the alien's people, either. His companion had told a far different story about the war, one that made a lot of sense—one where the aliens were merely defending themselves—but try explaining that to an angry soldier out for revenge.

Brex struggled to find a way out, but he couldn't see one. There was no escape route and no way to convince anyone that the monster wasn't a culpable war criminal. The only choice left was to help these soldiers either capture or kill his friend. What was the better alternative?

Death was a certainty. If not these soldiers, then somebody else in the military hierarchy would see to it. But if the monster were brought in alive, there would be interrogation, probably torture. The angry men and women of war would force any information they could out of their perceived enemy, and then enact as much vengeance as possible. Brex wondered if a similar fate didn't await him, as well.

His choice was simple—did he want his friend to die sooner or later? Quickly, or slowly? It was a damned, lousy choice.

"If you want him alive, you'll have to wait," Brex said, even as he continued to weigh his options. "He'll be back, sooner or later, but if you go out after him I don't know how he'll respond. If you confront him here, he might go peacefully."

Commander Wu nodded, then turned to his fellow soldiers. "Tinsler, Bing, you two scout around outside, see if you can get a bead on the monster, but don't engage. Observe and report back. Ravi, you hang back with me."

Brex sat down by his fire, and Wu crouched down across from him. They sat in silence, sharing the warmth, waiting for the monster's return. Ravi stood at the curtain of branches that served as a door, staring out at the snowy wilderness, attentive, as though the enemy might strike at any minute.

As the midday sun started its afternoon decline, the firewood began to run out, and Wu received a message over his earpiece. "Acknowledged," he answered tapping his ear. He turned back to Brex, saying, "Well, seems like your little monster is almost here. Have you decided how you'd like this to go down?"

Brex had considered it, and his indecision was at an end. "Don't kill him. I'll help you take him peacefully," he said, knowing how much he wanted life for both himself and his friend. Death was so final, with no hope for anything more. There was always a chance for something better, no matter how unlikely, so long as you were alive.

As the monster neared the shelter, Ravi stepped away from the opening. Wu and his fellow soldier took up positions on either side of the entrance and stood ready to ambush. Brex stayed by the fire and stared forward, praying there would be no bloodshed.

A rustling sounded as the branches were pushed aside, and the monster entered, covered head to toe in animal furs, carrying a thirty-pound Waxsipper on his shoulder. The large rodent looked like the bastard son of a rabbit and a red squirrel—not that Brex knew what either of those creatures were, having grown up exclusively on Bellaris IV.

Before the monster could set down his latest catch, Wu shot him. A flash of light blasted out of the commander's rifle and soaked into the target at point-blank range, dropping him in an instant.

Brex jumped from his seat by the fire, bewildered. "What have you done?"

Wu looked at him dispassionately. "Playing it safe. Stun shot. Puts him to sleep nice and quick."

"I thought you were going to have me talk to him, get him to cooperate," Brex said.

"That was *your* test," Wu replied. "Had to see if you were going to cooperate. If you hadn't, we would've shot you both, and your debriefing would be a lot harsher."

The bitter truth sank in, and Brex was left with little contempt for the ruse. He understood their need to know. It was almost comforting to know they didn't automatically consider him a traitor or enemy. Perhaps there was a chance, after all.

As Ravi grabbed the unconscious monster, Brex felt relieved that the soldiers hadn't shot him as well, knowing the limits of the *stun* setting on modern military firearms. The jolt necessary to instantly incapacitate sometimes left permanent nerve damage. It was a flaw that could have been worked out, but the military hierarchy wasn't interested in fixing their non-lethal weapons. It was unspoken doctrine—anyone who made a soldier fire his weapon should suffer the consequences.

"Let's move," Wu ordered, motioning toward the entrance with his rifle.

Brex fell in line, heading out into the frigid afternoon air. Squinting in the sunlight, a hissing caught his ear as an unnatural wind arose, blowing snow in a circular motion. A dark shadow appeared as a transport descended, landing a hundred yards from the shelter. The shiny, metal flyer came to a stop and lowered it's broad boarding ramp, inviting passengers to enter.

They crossed the short distance quickly, but as they reached the ramp Wu halted, pressing a finger to his ear. "Yes? I see. We're on our way."

"Commander?" Ravi asked as Tinsler and Bing approached the ramp.

"We've got incoming," Wu answered.

• • •

The transport made a mad dash for the Confederation Star Carrier *Wen Denning*, one of seven large warships in high orbit around Bellaris IV. As soon as the craft touched down in the ship's fighter bay, Wu and his men were on their feet, rushing Brex and his companion out.

The bay was massive and largely empty. A standard carrier had a fighter compliment in the hundreds, yet only a handful of disabled craft remained inside. Brex knew that the fighters would be scrambled, sent out to intercept the oncoming enemy. It was unnerving to be in the thick of the fight. He'd never signed up for combat. He was a technician who worked behind the lines. His combat training was limited, and his nerves were unaccustomed to the stress. Though, in light of his current predicament, the battle was a welcome reprieve from his pending interrogation.

Commander Wu marched his men across the vacant flight deck, and as they reached the doors to the troop lift a violent shake knocked everyone off their feet. As the shaking subsided, gravity vanished.

"Magnetize!" Wu ordered as he grabbed Brex roughly by the arm to prevent him from drifting away.

Thud, thud, thunk, the soldier's boots clicked down onto the metal deck.

Checking the lift, Wu shouted, "Let's move it before anything else goes offline!"

The soldiers rushed into the lift and Wu hit the command panel, sending them into motion. After only a few seconds, the compartment came to a halt and the lift doors opened to reveal a shimmering, silver hallway lined with doors.

The soldiers marched down the hall, as Brex floated behind Wu like a kite. Without mag-boots or artificial gravity there was nothing to hold him down, save for the commander's cold grip.

Another violent quake hit the ship, tossing everyone into a side wall. As the shake subsided, Wu received a new communication.

"I'm on Epsi deck, escorting the prisoners," Wu answered the phantom voice in his ear. "No, sir...yes... aye, sir, I will comply." Tapping his ear to end the conversation, he turned to his men, saying, "Back to the lift. We're heading to the bridge."

The second lift ride took a bit longer, and was periled by repeated quakes. The ship was taking a real pounding, and it was only getting worse.

As the lift stopped, its doors opened again, revealing the carrier's command center. Things were frantic, on the verge of chaos as personnel scurried about, performing a myriad array of duties in the heat of battle.

Before stepping onto the bridge, Wu ordered his men to shut off their mag-boots. The bridge had its own auxiliary gravity system, granting those in control the luxury of their own body weight at the worst of times.

Once Wu had his feet firmly planted on the bridge, he yanked Brex out of the lift, exposing the young technician to the full force of gravity. Brex fell to the floor, hard, and the soldiers escorting him chuckled slightly at the sight. Wu picked Brex up and marched him along further into the room.

"General Aday, may I present Tech Second Class Brex Katrine and his monster," Wu announced as he approached the command core, a circular dais in the center of the room.

"Thank you, Commander," a grizzled figure replied, looking up from the large computer display in the center of the command dais.

Wu shoved Brex forward, slamming him into the command display as Ravi tossed the monster to the deck unceremoniously like a sack of rocks.

"That's enough, Commander," General Aday snapped. He walked over to Brex, who was picking himself up off the deck. "Are you okay, lad?"

Brex nodded, not knowing what to think of the General's show of concern.

"I take it you've been through a special kind of hell," General Aday remarked, "but we don't have much time."

"Time?" Brex asked. "Time for what?"

"The enemy is upon us, and you may be our only hope." General Aday stepped over to the unconscious monster. "You've befriended one of them, learned to communicate with it. You can talk to our enemy, ask them to stop!"

"Are you out of your mind?" Commander Wu shouted, clearly shocked by the revelation. "We need to be fighting, not talking!"

"Watch your tongue, Commander! And know your place."

"They are monsters!" He emphasized each word as he spoke.

"Are they?" General Aday asked. "I don't know anymore. At this point, we'd better hope they're not. You know the extent of our losses. This carrier group is all that we have left, and if we can't persuade our enemy to cease fire here and now, we are lost!"

"How many ships are out there?" Ravi asked.

"Sensors are jammed, but our earlier scans revealed at least twenty battle cruisers converging on our position. That's three-to-one odds, in their favor. They've beaten us in battle with those odds reversed!

There is no chance of winning in combat. We have to negotiate. That's why I was assigned to command the remnants of the fleet—to seek an alternative to death."

"What do you want me to do?" Brex interjected.

"You can communicate with them. Talk to them for us, please."

"I can't," Brex said nervously. "I don't know how. I can't speak their language."

"But you can communicate," General Aday persisted.

"Yes, with him," Brex clarified, pointing to his friend. "He can understand what I say, but his speech is far too mumbly to comprehend. We worked out a form of non-verbal sign language, that's all."

"Then we'll talk through him," the general said. "Med-tech Vantz, wake this creature up."

One of the standers-by sprang into action, retrieving a small medical kit from under a control console. As the ship shook from another hit, Vantz dug out a syringe and filled it with a stimulant. Kneeling down by the monster, he looked to Brex, saying, "You know this creature better than anyone. Do you have any idea how much I should use?"

"A standard dose, I believe," Brex said, having a limited knowledge of his friend's physiology. "Of course, none of this would be necessary if your soldiers had let me talk to him first, rather than taking a preemptive shot."

"My orders were to bring you in," Wu challenged. "There was no mention of handing our fate over to your pet, you...traitor!"

"You're dismissed, Commander!" General Aday ordered.

Wu gave a rigid salute and stormed off the bridge with his men in tow.

As another quake subsided, the med-tech injected the stimulant into the monster's neck and within moments the creature began to stir.

"Quick, explain our situation," General Aday told Brex as the monster's eyes opened. "Tell him he will die if he can't call off the attack."

"He can understand you," Brex said.

"Where...are we?" the monster signed before rubbing his face.

Brex translated, and General Aday answered, "You're aboard the CSC *Wen Denning,* and we're under attack by your people."

"Have you talked to them?" the monster asked.

"They don't know how," Brex answered. "They've never really tried before now," he added, giving the surrounding personnel an indignant glare.

"This pointless fighting should end," the monster signed. *"Let me talk to my people. They will listen to me."*

After Brex translated his monster's request, one of the general's staff injected herself into the conversation. "Sir, if our roles were reversed, I'd probably tell my people to keep fighting, even if it meant sacrificing myself. How do we know that this thing isn't going to do just that, and assure our destruction?"

"He's my friend, and I trust him," Brex said.

"Indeed," General Aday answered, "and that trust is our only hope."

"Well, I *hope* that your *hope* isn't our undoing," the staffer added. "But even if he tells them to stand down, how do we know his people will listen?"

"Of course they'll listen," the monster signed. *"I am their ambassador."*

• • •

The flight deck of the CSC *Wen Denning* was packed with personnel, as the crew assembled to greet the officials from the enemy fleet. A first face-to-face meeting to pave the way for a lasting peace.

As the shuttle came to a landing in the center of the flight deck, Ambassador Howard Sadler stood front and center beside his alien savior, Brex. It had been a difficult two years, but at long last, his mission would bear fruit, and he would be a free man again.

For so many years, the Terran Stellar Republic had been under assault by mysterious aliens, warlike xenophobes who refused communication and seemed to prefer death in battle to surrender. The strange, high-pitched chatter Terran vessels intercepted failed to provide enough context for a translation matrix, and at every turn, these alien "monsters" attacked without known provocation.

After decades of minor skirmishes, the Stellar Congress finally agreed to a course of action. Communication had to be established, so a ship of diplomatic envoys was sent to one of the enemy's remote colony worlds, in the hopes that peace talks could be started. Sadly, the ship's stealth deflectors failed to sufficiently conceal its approach, and the enemy intercepted it with violent force, precluding a straightforward approach.

With the transport's systems failing, the diplomats had opted to teleport to the planet surface, in a last ditch effort to reach their destination. The diplomats were dematerialized and their energies stored inside the dozen capacitor modules, waiting for the ship to come in range of the planet. Unfortunately, the teleporter was knocked offline before they could get close enough, trapping the diplomats in limbo. There Howard Sadler's energy pattern remained until Brex's monumental discovery released him. Somehow, this odd outcast had built a rematerialization circuit, a feat unduplicated by his peers in the following years, leaving Sadler as Earth's only chance at establishing a dialog.

If not for Brex's anomalous behavior, the quest for peace would have died along with many more of the Vhelaran race.

The shuttle's hatch opened, and out stepped a handful of representatives of the Terran Defense Forces, duly authorized to negotiate the Vhelaran surrender.

"Captain Cooper," Sadler greeted the senior-most member of the group. "It's good to meet you in person."

"Same here," Cooper said, shaking Sadler's hand. Staring at the assembled group of Vhelarans, he added, "So, these are our monsters. Not too imposing, are they?"

"I suppose not," Sadler replied, looking over at his friend, Brex. The tall, wiry albino with scaly skin and oversized eyes appeared anything but threatening. The Vhelarans were amusing more than frightening, yet their race had a paranoia that bordered on insanity...at least, many of them did. Their desire to fight anyone they perceived to be a threat was a familiar trait, something humanity had struggled with so often throughout history.

How fateful that Earth's ambassador would encounter one Vhelaran who was willing to seek kinship over conflict.

Sadler wondered who the true monsters were, or if there were any at all.

ABOUT THE AUTHOR

MARTIN T. INGHAM is an author of fast-paced Science Fiction and Fantasy stories, and is currently the Senior Editor of Martinus Publishing. Influenced by the great writers of speculative fiction, including Asimov, Heinlein, & Herbert, Martin utilizes his unique wit and wisdom to craft adventures with his own unique voice. His stories are often complex, and filled with hidden philosophical insights that can be wholly ignored by those wishing to focus purely on the entertaining actions, leaving them accessible to a varied audience.

When he's not writing, Martin enjoys various hobbies, including numismatics, horology, and antique auto restoration. He currently resides in his hometown of Robbinston, Maine, with his four kids, Sylvia, Wyatt, Kathryn, & Lois.

Martin's latest novel series, "West of the Warlock," features the unique concept of blending Sword and Sorcery into the Wild West. The third volume in the series, "The Man Who Shot Thomas Edison," was released in 2014.

PRECIOUS IN THY SIGHT

KEVIN G. SUMMERS

HE DID IT in secret, in the dark hours of the night when nothing good ever happens. He did it in broad daylight, with the doors locked and the window shades drawn, whenever an opportunity presented itself. He would have been ashamed if his mother knew about this part of his life, but his mother was dust now and there was no one left to tell him that he was destroying himself. No one cared. It began as an impulse, but over time it evolved into an addiction, and eventually a fetish. It wasn't until he had driven everyone away, until the only thing that mattered was the behavior he thought of as his *Precious*, that John Galen realized he had a demon.

The first time he saw it was on a sweltering August night after a gig in Harlan, Kentucky. He was packing up his guitar and the rest of his equipment when a woman approached him from the crowd.

"Can I buy you a beer?" she asked.

She was wearing a plaid blouse that was just a little too short and a pair of Daisy Dukes that were just a little too tight. Her face was pretty enough and her body was about the best he could hope for in a town this size.

"Thank you," he said. "That would be wonderful."

She sauntered toward the bar like a cat, and Galen noticed the rose tattoo on her lower back—her tramp stamp. He took her back to his motel room and they fornicated with the lights off so Galen wouldn't have to look at her face. He thought her name was Candice, but he wasn't sure.

It was 2:22 a.m. when Galen awoke in the darkness. Candice lay beside him, sleeping soundly, and he wondered if she was the type that would sneak out at 6 a.m. or the kind that wanted to have breakfast and another roll in the sheets before she went back to whatever life she led here in this redneck town.

Galen felt like someone was watching him. He tried to tell himself that he was dreaming, but he couldn't shake the feeling no matter what he did. He turned slowly to a chair on the far side of the room and that's when he saw the demon sitting there, smiling in the darkness.

The sensation was uncanny, there was no other word for it. Galen was startled by the unexpected presence in the room and felt like jumping out of his skin, but he was paralyzed with fear. The figure in the chair seemed to be made of living shadow, and its eyes and mouth were nothing more than smudges of black on black, but Galen knew at once that it was looking at him and grinning horribly.

"Who are you? What do you want?"

He tried to speak but no words escaped his paralyzed lips. Still, the demon somehow understood his thoughts. It spoke in his mind, its voice low and terrible.

"Would it not feel good to put your hands around that whore's neck and choke the life out her?"

Galen was assaulted by the image of Candice's face as she struggled for breath. He tried to shake the thought away, but it was overwhelming.

"Kill her," said the demon. "Give her what she deserves."

Galen tried to resist, but no amount of will-power could overcome the demon who was rooted inside of him. He knew it was wrong to even think these thoughts, but he couldn't shake them. Candice's gasping face flashed on and off like a strobe light in the pleasure center of his brain, and slowly, very slowly, the notion of right and wrong faded. He wanted to hurt her because it made him feel good to think about hurting her.

He sat up in bed, rubbed his eyes, and took another look at the chair in the corner. The demon was still sitting there, watching voyeuristically at the scene unfolding before him. Galen knew there were demons in the world, but to see one and know that it dwelt inside of him like a parasite…that was a terrible thought. He had been a man of faith once upon a time, but that was long ago and far away. He had stood barefoot on the sacred ground of Israel and seen the places where Jesus walked upon the land, but it was so easy to turn your back on the Word. The demon smiled—its mouth like something out of a nightmare—and another wave of desire rippled through John Galen.

Hurt her.

Kill her.

Do it now.

Galen rolled on top of Candice and began kissing her face and neck. She stirred in her sleep as he rolled on top of her, and all the while he could hear the demon urging him on. It would be so easy to just tighten his grip and choke this poor woman to death. Galen wanted to do it, wanted that more than anything in the world. He reached for her throat.

"What are you doing?" Candice's voice was soft and sleepy.

"Nothing, I…"

"Get off me, I don't like that."

There was a moment when Galen hesitated, when all the power of the demon in his heart urged him to squeeze, but his sense of self-preservation was too strong. If he killed this woman he would be caught, that was a certainty, and he didn't want to go to jail. Galen rolled back to his side of the bed. He looked toward the chair in the corner of the room but the demon was gone.

"That's a creepy way to wake up," Candice said. "I know musicians can be into some freaky—"

"Get out."

"What?"

"You heard me, I said get out." Galen slipped out of bed, naked as Adam in the garden, and flipped on the light.

"Honey, I just didn't like…"

"It doesn't matter," Galen said, "you need to get out of here right now. I…I'm sorry. Just leave."

Candice threw the covers off and started gathering up her discarded clothing. It felt cruel to cast her out so suddenly, but the whole thing was just wrong and after he had come so close to murder, Galen knew he wouldn't be able to resist the demon a second time. He had to get the girl out of there and figure out what was happening to him.

"You're an asshole, you know that?" Candice was halfway into her clothes and she was steaming mad. "You think it's fun to choke a girl and then you get your panties in a wad when I tell you no? You're not much of a singer, even less of a guitar player, and you're about the worst lover I've ever had. You know that?"

The words stung, but Galen resisted the urge to lash out at her. She was right about all of it anyway. "Just get out of here," he said. "I'm sorry."

"Whatever, I hope you have a nice life, asshole."

She slammed the door on her way out and Galen was left alone in his motel room. He was thankful that he didn't have to spend the rest of the night trying to dispose of a dead body but that was a small consolation. He could feel the demon inside of him, twisting and gnawing in his brain like a maggot. He felt he might go mad if he thought about it too hard, and so he turned to his only comfort in the long, dark hours of the night—his *Precious*.

. . .

A year had passed and the demon had yet to resurface. Galen could still feel it inside of him, but he kept it at bay with every distraction under the sun. He drank too much, smoked too much, ate like a glutton, and binge-watched TV shows on Netflix. He snorted cocaine, and shot up with heroin, and downed countless prescription drugs which were easy enough to come by. He avoided women, terrified that whatever dwelt inside of him would seize control if he allowed himself to be intimate with a member of the fairer sex.

Galen was driving to a recording session in Nashville when he saw a flicker of movement in his rearview mirror. He looked closer and saw, to his horror, a woman sitting in the backseat...A woman who had been dead for ten years. He slammed on the brakes and his old Land Cruiser skidded to a stop in the middle of the road. The car behind him missed rear-ending him by inches, and the driver was blaring on the horn and flipping the bird as he drove around. Galen didn't care, he turned around in his seat to look at the woman who had been his lover once upon a time.

When he looked in her eyes he knew that this wasn't Lauren, but the demon wearing her skin.

"What's the matter, Darling...did you miss me?" It spoke with Lauren's voice, and the sound was like a dagger in Galen's heart. He was instantly transported back to the apartment he and Lauren shared a decade earlier in Fairfax, Virginia. They had known love and laughter in the two years they'd spent in each other's arms, and for a glimmer of time, he thought he had found a piece of happiness. But joy was fleeting and he ruined everything because he refused to give up his precious.

"You're not Lauren," Galen said. He took his foot off the break and touched the gas. The green Land Cruiser started rolling again down the highway toward Music City. He was in the suburb of Hendersonville, which was a bit of good luck considering he had just slammed on the brakes in the middle of a major road. If he had been in the city when he pulled that stunt he would have caused an accident for certain.

"I can be anyone you want me to be," said the demon. "Lauren...Shania Twain...your mother—"

"Stop. Please, why are you doing this to me?"

"I love you," said the demon, "and I want to give you what you want."

"I want you to go away," Galen said. "Get out of my head and leave me alone." He stole a glance at the monster in the rearview mirror. Lauren was sitting back there, smiling her terrible smile and staring at him with eyes that were cold and dead. He hated himself for what happened to her but there was nothing he could do about it now. Was there?

"You don't really mean that," said the demon wearing Lauren's skin. "Why don't you hit that school bus up there."

They were approaching an intersection, a four-way stop, and a big, yellow school bus was stopped to his right. The driver looked both ways, waited to be sure that no one was going to drive out of turn, and then rolled into the intersection.

Galen's foot shifted involuntarily on the brake. The Land Cruiser rolled forward an inch.

"Do it," said the demon. "Step on the gas and send those kids to meet Jesus. You'll walk away from the accident without even a scratch."

"Please," Galen said, "please, don't make me do this." His foot shifted again. He was trying to fight the monster in his head, but it was so, so difficult.

The demon didn't answer, only sat the in the back seat wearing Lauren's skin and watching him in the rearview mirror. Galen tried to resist, but the demon's suggestion overwhelmed him. He knew it was wrong, this thing the monster wanted him to do, but every neuron in his brain was firing, urging him to smash into the bus. The very thought of it, while revoltingly evil, gave him pleasure. He couldn't help himself.

Galen's foot went from the brake to the gas. He floored the pedal, and the Land Cruiser lurched away from the stop sign like a stock car at Daytona. The old truck's pick up was poor, and the engine strained as the automatic transmission climbed through the gears. It bore down on the school bus, and Galen was vaguely aware that the children inside were pointing at him and screaming in terror.

He knew he should pray, but the idea of speaking to God frightened John Galen. They didn't exactly have the best relationship these days, and the fact that he was carrying around a demon meant that God had abandoned him.

Didn't it?

The Land Cruiser missed by inches, and the bus stopped as soon as it passed through the intersection. Once the danger was passed, the pleasure center of Galen's brain shut down and absolute terror exploded inside of him. Whatever was inside of him, this demon, he couldn't control it. He had very nearly killed all those kids on the school bus, just as he had nearly killed that woman the year before. It was only a matter of time before his resistance slipped and he found himself with blood on his hands.

"Why are you doing this to me?" he shouted. He looked in the rearview mirror and saw that Lauren—the thing wearing Lauren's skin—was gone. He also noticed the flashing blue lights of a police cruiser in the rearview mirror.

Galen pulled off to the side of the road and the cop pulled up behind him. He thought about the recording session he had scheduled in Nashville in less than an hour, and he wondered if he was going to make it in time. Music was the one thing that let him forget his troubles for a little while—that and his *Precious*—but it seemed increasingly difficult to pick up his guitar and make the time. That didn't make any sense when he thought about it, because the music would just flow out of him as soon as he started strumming the chords, but just taking his guitar out of the case felt like the most difficult thing in the world sometimes.

The state trooper walked up beside the Land Cruiser and knocked on the window. Galen touched the button that lowered the glass and it disappeared inside the door.

"What in the blue hell were you doing back there?" asked the trooper. "Did you even see that bus?"

"Yes. I mean...no." Galen was a terrible liar, he knew it, and the demon wasn't back there now to help him get out of the situation. He felt his stomach twist into a knot.

"Either you did or you didn't," said the trooper. "Are you drunk?"

"No. No, sir. I...my foot slipped off the brake and I flew out into the intersection. I didn't mean to scare anyone. Is everyone ok?"

The trooper looked at him from behind a pair of mirrored sunglasses. When Galen saw his reflection in the glasses he noticed Lauren sitting in the passenger seat beside him. He turned to look at her and, sure enough, there she was. She smiled at him sweetly, keeping her mouth shut, and Galen had to force himself to remember that this wasn't really his old lover, but the demon that lived in his head.

"Call him a fascist pig," said the demon, "and spit on him."

Terror seized over Galen as he turned back to the officer. He tried to resist, but he heard the words come out of his mouth before he could control himself. He spat on the cop, and the next thing he knew he was being dragged from the car. Galen looked through the windshield as the state trooper bent him over the hood of his car and bound his hands behind his back. There was the demon, staring at him from the passenger seat and laughing like it was the funniest thing it had ever seen.

Galen wondered what was happening to him, where this demon came from, as he was being shoved into the back of the cruiser. Try as he might, he had no idea.

He spent the rest of that day in the Henderson-ville Jail, in a tiny holding cell with a single bed and a barred window that looked out over a parking lot. He sat there on the bed, wondering if they had changed the sheets since the last time they held a prisoner in here, and trying to pray to a god whom he had ignored for a lifetime. The words didn't come easily.

"Why did you let this happen to me?" he said in the darkness.

"It wasn't God," said a familiar voice, "it was you."

Galen turned and saw Lauren lying on the bed beside him. She was naked and as beautiful as he remembered, and it was the most natural thing in the world for him to reach out and touch her. She was as cold as ice.

"Who are you?"

"I'm Lauren, your lover."

"No, Lauren is dead. Who are you really? What's your name?"

"My name is Legion, for we are many."

The words were familiar, but Galen couldn't place them. "What are you? Why are you following me?

"I am an angel...your angel...and you chose me."

Galen had lived a long time in this world, and he had no memory of ever asking this supernatural creature to live in his head. "I don't understand," he said. "Where did you come from?"

Lauren sighed. "Are you sure you want to talk? There are other things we could do that might be a lot more...pleasurable." She touched him with her icy hand and Galen trembled in his soul. Her touch was both terrible and wonderful at the same time.

"Tell me," he pleaded. "I need to know."

"You found me online," said the demon. "You were looking at a certain website and there was a pop-up window. It said, 'Click yes and you'll never feel lonely again.' And you clicked yes."

Galen stared at her, incredulous. "I don't remember that."

"You were kind of distracted, but one little click and that's how you and me became we." Lauren smiled, revealing a mouth full of fangs. "You downloaded me through your eyes and into your brain, and now, here I am."

She ran her hands over her perfect body and Galen felt his resolve weaken. He reached for her again, and this time she was warm and soft. Lauren trembled under his hand as all sense of logic and rationality departed from Galen's mind. They fornicated in that little jail cell and it was wonderful and terrible at the same time. Afterward, they lay in each other's arms on the tiny bed.

"Why do you try to make me do horrible things?" Galen asked.

"Because I hate you," said Lauren.

"What? Why?"

"I hate you as I hate all life, and your suffering gives me pleasure." She leaned close to him and whispered in his ear. "Do you know why I took the form of your former lover?"

Galen felt a knife stick into his heart. He had been happy for a time when Lauren Preston had been his girl, but he ruined everything, just like he always did. "Please, I don't..."

"Lauren Preston wanted nothing more than to be your bride," said the demon, "even though you waited and waited and never worked up the guts to ask her. She would have said, 'yes' in a heartbeat, did you know that?"

Galen tried to fight back tears.

"You made her do things that she hated. You degraded her and still she loved you because her heart was full of goodness. You poisoned that goodness until every bit of hope she carried was nothing but ashes, and then you screwed her sister in the very bed you shared with Lauren. Women don't just get over something like that."

The demon laughed and the sound was like a fist closing around Galen's heart. He hated himself for the things he had done. Even at the time it was happening, he knew he was doing wrong, but he couldn't control himself. It was like he was possessed.

"It was you," he said. "You made me do those things. You caused this."

The thing wearing Lauren's skin smiled its terrible smile. "You downloaded me and gave me a place to dwell," it said. "I like to think that we did it all together."

Galen cried out in desperate anger and grabbed the demon by the throat. He wasn't even aware that he was making a low, guttural sound in this throat like an animal. Lauren struggled beneath him as he tried to snuff the demon out of existence. He closed his eyes for just a second, and when he opened them again he had the bed sheet wrapped around his neck and was hanging from the bars of his cell. Deputies were swarming around him like bees—one was trying to hold him up, and another was trying to cut the sheet with a pocket knife. In that bleary state of near-death, he saw Lauren sitting on the bed, smiling at him.

"Lauren left your apartment after she found her sister in your arms. She went back home to the house where she grew up and hung herself in the closet where she used to keep her dress-ups. It was all your fault."

Galen tried to deny it, but he couldn't speak. Even if he could, he knew that it was the truth. He had opened his heart to this monster and had been unable to control the demon that raged inside of him. In pride and self-indulgence he had chosen a life of bondage to this demon, and for the life of him he could not see how to break free.

• • •

John Galen was transported to a mental health facility in Knoxville, Tennessee, where he spent the next three and a half years looking at Rorschach patterns and eating anti-psychotic drugs and talking to a string of therapists, all of whom were convinced that his problems were entirely chemical in nature. These were men and women of science, who believed that demons were no more real than Santa Claus or the Tooth Fairy. Galen gave up trying to convince them what was really happening to him, and, after a while, even he began to accept their explanations for what was going on. He swallowed their drugs and felt nothing. No one came to see him and the world outside forgot that he even existed.

He had no idea what became of his worldly possessions. He had his guitar because it was with him in the Land Cruiser on the day he was arrested, but everything else was lost to him. He didn't care about the clothes and furniture in his apartment—he had lived long enough to know that those were all replaceable—but he had a box of old photographs that was dear to him, and it broke his heart to think that he would never again be able to look at the faces of the people he had loved in earlier part of his life. As for the future, Galen held no hope whatsoever that he would ever be able to leave this facility. His life was over now, and there was nothing left for him to do but sit on his bed and wait for the Day of the Lord.

He sat.

He waited.

Sometimes he would hold his guitar and pick the beginning of a tune. His fingers did it mechanically, finding the notes and filling up the empty space with sound that bordered on being music. He never sang because singing comes out of a person's heart and the cocktail of medication he consumed twice daily had built a wall around his heart that was taller and more impenetrable than the one President Trump was building along the Mexican border. He watched the shift in presidential power without emotion. He saw men speak as if they were going to change the world, but Galen had seen it all before and he knew that whatever happened one day, whatever they did, someone else would come along and undo it in two years or four or eight.

It didn't matter.

Nothing mattered.

Time wore on.

The demon still came around sometimes, and whenever it did Galen would have another episode and the doctors would increase his medication. He couldn't even pronounce some of the drugs they had him on, and could hardly move when the thing wearing Lauren's skin climbed on top of him and rode him in the cold, dark night. He found a word somewhere, perhaps in one of the novels down in the mental facility's pathetic excuse for a library.

Succubus.

Was that what this thing was...this demon that dwelt inside of him? It assumed a female shape, but somehow Galen understood that it was neither male nor female by nature. He lay in its arms one night, exhausted but unable to sleep, when the demon spoke in the darkness.

"I'm going to leave you for a time," it said.

The thought terrified Galen. He pleaded with the demon for it to stay even though he knew that it was destroying him.

"Fear not, our separation will be brief. There's something I want you to do for me, and you can't do it in here." Lauren's mouth opened in a grin, revealing the terrible blackness that swirled just below the surface of her skin. Galen wanted to scream but he could not.

He began to make rapid improvements, and it wasn't long before the administrators of the mental health facility felt that he was ready to be released back into the wide world outside. It was a chilly spring morning when he walked out the hospital with nothing but the clothes on his back and his guitar slung over one shoulder like a troubadour. He had a wad of prescriptions in his pocket and no means of paying for the drugs that, supposedly, would keep the demon that lived inside of him at bay. He headed for the highway, shivering all over as the cold seeped into his bones. He doubted anyone reputable would pick him up, but he had to get as far away from Knoxville as possible, and since he had no means of transportation, he had to hitchhike.

A semi picked him up an hour later and he was rolling north and east, toward the glittering white city where the King of America sat on his marble throne.

"Do you know where you're going to go when you die?"

The trucker was an older man, in the autumn of his middle age, and he looked like he had lived hard. Galen didn't expect him to be a Bible thumper, not by the look of him, and at first he wondered if the demon inside of him had assumed a new form. The demon had been quiet these past few months, wanting him to be free of the sanitarium, but Galen always knew that it was in there, biding its time.

"I don't know," he admitted.

"Have you met Jesus?"

Galen smiled in spite of himself. "I have, though it's been a long time."

The trucker launched into a message of evangelism, and Galen was taken back to the dusty road outside of Jerusalem that led to a hill called Golgotha. It was written in the Gospels that the Son of Man had given his apostles the ability to cast out demons, but Galen was skeptical that any of his followers could still wield the Holy Spirit in this way. It was doubtful, but still, wasn't it worth trying? He had, literally, nothing to lose.

That's when he looked up and saw his reflection in the mirror on his side of the truck. The demon, still wearing the shape of his lost lover, was sitting next to him, in between Galen and the driver. She was smiling as if she had just heard a joke that she found hilarious.

Galen turned to look at her, and he knew in his heart that if she told him to reach across the seat and strangle the driver he would be unable to stop himself. His heart trembled as the demon leaned close to him and and whispered in his ear.

"This man is going to leave you in a suburb of the White City. Once there, you're going to sell your prescriptions and use the money to purchase a Glock. It's an impressive weapon, you'll like the way it feels in your hands when you use it."

"Please, don't make me hurt anyone," Galen said in his mind. It was no use trying to fight the demon that lived within him, he had been broken by its superior will long before. Still, he had to try.

"You're going to do more than hurt people. There's a school field trip headed into the White City in two day's time. Middle schoolers." The demon grinned wickedly. "You're going to sacrifice them in my name.

• • •

It was dusk when Galen arrived in the town of Carmel, Virginia. The trucker left him in a Wal-Mart parking lot, and for that Galen was deeply grateful. The demon in his head had been telling him for hours that he should cut the poor man's throat and leave him on the side of the road, but thus far Galen had been able to resist the temptation. He wasn't sure if he could have resisted for much longer.

Standing in the parking lot, Galen realized that he had nowhere to lay his head that night, and while it was spring, the nights were still cold and he didn't fancy the idea of sleeping out of doors. Carmel was a suburb of Washington, D.C., a bedroom community that had once been an important town when the world was larger and less connected.

He started walking.

It was a Saturday night in a populated area, and it wasn't long before Galen found a wayside bar. He had no money in his pocket, but he had his prescriptions and he figured they might be almost as good.

The bar was called the King's Court Tavern. It was dark and narrow and reeked of decades of cigarette smoke that could never be washed out of the old floorboards. The place was nearly empty, and no waitress offered to show him to his seat when Galen darkened the doorway. He approached the bar, found a spot next to the only other customer in the tavern, and sat down. The man had a day's worth of stubble on his cheeks and was hunched over his drink like it was something precious to him. He looked like Gollum, and the sudden image in Galen's mind was painful.

My Precious.

"Hey there," Galen said as he sat down beside the man. He looked up and saw Lauren standing behind the bar, wiping a glass with a dirty rag. She winked at him and Galen's blood went icy cold.

"Lay your prescriptions on the bar," Lauren said, "and I'll work out the rest."

Galen closed his eyes and tried to resist, but he could not. This creature of pure evil lived inside of him—he had been foolish enough to invite her in—and he was powerless to resist whatever twisted command it uttered. He reached into his pocket and removed the prescriptions. He set three slightly crumpled pieces of paper on the glossy wood, and after a few moments, the man turned his head to look.

"How much do you want for those?" he asked.

Galen's eyes went to Lauren. "Tell him five hundred," she said.

"Five hundred dollars," said Galen.

The man stared at him for a long moment, sighed, and then reached for his wallet. He produced ten crisp fifty dollar bills and laid them on the bar. Galen took the money, counted it, and shoved it into the pocket where the prescriptions had been. The man grabbed the papers, slid off his bar stool, and was headed for the door all in the space of a few seconds. The transaction was done, and Galen was left sitting alone in the King's Court Tavern. It was like the whole thing had been set up for him, and maybe it had. If that man also had a demon in him, and by the look of him Galen thought that was likely, then perhaps the preternatural creatures had some way of communicating with one another. The thought was terrifying.

It wasn't long before an actual bartender appeared and apologized profusely that Galen had to wait for service. He pulled a beer from a tap behind the bar and served him the best fish and chips the wandering man had eaten in many a year. The fish was hot and crispy and the beer went down smooth. Galen thought of Jesus again, dining on his last supper with fools that hadn't understood a word he had said in three years. Jesus must have known what was coming—that a terrible death was waiting for him just up the road a ways—but there was nothing for him to do but eat his bread and drink his wine. For Galen, he understood that he would be powerless to stop this horror the demon wanted him to commit, and he was terribly sorry for what he was about to do.

There was a construction site a block away from the tavern, and Galen found the building unlocked that Saturday night. This place had been a cinema once upon a time, but a fire had gutted the old building leaving a blackened ruin. The new theater they were building on the site looked magnificent, and Galen wished he could see the finished product, but he doubted that he would ever come this way again. It was cold that night, but at least he was dry, and no one bothered Galen as he slept. He decided in the night that he would make one final effort to defy the demon that lived inside of him. He knew that the chances were slim, but he had to try. Resisting evil was the duty of every man, and Galen hoped—prayed—that there was someone in this town that could deliver him from his burden.

He awoke the next morning, grimy from a day of hard travel and a night of hard drinking. In a word, John Galen was unclean. He thought about the long chain of mistakes he had made that had brought him to this point and hoped that today he would meet the one the one man who could break that chain.

Galen slipped out of the theater and walked along the sidewalks in the slumbering town of Carmel, Virginia. He had seen a beautiful church on the way into town, and it wasn't hard for him to backtrack the route and find the place again. The building glittered in the light of the morning sun—it appeared almost golden in that light, and Galen wondered if the people that worshipped here ever noticed the beauty of the Lord's house as they scrambled for a parking space, hoping that the minister wouldn't go overtime and cause them to miss the football game.

An elaborate sign stood at the corner of the property. It read:

Carmel Bible Church
Rev. Dr. Van Gernhardt
Services: Saturday 4:00 p.m.
Sundays 9:00, 10:30, 12:00

Galen crossed the parking lot, in the cold morning air. There were only a handful of cars, and the wandering man suspected that these might belong to some deacons or even the Reverend Dr. Gernhardt. His heart swelled with hope and anticipation as he drew near to God's house—this was the answer to his problem, he was certain. All he had to do was find this minister and ask him to cast out the demon in Jesus's name.

He reached the glass front doors of the church and found, to his amazement, that they were locked. Galen pressed his face to the thick glass and saw men in suits moving about the sanctuary. A heavyset man was standing at the pulpit and fiddling with a microphone. He could see them as plain as day, and unless this glass was tinted, Galen figured that they could probably see him as well, but they didn't look at him. He balled his right hand into a fist and rapped once on the glass door.

The men in the sanctuary turned to look at him; the reverend stared at him from the pulpit with a look of annoyance on his stern face.

"They won't be able to help you," said a familiar voice.

Galen's eyes went from the people inside the sanctuary to the demon, who stood beside him in front of the church. Lauren's lips parted in a grin, revealing the needle-sharp teeth of the demon beneath her skin.

"You don't know that," Galen said. "I'll tell them what you've done to me and they'll cast you out. That's how the story of Legion ends, don't you know?"

Lauren laughed. "Look for Jesus all you want," she said, "but you won't find him here."

Galen rapped on the door again, this time a little harder, and one of the deacons headed for the door. He was wearing a dark suit with a red tie, and his face was hard. He reached the door, turned the bolt lock, and opened the glass just a crack.

"Worship isn't for another hour," he said. He closed the door and bolted it again.

The demon was holding its belly and laughing so hard that it had to sit down. Galen banged on the door again, hard enough this time that he thought the glass might shatter. The deacon, who was halfway back to the pulpit, returned to the door and opened it again. This time, the expression on his face was clearly anger.

"I told you, we're not open yet..."

"Please," Galen said, "I need your help."

The deacon looked skeptical.

"There's something wrong with me...something in my head. I think it's a demon, and you all can cast out demons, right? Please, I need your help."

The deacon rolled his eyes and sighed. "Van," he said, "this guy says he has a demon and he wants you to exorcise him."

The reverend laughed. Galen was able to hear because the sound was projected into the sanctuary speakers through the microphone he wore.

"Demons aren't real," said Dr. Gernhardt, "you know that, Ed. Tell him to pound sand."

Galen fell to his knees, desperate that his last chance at redemption not slip through his fingers. "Please...I need Jesus. He can save me...deliver me from this abomination. I need your help."

The deacon whose name was Ed closed the glass door in Galen's face and turned the lock. Tears fell from the wandering man's eyes and splashed upon the white concrete step in front of Carmel Bible Church. He had come here in search of a miracle, but it was clear to him now that Jesus wasn't here. Hope was gone, and all that remained was the demon wearing Lauren's skin. The creature stood, brushed itself off, and helped Galen to his feet.

"Come on," it said, "I know a place where you can get that gun."

He stumbled along the historic streets of Carmel, past Victorian homes that had stood for a century, and hipster shops that would be gone in a year. He passed through the nice suburbs, full of expensive McMansions that weren't quite as nice as the homes in the older part of town. He passed through middle class suburbs packed with durable houses that were built before the turn of the new millennium. And finally he came to the poor part of town, where obese children stared at him as he walked by. Galen felt a smoldering anger in his heart, and the demon that walked beside him was fanning the flames.

"Going to church didn't work out so well for you," it said. "Would you like to try another denomination or three before you admit that God has turned his back on you?"

The monster's words were like a slap in the face. Galen had been a man of faith once upon a time, but that was long ago and far away. He tried to pray every once in a while, but he was out of practice and the words did not come easily to him. The idea of bowing to anyone, even a god, was difficult for him, and he was beginning to accept the fact that God did not love him any more.

"It's so much worse than that," said the demon. "Not only does God not love you, he hates you. He wants to see you suffer."

"No..."

"Yes, you are cursed, that's why the followers of the Son of Man refused to even let you into his house. You are cursed, John Galen, and your soul belongs to no one but me."

Those words were poison for a man such a he, and the burden Galen carried grew heavier with every step. He had fallen so far from the person he wanted to be, fallen like lighting from Heaven, and Galen despaired in his heart. He was contemplating jumping in front of the next car that drove by when they stopped suddenly in front of a dilapidated house.

"This is the place," said the demon. "Go knock on the door and ask for Bray."

Galen obeyed without hesitation. He had managed to resist the creature in his head at the start of their relationship, but he knew now that all of his strength had gone. He knocked on the door and a pale woman appeared a few moments later. She was dark-eyed and wary, but she let Galen into the house as if she was expecting him. He stood in a cramped living room—the house had nothing so grand as a foyer—and waited until a heavyset man appeared from upstairs. He had long hair tucked under a baseball cap, and a beard that flowed down his chest like a wizard or a Pharasee. When Galen looked into Bray's eyes he saw nothing...no emotion whatsoever.

"How can I help you?" he asked.

"I need a gun," said Galen. "Maybe a Glock if you have one."

Bray's face betrayed no emotion as he spoke. "I have one. You've got five hundred?"

"I've got about four seventy-five." He spent the rest on supper and drinks the night before, and a small part of Galen hoped that the man would refuse the price.

He did not.

They made the deal and Galen left the house with a pistol tucked into his belt and a half dozen clips of ammunition—enough to kill seventy people if his aim was true. Somehow, he knew that it would be.

• • •

He had spent every dollar in his pocket, and so Galen was once again forced to use his thumb to catch a ride. He moved ever eastward, spending the rest of that Sunday creeping from suburb to suburb. He was hungry and cold and burdened by thoughts of what he was about to do. He knew it was wrong, but he couldn't help himself anymore. And in the midst of everything else, his thoughts turned ever to his *Precious*.

When this was all done, when the bodies of three score school children were scattered all around him, Galen wondered if the demon would let him delve into the *Precious* once again.

Galen spent that night in an alley in Washington, D.C., the white city that claimed to be the capital of the world. It wasn't the first to make such a claim, and he wondered how long it would be before Washington went the way of London and Rome and Babylon and Thera. It was only a matter of time.

He was starving when he awoke the next morning, but without any money he had no way to eat. He still had his guitar, and while he had sung for his supper many times, he had never heard of anyone singing for their breakfast.

The memory of a little compartment in the guitar case hit him like a ton of bricks. It was designed to hold picks and his capo, neither of which had seen much use these past few years, but Galen often kept some cash secreted away in that compartment as well—rainy day money for situations just like this one. He set the case on the ground and opened the latches one by one. The lid lifted up on its hinges, revealing the 1968 Gibson J50 that was his only possession in the world. It was a beautiful instrument, a classic that held its tune no matter how much or how little he played it. His fingers hovered over the strings, longing to bring their sweet sounds to life, but he resisted. Instead he lifted up the guitar and opened the compartment under its neck. There was a twenty dollar bill folded up inside. Galen removed the twenty, stuffed it into his pocket, and was setting the guitar back in its place when a voice spoke up behind him.

"That's a beauty, Mister. Can you play that thing?"

Galen turned to see a shabby-looking man standing in the alley behind him. His clothes were threadbare and he wore no shoes in spite of the cold morning. He was thin to the point of starvation and his eyes were set deep in his their sockets. He seemed familiar somehow, but Galen couldn't place him.

"I used to play," he said. "Now I just carry it around. A reminder, I suppose, of my old life."

"Have you got any change?" asked the stranger. He held out a styrofoam cup and gave it a little shake.

Galen thought about the twenty in his pocket. He was hungry, but this man clearly was as well. It was nothing, a token gesture, but the idea of doing a kindness to a stranger pleased him somehow. He fished the folded bill from his pocket and dropped it in the man's cup."

The homeless man smiled. "I'd love to hear you play. You could spare a minute to pick something for me, couldn't you?"

Galen thought about the ache in his belly and the weight of the gun tucked into his belt. Every step carried him closer to an act of terrible evil and he was in no hurry. He reached into the case and lifted out the guitar. He slid the strap over his shoulder, formed the C chord with his left hand, and strummed the strings one time to see if it was in tune. The sound was as sweet as honey.

"What do you want to hear?"

The homeless man smiled. "Oh, anything."

Galen closed his eyes and scanned through the musical library that was locked away in his head. He knew hundreds of songs, but he was having a difficult time dredging one up out of his memory. He had hardly played a note since his demon surfaced, and there had been a time when his music was more precious to him than anything else.

Precious.

The wandering man formed a few chords and then began to pick a slow tune on the old Gibson. He closed his eyes as he slipped deeper into the song, and after a few moments, he began to sing.

Precious Lord, take my hand, lead me on, let me stand...

I'm tired, I'm weak, I'm alone.

Through the storm, through the night, Lead me on to the light...

Take my hand, Precious Lord, lead me home.

There were tears in Galen's eyes as he looked up at the stranger, and suddenly he recognized him. *He knew this man.* Galen was about to speak when the demon inside of him came up screaming to the surface of his mind.

He cried out and fell to his knees before the homeless man, and with a loud voice said, "What have I to do with you, Jesus, Son of the Most High God?"

The stranger just stared at him, his eyes deep pools of terrible sorrow. "Come out of him," he said in a calm, quiet voice that was almost a whisper.

Galen coughed violently, and from his mouth poured an oily, black smoke that took shape beside him in the alley. The demon that had tormented him no longer wore the skin of his former lover like a mask, but seemed instead to be made of living shadow. It stared at him for a moment, and Galen saw no anger or hatred in the creature's empty eyes, but only fear.

"I beg you," said the demon, "do not torment me."

The homeless man asked him, saying "What is your name?"

"My name is Legion," said the demon, "for we are many."

"Your true name..." said the man, Jesus.

The demon uttered something guttural, unpronounceable, and then broke into a fit of whimpering sobs. The creature was terrified.

The homeless man reached across the empty gulf between them and touched the shadowy demon. The monster screamed in agony as its body burned away like fog in the sunshine. The stranger who wasn't a stranger turned to look at Galen. He smiled. "That was some nice singing," he said. "You should do more gospel songs."

Still on his knees in the cold alley, Galen struggled to find his words. "I...I'm sorry," he said at last.

"I forgive you."

Galen thought of the bitter trial that had been his long life. He had invited the demon into his heart and mind, and had sinned continually since the day he was born. He thought about the last time he had seen this Son of Man, and the curse that had hung around his neck like an albatross. Surely, Jesus could not forgive him for all of that.

"I can," said the stranger, as if he had heard Galen's thoughts. "I can and I do, but you still must reap what you have sown."

Still weeping, still overwhelmed that he was free from the demon that had plagued him, Galen slid his guitar onto his back and bowed before his savior. When he looked up, the homeless man was gone.

• • •

John Galen threw the gun into the Potomac River and thanked the Son of Man that things had not ended up differently. He was free at last, and though he was tempted even now, he vowed that he would never again return to the thing he did in secret...the thing that had invited a demon into his mind. The gun was a physical object, something he could touch, but in his heart Galen was tossing his *Precious* into the wide river below.

He crossed the bridge into Virginia on foot, and began a slow trek westward that afternoon, hitching his way from town to town, picking tunes in bars and restaurants and little wayside honky-tonks to pay his way. He wandered the nation and the world, for such was his burden, and sometimes, when he rode in the back of a pickup with the wind whipping through his hair or when he played an A.P. Carter song that no one had heard for decades, the wandering man smiled and thought that his burden wasn't so heavy after all.

ABOUT THE AUTHOR

KEVIN G. SUMMERS is the author of the critically acclaimed short story ISOLATION WARD 4, as well as
several other stories set in the Star Trek universe. His
short story THE BELL CURSE was the very first tale
published in The World of Kurt Vonnegut under the
Kindle Worlds imprint. He is the co-author of LEG-
ENDARIUM with Michael Bunker, and, most recently,
THE BLEAK DECEMBER. Kevin lives in an 100-year old
farmhouse in Amissville, Virginia with his beautiful
wife Rachel and their children.

You can write to Kevin c/o The Crowfoot Farm,
Amissville, Rappahannock County,Virginia, United
States of America, Continent of North America, West-
ern Hemisphere, the Earth, the Solar System, the Universe, the Mind of God; or you can visit his website:
www.kevingsummers.com.